Brooklyn Graves

Books by Triss Stein

The Erica Donato Mysteries
Brooklyn Bones
Brooklyn Graves

Brooklyn Graves

An Erica Donato Mystery

Triss Stein

Poisoned Pen Press

First Edition 2014

10 9 8 7 6 5 4 3 2 1

Library of Congress Catalog Card Number: 2013941229

ISBN: 9781464202179   Hardcover
       9781464202193   Trade Paperback

Poisoned Pen Press
6962 E. First Ave., Ste. 103
Scottsdale, AZ 85251
www.poisonedpenpress.com
info@poisonedpenpress.com

Printed in the United States of America

For Miriam and Carolyn,
who have grown up a lot faster than Chris.

Acknowledgments

Deepest thanks again to Mary Darby and Jane Olson, writing group partners and cheerleaders, and to Bob, as always.

Chapter One

The day my friend Dima was killed, I was thinking about Tiffany. Of course that was before I heard the dreadful news.

Say Tiffany to most New Yorkers and they immediately see a box covered with glazed paper in a shade of blue that has been saying Tiffany since 1845. Maybe it holds a diamond engagement ring or the emerald earrings that will begin an affair or end a marriage, or perhaps the silver key chain that says, with that touch of Tiffany & Company class, thank you for another year of hard work.

Myself, I saw a cemetery. Not just any cemetery, mind you, but a famously beautiful one, the eternal resting place of the deceased rich and famous, a National Historic Landmark, Green-Wood Cemetery. Yes, a few of the founding Mr. Tiffanies, including the great Louis Comfort himself, were buried there under surprisingly simple stones, but I was not going to visit his grave. I was going to visit his work.

That was not my plan when I started this day. I work part-time at the Brooklyn Historical Museum, and I was worryingly behind on an assignment. The job was only one of the many balls I kept up in the air, so sometimes one of them knocked another to the floor. My plan for that day was to power-through and get entirely caught up.

Those balls began dropping all over the room the moment I walked into the cubicle I share with other part-time assistants and interns. I arrived late due to the rain snarling up the traffic. Eliot, my boss, was already there leaving a note on my desk.

"Erica. Glad you are here. Did you by any chance drive today?"

Driving is the least sane way to get from my neighborhood, Park Slope, where street parking is only difficult, to my work neighborhood, Brooklyn Heights, where it is impossible. Sometimes I do it anyway because I have later errands. Or because I have temporarily lost my mind. He knew that.

"We have a distinguished visitor today, one of the great experts on Tiffany, and he needs some chauffeuring around and some note-taking assistance at Green-Wood Cemetery. It involves Tiffany windows. You know how to get there, right? It's near where you live? Sarah is the logical choice, in fact, but she is out with the flu."

Denying I had my car was a tempting option, but Eliot has been a great boss and mentor. I owed him.

"I did drive," I answer, "but my car is not exactly a luxury ride." My car, in fact, is a twelve-year-old Civic with pothole-damaged shocks and a backseat covered with work papers, school papers, daughter papers. A lot like my house.

"You are a lifesaver. Come be introduced in the conference room at ten, and join the meeting. It's not exactly your field, but I promise it will be interesting." He left without telling me anything more.

One more ball hit the floor, but my job is only a small step above intern. The tiny salary is useful; the flexible work hours are necessary; the experience will make me a little more employable when I finally finish my PhD. Maybe. Maybe I could take home my sure-to-be-unfinished work and fit it in with dinner, my schoolwork, my teenage daughter's schoolwork. Oh, yes, and maybe sleep.

I hurried up the institutional-steel back-stairway, through a fire door and out into the oak-paneled magnificence of the original building.

Eliot was in the conference room along with a chunky in a checked flannel shirt, her pepper-and-salt hair in braid. Also sitting at the table was a tall, thin silver-haired in an elegant navy suit, a tie even I knew was silk, and cuff links even I could guess were gold. The distinguished expert? The rest of the crowd was the head curator, some department heads, and the museum's managing director—all heavy hitters. I wished I had spent a little more time tidying myself up, and took a seat as invisibly as I could. My boss smiled at me and passed me a note. "Her name is Bright Skye (!!!). She has a story."

Three large liquor cartons stood on the conference table beside the woman who was explaining in a soft, tentative voice: "...so you see, just by accident in a doctor's office, I read that you have a Tiffany collection here. I have been away from New York for a long, long time. I live in the desert near Sedona now. I wasn't even sure I could find you, but I had already found this." She gestured to the boxes. "I didn't know what it was at first, and I'm still not exactly sure, but when I read about your collection, I realized someone might want these things, and they might be valuable, and I came to see you to find out it they are worth anything."

She stopped abruptly, as if she had run out of words.

"Thank you," Eliot said politely. "You showed us a promising folder of samples when you first contacted us, so perhaps now you could show that to everyone? And tell us where they came from?"

"I'm cleaning out my mother's big old house, over in the Midwood neighborhood. It's been in her family since it was built, maybe about a hundred years ago, I guess. Maybe more. And there's about a hundred years of junk, too. I found this in the attic behind all the other junk. There's a whole box of letters and other things. There are some sketchbooks, I guess, and a pouch of jewelry with pins and bracelets and little pieces of colored glass. I don't even know what they are called. I don't know anything about all this kind of stuff, but I saw the name Tiffany in the letters a lot of times. And these pictures seem very nice."

She shook out the contents of a large envelope. The drab table was suddenly covered in a rainbow— pages of watercolors, brilliantly glowing. They were familiar Tiffany designs: lacy red dragonflies, exuberantly blooming wisteria in vivid lavender blue, rosy cherry blossoms, daffodils that radiated sunshine, pale opalescent magnolias and shimmering blue-green peacock feathers.

The entire room seemed to take on the glow. I couldn't stop staring. "Very nice" didn't even come close.

The well-dressed expert, who seemed to have appointed himself in charge, was the first to reach for some of the papers, whipping out a pair of white archivist's gloves to protect the paper from any damage.

"Hmm," he said. "Certainly the style and colors are right. Some of these are very well-known—the wisteria would scream Tiffany even in China! But some, I don't know." He was talking quietly and quickly, murmuring as if to himself, his face flushed with excitement. "I've never seen them before. Perhaps never produced? And the signature is simply unknown, at least to me. Maude Cooper? But if even I have never seen it—and I've seen everything—it's extraordinary, if true. Extraordinary."

He snapped out of his reverie and looked directly at the owner of the papers. "This Maude Cooper. Who was she? Come on, woman, you must have some idea."

Bright Skye whispered, "No, I have no idea at all. I think my grandmother had some Cooper relatives, but I've never heard about a Maude that I remember. My mother's family name was Updike before she was married a few times."

"And, umm, Skye was one of those married names?"

She flushed and whispered, "No, that is my own true name that I found."

Goodness, I thought, what a wimp. A New Age wimp at that.

He sighed deeply and turned to the museum director. "You spoke the truth. This is indeed very interesting and may even be of real importance, possibly even exceptional importance. Or not. Of course I want to be involved. Of course. I'd never forgive you if I were not included."

"Just what we were hoping to hear you say." He was all smiles. "Our staff has some thoughts, but we felt we needed more true expertise. Ladies and gentlemen, for any latecomers, let me introduce Dr. Thomas Flint, who is probably the leading expert on the artwork of the Tiffany studio. We are lucky he has consented to join us for this project."

"I don't know about that 'probably.'" He smiled stiffly. Was that meant to be a joke? "Yes, yes, but unfortunately I need to leave today for a conference in Rome, and I have an appointment at Green-Wood Cemetery first. I must verify a few details for my presentation. Really, I had to squeeze you in.

"Let's do this. Your driver gets me there and back here efficiently. Give me a room for an hour and let me see what I can make of this. While I'm abroad you take care of basic preliminary cataloguing and physical preservation. I already see terrible damage. Dear lord, they have been in an attic for a century! I'll send my assistant over to help tomorrow. When I return next week, we will be ready to begin a full analysis. A good plan, don't you think?"

An excellent plan, they all thought, and he was given the conference room on the spot.

A small voice rose from the end of the table.

"Do you think that these papers would be valuable? And the jewelry? I mean, for money?" It was Ms. Skye. She had been completely forgotten in the excitement.

Flint turned to her and said, "Did you understand that I am an expert on everything about Tiffany? His works and his life? This may indeed be very valuable, or perhaps it is not what it seems. It will take us some time to work that out."

"But I was hoping..." She said it softly, and then she looked away, her voice fading. "I could use the money."

"Miss...Skye, is it?" He raised one eyebrow as he said her name. "May we—that is, the museum—borrow the contents of these cartons for a few weeks? They will take excellent care of it, you can be sure of that, better care than it has had for decades in your attic, and then we will have an answer for you."

"I guess so. I mean, I have no use for it." She fiddled with the end of her braid, and then said, "I don't like old things, personally."

"You will be given a receipt for the items, and they will be kept locked up here. Yes?" He looked over at the director, who said, "Absolutely."

Ms. Skye drifted off, escorted by the director's assistant, who was explaining what needed to be signed.

Eliot motioned me over to meet the intimidating Dr. Flint.

"This is Erica Donato. Erica, Dr. Thomas Flint. Erica here will drive you, in her own car, and provide all the assistance you need."

He frowned. "What happened to Sarah? She was a student of mine and she is reasonably capable."

"Down with the flu."

"Then you'll have to do, I suppose. And you are also a decorative arts specialist, I hope?'

"No, I am an urban historian. Historian-in-training, really. But I'll be happy to assist today." It seemed like the right thing to say.

His cool blue eyes got much cooler. I added quickly, "I'll try not to ask foolish questions."

"See that you don't."

And that is how I ended up sucking down coffee in my car, peering though the streaming window, hoping the puddles were not deep enough to damage my old engine and hoping I had mastered taking pictures with the museum's camera.

It was raining too hard to look over the spectacularly Gothic stone gate. We splashed our way into the visitors center and were greeted by a woman Flint's age, somewhere in late middle age on the verge of old. My quick glance took in that she was small, gray-haired, no makeup, wrapped in a faded beige raincoat, with faded khakis and stout orthopedic shoes showing below. She reminded me of the older women of my youth, before they all discovered gyms and plastic surgery. Mrs. Mercer, she told us.

"I'm so sorry. I'm so very sorry." She kept repeating it. "There has been a problem. The cemetery is closed to all visitors this morning. I cannot take you…"

"All the arrangements were made for me personally by Dr. Reade," said Dr. Flint. "Just call her and get this straightened out. I don't have any more time to waste. Give me a phone and I'll call her myself."

I stopped in my tracks. No one even noticed me.

"Dr. Reade is very busy today. I would not dream of disturbing her."

"Well, I would! Her office is still in the administrative building over there?" He gestured with his right arm.

She nodded. "But…but…"

"Come along! If I can find Nancy Reade, perhaps I can rescue this monumentally wasted morning."

We stepped outside to find the rain had stopped and bright rays of sunlight were streaming out from under the massive dark clouds. I always think that particular phenomenon looks like a Renaissance painting of a deity at work. The massive gate with its pointed arches and soaring towers provided a suitable backdrop, too, but Dr. Flint did not pause to look at it, and I had to hustle to keep up with his long, furious stride. The drab woman from the office trailed behind, but we did not get very far.

A man in work clothes stopped us where the road curves up the hill into the cemetery itself.

"Sorry, sir. No one is allowed to enter right now."

"I had an appointment. I am a personal friend of Dr. Reade and several of the trustees as well, and I have important work to do here today."

"Sorry, sir. No one is allowed in."

Behind us I heard the lady from the office take a deep breath, but ahead of us I could see a group coming in our direction. Dr. Flint quickly walked over to a tall woman with a Burberry umbrella. She looked elegant and stressed.

"Nancy, what is the meaning of this? I had an appointment and as you know very well, I don't have time to waste, here or anywhere."

She stopped her group with a lifted hand, and drew Dr. Flint away from them.

"Oh, Thomas, we are dealing with an unexpected problem today. We had to close for a while. It is a…a safety issue. Of course I will personally reschedule your visit as soon as we… um…get this…um…resolved."

"That is not helpful. I leave for Rome tonight. I came to confirm some old notes on Tiffany's work here. I have a presentation coming up."

I could swear she turned pale.

"Surely you can make an exception for someone like me, whose work you know so well? Under the circumstances?" The tone was not as polite as the words.

She looked back nervously and said, "Tom, you know I would, if it was just up to me—of course we know you—but there are other issues."

She returned to her group and finally motioned Flint over. I followed behind him, and the lady from the office trotted along, too.

"We will allow you in, but only under escort from our security staff. One of the locations you wanted to see is…is where the problem is. There has been a collapse, a dangerous situation, so you cannot go there at all, and you cannot leave the paths anywhere. Will that be of any use to you?"

The red spots on his cheeks got redder, but he said, "Better than nothing. I suppose I'll just have to write around whatever is missing."

"Mrs. Mercer can take you to the other site, as planned. The Konick Mausoleum is the one off-limits."

Mrs. Mercer nodded and led the way, but Dr. Flint took Dr. Reade by the arm, gently leading her from the others, and whispered urgently. She whispered back, looked apologetic, shook her head. He looked furious. He stalked off into the cemetery itself. I hustled to keep up with his long legs, and Mrs. Mercer, the guide who should have been leading us, trailed behind, along with the cemetery's rent-a-cop security guard. Our parade would have been funny if tensions had not been so high.

The guard, an older man and not in the best of shape, did eventually outpace us all and stopped Dr. Flint with his bulk planted across the path.

"The other way, sir."

He led us around a lake with flocks of birds, including brilliantly blue teals, some stately Canada geese, and a pair of swans as perfect as Dresden china ornaments. With the sun now shining, it was lovely.

Dr. Flint went on ahead, but Mrs. Mercer stopped me and pointed. "There. In the reeds."

It was a long-legged white bird with a curved neck and a trailing headpiece of feathers, an egret or heron. It was standing as still as one of the cemetery stones, looking like a Japanese print, right here, unbelievably, in the heart of Brooklyn, just a few minutes' walk from the truck traffic on a six-lane avenue. I was transfixed.

With a light touch on my arm she moved me back onto the path. The trees were in October gold, and with the unexpected sunlight glinting off the wet leaves and the polished stone chapels, there really was something magical about the place. It was a far cry from the bleak cities of gravestones where my mother and my husband were buried.

That was no accident, as I knew very well. Green-Wood had been designed from the beginning to be a kind of park, a rambling, pastoral, social environment meant as much for recreation by the living as for as interment of the dead. The living used to come in their carriages for scenic drives and picnics. It was a weird thought, but I know Victorians thought about death differently. On a day like this I thought the designers would have to be proud. Were their ghosts hanging around, satisfied to see that their work was in good hands, still valued and cared for?

Actually, I had no idea if they were even buried here, and I gave myself a little mental slap. The rare birds, the fanciful architecture, and the golden forest might have looked like an illustration from a fairy tale, but I was here to work, not to fantasize.

I stepped into a puddle, soaking my shoe to my ankle, shocking me out of my daydream. Dr. Flint stopped abruptly and pointed across the road to one of the oddest mausoleums we had seen so far. It was made of mixed red-and-yellow brick, with a Dutch-style stepped roof. Elaborate stone columns added a formal touch, but the effect was sadly diminished because so many of them were broken, and the wrought-iron gate was falling off its hinges. At the back, a number of people were milling around with ladders and tools and putting up some kind of scaffolding. From our perch, it was impossible to see that side clearly.

"That was to have been our first stop. You." He meant me. "Come here with that camera. Get as close as you can." He glanced at the guard. "Take photos of the windows as well as you can, not that it matters. None of them will be useful to me from here. It's meant to be viewed from the inside, with light coming in." He turned back to the guard. "What in the world are those workers doing?"

The guard shrugged, and Flint barked out, "Oh, give up the Sergeant Friday pretense. That shabby building happens to hold exceptional pieces of Tiffany glassmaking. I should be there if there is a building problem. Imagine if the workers do damage. It would be a disaster. Irreplaceable."

He muttered, "Fools, all of them. You!" He meant Mrs. Mercer or me or both of us. "Keep on top of this while I am out of town." I guessed he meant that for me. "If I had more time, Nancy Reade would have her ears sizzled."

"Perhaps we should move on to our other destination?" Mrs. Mercer could barely get the words out, she was so nervous.

"Yes, let's at least get one thing done. Come along. You. Are you taking notes? Describe what we have seen here, and note that this is the Konick Mausoleum. Badly neglected."

I whipped out a notebook, wishing I had an iPhone. Mrs. Mercer was standing next to me.

"Yes, the neglect is sad, isn't it? I prepared for this tour by looking it up yesterday. The family has quite disappeared or died out."

"What do you…?" I started to ask, but she guessed where my question was going.

"In the old days," she said, "it would have been torn down, I'm told. Shocking, isn't it? Now the cemetery will preserve it. Eventually."

"Does it really have wonderful windows?"

"I should say it does! They are not very well-known, and it's a shame for you to miss them, but at least you'll see one here."

We had reached our destination. This one was a miniature Greek temple, white marble, with columns topped with curly decorations whose names I didn't know. Two limestone steps up and the door had been opened for us. I was certainly curious. I had never been inside anything like this.

Facing us, above what I thought must be the tomb, was a huge stained-glass window: a redheaded Jesus in a field of shimmering white flowers, backed by a glowing red and yellow sky.

I know I gasped. I'd never been so close to anything that large and that magnificent. The glass had the shimmering effect Tiffany was famous for. Even I knew that. Were the flowers lilies? Was the sun rising or setting?

"His work doesn't become less wonderful with familiarity." Flint's tone seemed almost approving. "Now, you. What I need is close-ups of that border. Borders are very unclear in my working collection of pictures, and I need the information for my speech. And make notes. I would know the origin, but I can't say the same for my assistants."

He took some measurements, made some notes himself, motioned to me to take a few more angles. I hoped I knew what I was doing.

There was a plaque with information. This was the tomb of Octavios Knight, the Silver King of Montana, and his wife, Anne, who became New Yorkers after they got rich. I had never heard of them, but here was a true work of art they had brought into existence.

And that was it. Flint led the way out and down the hill to the parking lot. Before we could make our escape, a very young woman came up to us. "You are Dr. Flint? I must ask that you not discuss the problems with anyone. We prefer to handle it all privately."

Flint lifted an eyebrow. "Since we have been told precisely nothing, that will not be a problem."

The young woman seemed to collapse, just a little, from her rigid posture.

Mercer muttered to me, "That twelve-year-old child is our new public relations pro. I'm sure she thought her job would be getting journalists to write happy stories about our beauty and history."

The young woman said, "That is good news. I was not sure, when I saw you talking to Dr. Reade. But you must not mention anything you've seen to anyone. Is that fully understood?"

Mercer nodded, but Professor Flint said, "You misunderstand. I am not an employee. You have no authority whatsoever with me, none at all."

The woman looked even more stressed. "If you have any respect for Green-Wood as an organization, please help us here?" She tried a placating smile. "We do have a problem today, and we will handle it appropriately, but who knows what some idiot may want to make public? A blog? Local news?" She shuddered.

"Of course. All you had to do was ask." There was the tiniest emphasis on the word *ask*. "I would certainly agree to anything Nancy Reade asked."

"She is just a bit preoccupied just now."

"Yes, I suppose so. I wouldn't deal with that gossipy trash, even without being asked, and I hope I can speak for my scholar colleague here as well." He was looking at me. Now I was his colleague? I nodded. Of course.

Not another word was said until we were back in the suitably old and elegant part of Brooklyn where our museum is housed in a suitably old and elegant Victorian mansion. I paused at the main door to let my passenger out before tackling the unsuitably modern problem of finding street parking. He said, "I plan to keep quiet about this puzzling morning, and I certainly hope you will too."

"I don't see why…"

"Oh, for heaven's sake. Trust me on this. The museum and scholarly worlds are endlessly gossipy. They are a bunch of old women of all sexes. Let them all learn something happened from public sources. It's probably all a tempest in a teapot anyway."

"I don't think…"

He gave me a stern look. "Do you want to spend the rest of the morning pandering to their curiosity? I don't care to waste my valuable time that way."

I had to agree. I did not value his time as highly as he did, but I did value my own.

"I need you in a thirty-second meeting inside. Garage the car. There is no time to waste."

He waited while I left the car at a commercial garage, hoping I would be reimbursed for the shocking fee. Once again I followed, struggling to keep up, as he hustled to the director's office, picking Eliot up along the way.

He spun a vague excuse about being delayed at Green-Wood, and quickly set up a plan for the rest of the week.

I turned to leave, along with some other junior staff, when Flint barked, "You! Donadio, wasn't it?"

"Donato."

"Yes, whatever. You said you are a historian. Think you can create a reliable record of what's here?"

"Yes, of course, but…"

"Good. I'll ask for you to work on this for now. You kept your head this morning. That gave me a hunch you might be competent, even if you don't know anything about Tiffany."

I didn't know which I wanted to argue about first, that I had other work to do or that I did, too, know something about Tiffany. It wouldn't have mattered. He was already ushering me out of the room. "My airport car will be here in just minutes now."

Eliot gently took my arm and led me out. As soon as we were out of hearing range, I exploded. "I have other work to do—that whole new project for the school visits. And this Flint? I was with him this morning at Green-Wood. What a…"

"Yes, yes, an arrogant son of a bitch." He smiled sympathetically. "I've known him for years. But you are overlooking how high-profile this could be, if, of course, it turns out to be what it seems." He was still smiling. "I'm doing you a big favor to allow you to become involved."

"Do I have a choice? I don't, do I?"

"Nope. You'll be grateful when this is published and your name is on it."

"But…" Something told me Flint was not the glory-sharing type.

Eliot stopped me with an upheld hand. "I'll make sure of that. It will be the price for us doing some of his grunt work for him, and he did promise some help. He left in a hurry but said he'd e-mail us some instructions, and a copy to his assistant and it will all be ready tomorrow. Set aside your other work, just until Flint gets back. I'll make it all right. Oh, and put in a voucher for the parking today." He winked.

There would be no more work today, not for me. I didn't care who gave me another task. I was going out for a walk in the fresh, rain-washed air. If my walk just happened to take me past my daughter's school, and it was time for her to be coming out, so much the better. I admitted to myself she might not see it that way. What high school sophomore wants to leave school with her friends and find Mom outside? Invading her world? As if she needed to be picked up? I didn't care; I wanted to see her, whether she wanted to see me or not.

Unlike the noisy flood of younger classes, upper-school students usually came out in discrete, chattering groups. Today, no one was chattering. As I stood across the street, on the alert for Chris or her friends, I thought some of the students were crying.

There they were. Chris, fashionably sloppy and almost as tall as I am now, and her neighborhood best friend Melanie. Two other familiar faces were right behind. And they were definitely crying. I wove my way across the street, through the stalled traffic on the school block.

Chris walked right into my arms and sobbed, "I guess you heard."

I held her tight and glanced over her head at her friends. One patted her shoulder, the others were standing by, arm-in-arm. They all looked teary.

"What in the world is going on?" I asked

"I thought you must have heard, somehow." Chris' sobs slowed down enough for her to talk. "Isn't that why you came?"

"Uh, no, I was just walking by. Suppose someone explains?"

They all grew a shade paler at the thought, and Chris finally took a deep breath.

"Alex wasn't in school today and nobody heard from him, and Natalya wasn't in the office, either. We thought, maybe, his grandmother? She's pretty old. Then, later, like in Latin, there was an announcement." Her friends waited, breathless, while she brushed the tears from her eyes. "It said his father had died and Natalya would be out of the office for the rest of the week. And that's all."

Melanie prompted her. "They said we would have an assembly first thing tomorrow to talk about it, to determine the appropriate school community response. You know how they talk, blah, blah."

And that was how I learned Dima had died.

Alex and Chris have been friends since first grade. Natalya, his mother, was the secretary in the upper-school office. And Dima was the chief school custodian, handyman, friend to everyone in the school community, a vigorous man in his forties who could fix anything, build anything. I had a sudden picture of him walking the school roof to repair a leak.

One part of my mind said he could not possibly be dead, just like that, that it was impossible, but another part said, "You know better. You know better than most."

"That's all? There was no more information?" A stupid thing to say to these grieving girls; my mouth was moving on autopilot.

The girls all shook their heads, solemnly. Then one of them said, "But you know, it felt all day like there was something. Didn't it? Teachers looked weird and, I don't know, it just felt like there is more that they aren't telling us. Something they don't want us to know, right?"

"It wouldn't be helpful to spread stories like that, Heather." I hoped I'd said it gently. "I know you are all very upset, but wait until someone really knows the facts."

"Wait, wait, I have a text." Melanie turned the annoying tune off and consulted her phone. "Dan. Alex's best friend."

She turned even paler and passed her phone around. Each girl gasped as she read it.

I was last. "Alex's dad killed. Not accident. More later."

Chapter Two

I had to blink and read it a second time and then a third. It was the girls' sobbing again that brought me back to the moment.

I was shaking right down to my damp, worn-out loafers, but I was the grown-up here.

"Come on, girls." I kept my arm around Chris. "We can't talk here on the street. Hot chocolate?"

"Thank you, but..." All the girls had plans. School activities had been cancelled, but there were other responsibilities—babysitting, lab notes to do together, allergist appointment.

"Chris, honey, I'm going to skip out on work and go home. I just need to go back for a few minutes. Do you want to wait?"

She was blinking back tears. "I'll go home with Mel and see you later." They walked off, supportive arms around each other's shoulders.

Everyone at the school knew Natalya and Dima. Their school jobs made it possible to send their son to this excellent—and expensive—private school. Russian immigrants, they lived for their only child's future. This would affect the school world in ways I could not even imagine.

I returned to my cubicle in a fog, collected some items, and sent a terse message to Eliot that I was taking off for the rest of the day. I wanted a stiff drink, and the chance to dial my mind all the way down to "off." I resolved to think about Dima and his family when I knew something. I would not let it take over all my thoughts right now.

Of course that didn't work out.

We had become acquainted years ago. Our children were best friends when they still wore nametags for class outings. And we became friends as parents, perhaps because I was almost as lost in this world as they were. Our children were scholarship kids in a rich kids' school.

I could not forget that Alex and Chris now had another bond: young people whose fathers had died. And I would have to reach out to Natalya soon. As I drove home, a giant headache was forming behind my eyes.

I told myself I had work to do. I was falling behind. I only worked at the museum part-time, with the rest of my week supposedly devoted to writing my dissertation on urban history. I was examining the effects of new immigration on old neighborhoods and comparing changes from overseas immigration to changes from gentrification. It was the old yet always current story of life in Brooklyn.

It seemed like a good idea at the time. I lived in a neighborhood that was the perfect laboratory for it. The heart of Park Slope had been the height of elegance when new, with mansions on the park and modest homes at the edges. Then it deteriorated badly in the post-World War II decades. Later it was rediscovered, rebuilt, and gentrified to a fare-thee-well, with chic restaurants replacing the bars where old men drank beer at eleven in the morning. It had been through all the cycles.

I, myself, am not a gentrifier. Not even close. My shabby house is at the still-kind-of-gritty, not-really-renovated end of the neighborhood—a long way from the official historic district and out of zoning for the excellent public schools.

I'm a kind of immigrant, though, even if my trip was nothing compared to Natalya and Dima's. My home turf was a completely different Brooklyn, only a few miles away but another world, where a trip to Manhattan was a twice-a-year excursion; college was a short bus ride away, just like high school; moms stayed at home if they could and dads were cops or cab drivers; and most people married and settled down around the corner from their parents. I was happy with that life. too, until I had to move away from those memories and build new ones.

Sometimes I feel a bit like a stranger in a strange land, but my daughter has no other memories. She takes the subway with her friends to Manhattan concerts, has been eating dim sum with chopsticks since she was six, and knows how to order ballet tickets. She doesn't think twice about it. And living where we do, she also doesn't think twice about families with different languages, different colors—even in one family—or families with adopted children or with two moms, or two dads.

Thinking about Chris brought me back to Alex to Natalya to Dima. That was when I gave up on work and curled up under my down comforter, thinking about my friend and what she was feeling right now.

I woke when I heard Chris' backpack hit the floor downstairs.

"Chris?" I was confused. How long had I slept? "I'm up here, honey."

She came clattering up the stairs and into the dark room, flipping on the light as she did. She opened one of the built-in shutters, too, folding it back into its slot, but the light from outside was dim.

"Chris? Is it night? How late is it?"

"Nope, it's dark because it's pouring again. But it is dinner-time. Aren't you getting up?'

"Oh. Sure. Let me go splash some water on my face." I hugged her as I went past. "I am so glad you're here."

She hugged back briefly, in that teenage way of not wanting to show she needed one.

I returned with my eyes wide open and my brain almost back on. "Ok. Let's warm up some chicken soup for supper and then tell me what's going on."

It was canned soup with leftover supermarket barbecue chicken added—I have no time for making homemade soups—but the comforting smells filled the kitchen anyway.

"Is there news from Alex?"

"No."

"Or Natalya?"

She shook her head. "That assembly at school tomorrow? I guess they'll tell us more then."

To each of the two steaming bowls on the kitchen counter, I added a fluffy dumpling, a matzo ball—right out of the freezer, but filling and familiar. We ate in silence. I could tell Chris wanted to talk, and I waited.

"What was it like?" She was looking into her soup bowl, chasing down a slice of carrot. "I want to know what it's like for Alex."

My mom "Danger" light went on. This felt like thin ice.

"What do you mean?"

"Mom, you know. When my own father…"

She doesn't remember. She was three. We were too young to have a baby, too poor, and too stupid to be anything but happy. She was a honeymoon baby and I was twenty-four when he was killed.

If she was asking, I had to answer her. It had been a long time since she asked me. Much as I wanted to run far away, maybe we were both ready. Anyway, ready or not, I had to answer her.

"He was a firefighter, a dangerous job. We talked about that when he started, but he loved being active and we knew a desk job just was not for him. Then he went and died so stupidly, hit by a drunk driver while he was riding his bike."

Chris nodded. She knew this part.

"I remember, it was a beautiful day, and I said, 'Sure, go for a ride. Enjoy your day off.' Later, I felt like 'how could the sun still be shining?'"

"Mom, we don't have to, if you can't…"

"I'm okay." If I wasn't I had to be a mom now and fake it. "The police came to the door and told me there was an accident. I kind of fell apart and I remember being embarrassed, but they were used to that. My friend down the hall came for you and they took me to the hospital. And they didn't tell me, but from the way they looked, I guessed he was already gone, and I was right. I saw him, and touched him but it…it wasn't him."

I had to stop.

"And then?"

"You know, after that it's kind of a blur. Soon his parents were there, and my parents, and I went back to Grandma and Grandpa's house with them. Really, I was in shock for a long time. You know I wasn't even ten years older than you are now."

Chris was silent for a long time before the next question. "Where was I?"

"Someone brought you over there. They had a bed for you in their house, and we just stayed for a while. Quite a while."

"It's different for Alex, I guess. I mean he knows everything that's happening. I don't even remember when I had a father. Did I even know something happened?"

"Yes and no. We could not really explain it to you, but you knew everything was different, and you had your tantrums. You knew your daddy wasn't there and you didn't understand where he had gone."

I could not tell her about the times, when I thought I would actually, literally, die of the grief. And how, when she was an inconsolable three-year-old wailing, "I want Daddy! I want Daddy!" I did not know how I could go on.

Another long silence, and then, "That will be something I will always share with Alex, isn't it? Missing fathers?"

I held her hands for both our sakes. "You might want to think about how to be a good friend right now."

She nodded, withdrew her hands, and went upstairs without another word.

Me, I was exhausted both physically and mentally. This day felt endless. Yet my mind was jumping all over, and I found myself wandering from living room to kitchen, peering into the refrigerator and then closing it, picking up the phone and putting it down again. I had twelve people on speed dial; I didn't feel like talking to any of them. I didn't know what I wanted.

My restless eyes fell on the daypack I carry to work and school, then on the books about Tiffany I had been given that afternoon. Funny how long ago it seemed now. Not so funny, really.

Sometimes, when nothing else makes sense, work is the anchor. I had to learn that lesson a long time ago, so I pulled out the books and notebooks and curled up on the couch, prepared to spend an hour or two tightly focused on learning something new about Tiffany. It didn't matter what—anything that would be, one, useful for my work and, two, not at all related to my real life. I would work for an hour, clear my head, and with luck, unwind enough to fall asleep.

Instead, I got lost in Tiffany's time and place, turn-of-the-last-century New York, when a woman daring to take part in the new bicycling craze had to manage ankle-length skirts, when the opening of the first subway line had the entire city excited, and young Teddy Roosevelt was running for governor. Women still couldn't vote, and yet, I learned, there was a whole team of women working for Tiffany, living independently and making art. They were the "New Women" of a century ago. I couldn't stop reading and I couldn't wait to dig into our just-found collection of letters to see if the previously unknown Maude Cooper was one of them.

Hours later, I woke up on the couch, facedown on the open books and my head full of glowing stained-glass flowers and young women in Gibson Girl shirtwaists and enormous hats trimmed with glowing flowers and feathers. But in my dreams, they all seemed to be walking around a glowing stained-glass cemetery.

Chris was gently shaking me.

"Wake up. Why are you here? "

"Why are you here? Middle of the night? Why are you up?" Her face was white in the lamplight.

"It's almost morning. Alex sent a note to all his friends."

She handed me the phone. The message wasn't in text-speak but written out.

"Up all night. Can't sleep. Dad shot. We found him on our lawn yesterday AM."

I dropped the phone as if it burned. I could not make my mind process this horrifying piece of news. I grew up around cops, and anyone who's ever watched a cop show on TV would have the same thought: This looks like an ugly message from some very ugly people. How could that possibly be about Dima, who was the nicest man and a straight arrow if there ever was one?

What could I possibly say to Chris about this? Nothing this evil had ever touched her life. Then I saw she was not looking to me. She was madly texting, so her friends were up, too, looking to each other for some measure of comfort.

Gray light was reaching into the house, so it was already dawn. No point in going back to bed. I made a pot of coffee and even poured a mug for Chris. This was no ordinary morning. I found pancake mix way in the back of a cupboard and threw together a stack of them.

She was ready for school early instead of the usual mad rush, and Melanie stopped by to walk to the subway together. I was awake now, and two mugs of coffee insured I would not go back to sleep. I might as well go to work early too.

◇◇◇

Before I left home I had an e-mail from a Ryan Ames with the subject line "Dr. Thomas Flint assistant." I briefly considered a quick delete, followed by a claim that it had never arrived. I did not want to deal with any of this today.

Nope, I knew I had to be a grown-up.

It said "Professor Flint wants us to meet as soon as possible to begin working on the information you discussed. I will be at the museum at noon sharp today."

Oh, I could hardly wait. He sounded as arrogant as his boss. What if I did not work that day? What if I had other plans? Or—heaven forbid—other responsibilities?

He was there on the museum steps when I went down to look for him. From inside the long hall, he actually looked kind of scary, not in Flint's "I know everything, you peasant," style, but more in an "avoid him late at night on a dark street" style. He was tall and thin, with a long black raincoat heavily decorated with looping chains. Part of his head was shaved and tattooed and I flinched just thinking of the pain involved. Not only would I avoid him on a dark street, I certainly would not want my daughter to know him.

Then I opened the door and he said hello in a voice that was scarcely louder than a whisper. It was extra muted because he was looking at the ground. When he looked up I was surprised to see the timid expression in his eyes. I couldn't match it with either his boss' arrogance or the macho swagger of his own appearance. He looked exactly like a child who hoped you would like him but wasn't expecting you to.

I smiled and he smiled back. He looked relieved. Let's say I was confused. I hid it well by escorting him into my tiny cubicle and clearing some books stacked on the one extra chair.

"I understand that you are Dr. Flint's assistant, but what does that mean, exactly? And did he tell you what he expects you to do here?" My computer powered on and I added, "Ah, let's see if he sent me anything. He said he would."

"I sent it. He doesn't know how to use e-mail. He dictated it."

Two pages of crisp directive, laying out all our tasks until Flint returned. He suspected Maude Cooper might be a previously unknown "Tiffany girl," one of the girls who worked in Tiffany's all-female design studio. His ultimate goal would be to determine how much new information her papers held, if any, and what their scholarly value could be. He conceded there might be some monetary value, too, but that did not seem to interest him very much.

Our assignment, young Ryan's and mine, was to aid him in this by doing pretty much just what I would have done anyway: organize, record, and describe the jumbled contents of the boxes, then start the research to see what we could learn about it. He included a list of sources to consult. Because no one here at the museum with its fine library would have known enough to do that.

"That's what he said, word for word. My job is to do anything Dr. Flint needs done. Mainly I do his computer tech work, write up his notes, organize his paperwork, but I do everything—bring his coffee, get his dry cleaning, pick up airline tickets." He turned pink. "I know how it sounds, but I'm not just a gofer."

"Oh, I know, I know. I started here as an intern myself, possible the oldest they ever had, and I'm still only a very junior part-timer. But—" I paused, trying to ask the obvious without being obvious. "Are you—um—very interested in Tiffany? Or period decorative art in general? I mean…"

He said with great dignity, "I am a third-year painting student at Pratt. I can appreciate all forms of art." Then he smiled a little sheepishly. "But no, my goal is to become the next Dave McKean." He saw my blank face, and explained, "He does dark, scary, beautiful art. He's illustrated Neal Gaiman's books. He's the best in two generations." He turned a little pink again. "Or ever, really. Yes, I would say ever. He's my idol."

He added hastily, "Dr. Flint didn't hire me for my art but for my tech skills. I'm his tame geek. But he doesn't know I'm interested in graphic art. Please don't mention it?"

"I see," I said, though I didn't, really. Then I imagined Dr. Flint with a comic book—pardon me, a graphic novel—in his hands, and I did see it, quite clearly.

After I retrieved the cartons from their place under lock and key, we dug in and found a haphazard mess. No need to keep the contents in original order as there clearly was none. We spread out at a worktable, dividing the contents by type for starters: one pile for letters, one pile for art, and one pile for "whatever." The couple of books that looked like diaries were set aside on their own.

Ryan had a template already set up on his laptop and could type a lot faster than I could, so I dictated content and he keyed away. His questions were right on the mark and I was beginning to see why Flint hired him.

It took most of the morning just to list the letters in the first box. When I led him into the staff room for a coffee break, I said, "I just have to ask. How the heck did you and Flint get together? I don't mean to be nosy…"

He ducked his head. "I guess we are an odd couple. Actually Dr. Flint says it all the time. Sometimes I think he is laughing at me."

That seemed more than likely.

I handed him coffee, watched him pour in four packets of sugar and passed him my personal supply of cookies. He inhaled three, making me wonder if he'd any breakfast, before he went on. "I was working for the computer lab at Pratt and Flint begged my boss to send him someone to fix a computer problem in a hurry. He isn't a Pratt professor but I guess he had some pull."

"I gather you succeeded."

He looked at me with his very first hint of humor. "He'd accidentally closed a screen and thought he'd lost his whole manuscript. Turned out his last assistant—actually, his last three—had quit suddenly, he had a deadline, and was in complete panic." He shook his head. "Brilliant man but barely knows how to turn his computer on. Pathetic in this day and age. Who uses file cards for notes?"

"Now I see what you mean by 'tame geek!' You're his own personal tech support department?"

"Kind of. He was just convinced that I was a genius and offered to overlook what he calls my inappropriate sense of style."

"He didn't say that!"

"Yes, he did. Why not?" He didn't seem offended. "He says I don't look scholarly or like a gentleman. I guess before me he had a few girls in pearls working for him, but they didn't like doing his errands and they didn't need the money. I do. I mean, I need the money and, you know, I can deal with the rest." He flushed. "I'm learning a lot about, um, how to conduct myself. I can see it makes a difference in his work, you know, how people think of him. And even how to dress right."

He said it with a straight face, and not a hint of irony. I struggled to keep a straight face of my own, wondering how he had looked before becoming acquainted with the suave Dr. Flint.

We went back to work. Ryan went to discuss scanner capabilities so he could create a digital record of the art, while I began to read the letters. I told myself it was a quick overview for now. I was not going to waste a lot of time today getting sucked into reading them in detail.

Of course I got sucked in. How could I not?

She was a lively letter writer, obviously thrilled to be in New York, and writing so often to her mother and sister back in Illinois it would take us days to read them all. We would have to try to piece together her history, because she did not need to include the background details for her letters home. Instead, she seemed determined to take her mother and sisters along on her adventures.

A note to myself in parentheses—if she sent the letters to her family in Illinois how did they end up in a house in Brooklyn? Find out.

She wrote all about her boardinghouse and included sketches of her fellow boarders, telling her sister how much fun it was to be surrounded by such creative and sociable people and assuring her mother how very respectable they all were, how high the housekeeping standards were, and that the promised "excellent daily breakfast and dinner" were really provided. She included a sample menu.

She told them about seeing the great Maude Adams in *Peter Pan*, including a charming sketch in colored pencil of her costume, and joked about making Maude Cooper as famous a name someday. She saw the "divine" Madam Schuman-Heinke in *Das Rheingold*, in company with a crowd from the boardinghouse. She wrote to her sister—but not to her mother!—about using a long, sharp hatpin to discourage a "masher" on the streetcar. She began a painting class at the Art Students League and was happy to be back among the easels and oils.

She was in awe of Clara Driscoll, who ran the all-female design studio and declared Driscoll to be her idol, the person she aspired to become. She described her early assignments, cutting glass for small projects, and the joy of using her Art Institute training, and sent watercolor sketches that looked like familiar Tiffany designs. She confessed her passionate desire for her talent to be recognized.

Her world itself was different in every detail from mine. The Wright brothers would not take to the sky for a few more years, penicillin was decades in the future, and the city pollution problem was created by the vast number of horses on the street. Only half the states had child labor laws. A lady began dressing by lacing up her corset and adding layers of petticoats.

And yet, she did not seem so different from me. She was a young woman making her way in the world. I knew her. I could not wait to read more and know her better.

Absorbed as I was, at the back of my mind I was always thinking about Dima, Natalya, Alex, and about all the people who knew them at Chris' school. What was happening there today? Could I find a moment to sneak away and meet Chris at lunchtime or the end of the school day?

In the end, Chris came to me, dropping in after an early dismissal. She shook her head. "We had an assembly. I told you we would. Middle- and upper-school. I guess the little ones had their own. Herbert talked and talked, like always."

This is artsy private school. The headmaster is called by his first name and so are the teachers. It took me a long time to get used to that.

"And?"

"Oh, he said they don't know anything about what happened, but that other people will cover for Natalya this week in the office. And Alex is still out too.' And we all send our best wishes to both of them. We will come together as a community to honor a man so beloved,' blah, blah—you know how he talks. Not that it isn't true, though. So now there is a committee to figure out what we should do. And then everyone who wanted to was allowed to say something. Sharing! So people who don't even know Alex and were never nice to Dima, even, just had to get up there and talk. Sickening. I hate drama llamas! And then they said counselors will add sessions in case anyone is feeling frightened. Or whatever.

"Well, so, we want to go see Alex tonight, just for a little while."

"Oh, Chris, I don't know about that. It is so soon, they are still in shock. Are you sure it's okay, having visitors tonight? Maybe they want to be alone."

"Mom, Alex asked us to. We all got texted. He needs his friends, like you said last night. So could you drive me and Mel and maybe Roger and Sean?"

"Okay, if he asked you to come. If you don't mind crowding. If it's still raining, I'll even pick them up."

I threw together a meal, and Chris connected with her friends and declared herself ready to roll. I wasn't sure her sloppy school clothes were quite right for a condolence call but decided it wasn't worth a fight; this evening would be hard enough for a teenager without that. First rule of parenting a teen: Pick your battles. Sometimes I even managed to remember that. Not always.

Soon there were there three equally sloppy but wide-eyed, sober youngsters in my car, and we were winding our way through the evening traffic on Ocean Parkway headed to the other side of Brooklyn, right out to one of urban Brooklyn's very own beaches. The car was filled with the sugar and oil smell of fresh doughnuts, Alex's favorite food.

Chapter Three

I knew how to get there—just drive to the end of Ocean Parkway and stop at the ocean—and then turn onto a side street crowded with modest homes and worn brick apartment buildings. Their home was a modest stucco two-family house, one up and one down, standing in a row with others exactly like it separated by narrow driveways. It was an old house, a little tired-looking, but clean and cared for. I remembered Dima painting the woodwork and planting rosebushes in the tiny front garden. There was no crime scene tape now, but I saw some ripped pieces of it caught in the shrubbery.

"You can go ahead. Alex might have wanted you, but I am afraid I'd be intruding."

"Mom?"

"It's not the moment for Natalya to be entertaining guests. I'll park when I can, go have a cup of coffee, and meet you in front in an hour, okay? That's long enough for this type of visit, and it's a school night, too."

They tumbled out, unusually silent. I added, "Chris, you can call if you want to leave sooner." I watched as they went up the walk, girls holding hands and the boys squaring their shoulders before they rang the bell, trying so hard to be grown up.

I sat in the car, music on, thinking about the very different last time I had driven Chris out here, for another classmate's gigantic sixteenth birthday party at a gaudy Russian restaurant.

I tried to occupy my mind with watching for a parking space and wondering if I would have time for a short walk on the boardwalk along the beach. Sea air and the soothing sound of the waves suddenly seemed very appealing.

I jumped when Chris knocked on the car window and motioned me to roll it down.

"It's awful. The house is full of people speaking Russian and crying, but we are hanging out in Alex's room. Natalya isn't crying, but she looks awful and she says come right up, don't sit in the car."

"I don't know. I'm not dressed for it and I'm empty-handed. People bring food..." The excuses tumbled out.

"Mom, she really meant it. And quick! There's a spot opening up."

She pointed down the block and I sped away to grab it the second it was vacated. Chris had gone back inside, and as I approached the front door Natalya stepped out. She stood under the light over the front door, and I could see her shiver in the chilly night air, hug herself, take out a cigarette. She came down the walk to meet me and took both my hands in her own cold ones.

"I thank you for coming, Erica! I had to get away for a moment." She shivered again. "My house is full of crazy people. All the drama. Turns all your insides into opera. You know?" She put her arm around my shoulders and said, "Come. We talk ourselves, here, on the steps."

Her face was a decade older, a fierce mask. "No mistake. My heart is broken and I know it will not mend, not in my whole life. You know too, don't you?"

"Yes, I do. It will be better someday, I promise, but I won't lie to you. It won't be right away."

She said with chilly calm, "I have no need for it to be better. As long as it hurts, my Dima will be alive in my heart. But I do not need to make a spectacle of my feelings for a houseful of his relatives. They are my feelings, mine alone, and Alex's." She went silent. "They think I am cold, but they know nothing. If I could, I would crawl into a bottle of vodka and never come out."

I'd never seen Natalya take a drink and she was generally critical of anyone who liked it too much.

"For now, I am angry and that keeps me standing. Standing up? Will keep me going. Later, later, I can go to pieces."

I hugged her. What else could I do?

She shivered. "He has a second job, Dima. Had. Had a second job. Did you know? And sometimes he went straight from his night job to breakfast out and to his day job at school. So I did not think anything, when he was not at home this morning. Then. I stepped out to see how the weather looked. He was there." She pointed. "Right there. Lying there, all crumpled up, my Dima. I found him. I screamed. I ran to him." She shuddered. "I knew when I touched him. People came, called EMS, but I knew." A long shuddering breath. "I am like an ice statue now, frozen at that moment. You know? Except I still see…"

She lifted her head from my shoulder at last, and looked at me with a fierce expression. "The police came, they talk, they say no chance it was an accident. As if I did not know that. Someone put a bullet in his head and left him here, at home, so we could find him. They ask, those cops, did he have enemies? Only one. I told them to start with his no-good brother."

She gestured at the house. "They don't know I said it. Oh, they would be angry. The good name of the family. Mama's darling baby boy. Dima worked himself to death for all of them and they care more about baby brother. That…that…" She ended with a string of Russian words. I didn't need a translator to know they were curses. "I have no one here now, no one, only my Alex."

She pointed to the driveway which was dominated by a black Mercedes SUV that made the house look even older and smaller, and made my own car look like a tin can.

"My brother-in-law, the big shot with the big shot car and no job. We have our guesses about where that came from, but no proof. Dima tried, he tried so hard, he did everything…brought him here, tried to get him to go to school."

"That was Dima, wasn't it? He took care of everyone. He had a big heart."

"Mine is not so big, but I learned from him. But with this one, his own brother, nothing, nothing worked."

A young man wearing a slick black leather jacket walked from the house, keys in hand.

Natalya jumped up, walked right up to him and shoved him in the shoulder.

"You have some nerve, coming here!"

"What?" he said, holding her arms to prevent another shove. "What? My beloved older brother is dead and I should not come to comfort my mother?"

"Don't put on your act with me, you lying sneak. She's fooled, but I am not." She struggled out of his grip.

"Natasha, Natasha," he said softly. "Dima is gone. Is it not time to let go of the past?"

"Do not call me by a pet name. You have not the right. Get off my property now!"

He chucked her under the chin, and said softly, "You cannot keep me from my mother." He stepped back and added, "You know I will be back."

"You can take your mother to move in with you—oh, you wouldn't like that so much, would you?—but I can and will keep you out of my house." She said it in a soft voice that was so furious it could have been shouting. I could hardly believe this was happening in her driveway, in front of me and any neighbor who happened to be on the street.

He just got into his car and backed out so quickly his tires squealed. She went from red and furious to white and collapsing, sitting on her porch steps, head on her knees. I sat down beside her, my hand on her arm.

"Natalya, what is it? How can I help?"

"My Dima is gone, and this—this—is what I have left of him, this rotten brother." She wiped tears off her face with a furious movement of both hands.

She stood up and stumbled her way back to the front door, moving blindly, groping for the doorknob.

I thought I had better go with her, but she stopped herself at the door, wiped the tears from her face, and tidied her hair.

"Thank you for sitting with me, Erica. I am in control of myself now. I send everyone home and Alex and I must have some sleep. My cousin the doctor left us some pills for sleeping without nightmares."

"Natalya, I am so, so sorry. Can I do anything else for you?" It was dawning on me that though she was surrounded by family, she seemed to be lonely.

"You know. You know! You understand. If I could just talk from my heart..."

"Any time."

She nodded, wearily, looking as if she had already taken a pill.

"I will call you soon, when I am thinking a little clearly. More clearly."

She closed her eyes and then snapped them open again. "I will send your kids out now, and everyone else too. We have had enough, Alex and me."

She turned back to the house, straightening her back and curling her hands into little fists.

Just a minute later my passengers came out and got in the car without a word. They looked stunned. This was the only silent ride I'd ever taken with Chris and her talkative friends. Usually they sound like little birds, chattering away.

The silence was fine with me. My thoughts kept chasing each other around, past and present colliding over good men dead too soon. I thought of the Natalya I had seen tonight when shock and grief had ripped the doors open on the side of her she kept tightly shut. I knew a woman who was witty and adventurous and playful, in love with New York, in love with fashion, passionate about her husband and her child. She kept the doors tightly closed on the dark days in her life.

When we were back in our own house, Chris hugged me hard, turned and came back for another hug before she went to her room without a word. In the morning she flew out the door, late as usual, and I settled in to work at home. I would call Natalya later, I thought, but now she would be sleeping. I hoped she would be sleeping, blessedly oblivious for many hours. Thank goodness for sleep meds.

My plan was to do my own work, chain myself to the computer, and make some real progress. Not think about Chris or Dima or Tiffany for a few hours.

The only flaw was that Tiffany was thinking about me. Not really Tiffany of course, but his fans. My work e-mail had a badly typed, all caps message from Dr. Flint, insisting I return to Green-Wood to collect the information he still needed. He wrote: "IF SIND TODAY, CAN STILL UES. FAX TO HOTL? ASAP" Evidently he did not realize I could send it all digitally. I also noticed there was no "please" anywhere in there.

Young Ryan was also very definitely thinking about Tiffany. And me. He was contacting me every five minutes with questions that ranged from panic about Flint to background about Tiffany. Maybe it only felt like every five minutes, but it was enough to blow my concentration into confetti. By midday, I gave up. I was going to make myself unavailable.

I would go back to Green-Wood but I could keep my phone off. With any luck, I told myself, I could calm both Ryan and Flint, the power behind the curtain, by going to see the window we had missed the other day.

I was glad to have a little time to myself. Today my own memories of my husband came flooding in. It took me by surprise, after all this time, but I knew it was set off by Dima's death. After a while, I stopped seeing the stones and the mausoleums and only thought about my Jeff dying in a park kind of like this, under the trees.

I'd met him at my best friend's Sweet Sixteen barbecue. To this day, he comes back to me with warm summer nights, the radio playing "Heaven is a Place on Earth," and the smell of grilling hot dogs. We were deaf to all concerns from my Jewish parents and his Italian ones. We knew we belonged together.

Brooklyn girls are nothing if not tough.

After the accident, I remade my life and in the process I accidentally became a scholar. When I went back to school to become a high school teacher because I thought it offered a better future for us, my professors encouraged me, and I got some fellowships, and then I started a PhD program at City College. Now I go to museums and antique shows—for fun! And I read scholarly journals and even understand them. I have fallen into a life that my Jeff didn't even know existed, a bigger life in some ways, and I am fine with it.

Yet some days, I'd give it all up—everything I am now, everything I have—for just one summer night in the back seat of his battered Toyota, parked at Rockaway Beach with the sound of the surf rushing in and out.

As I reached the hill I didn't know if I was crying for myself or for what Natalya would have to live through. She would, though, just as I had. If Brooklyn girls are tough, Russian women have backbones of steel. Still, I would not tell her I still miss Jeff.

One more bend in the path brought me to the crumbling building I could not get to see the other day. A tall metal fence, now rusty, and a small garden, now filled with overgrown evergreens and weeds surrounding it. The elaborately wrought gate was open, hanging on its hinges, and the caution signs were gone, so I went right up the front steps, walking carefully over the broken marble. I pushed on the massive bronze door, gently at first, and then harder, until it finally squealed and slowly opened just a crack. Just enough.

I was assaulted by a damp, musty, moldy odor before my eyes had even adjusted enough to see anything. The light was dim, coming through a great rear window that had not been cleaned in, I guessed, decades. How strange to be in a chapel like this for the second time in a few days, when I had never even been near one before.

There were two marble benches and a carved marble altar. Or was it, actually, the sarcophagus for the people who had built this memorial? There were some memorial tablets on the walls, but they were too dirty, and the light was too dim, for me to read them. Certainly they were in memory of the rich people who intended to establish their social position in death as well as in life.

I turned to look at the great window. It was far too grimy to have the glorious effect it should have, but where the sun pierced through the dirt, brilliant rainbow fragments of color splashed across the dingy marble floor. I could see chips and scrapes around the frame, some ugly scratches in the dust on the glass, some bending of the leading.

I looked up and up, as the window rose at least six feet above me. I could not make out what was depicted—I really would have to ask to see a reproduction—but it seemed complex and dramatic. Repeated patches in shades of blue suggested maybe a lake or river, or perhaps it was the sky.

One side wall was plain white plaster now grimy and cracked. On the other, there were wooden boards covering an empty space. So that was it, all the problem from the other day. A window was broken? Or removed because it was unsafe? Could the metal frame have become weakened, or rusted? I had no idea, but I knew someone who might. I would call him later. I was curious now. Ahhh, maybe someone was hurt when it fell out.

It was fascinating but also a little creepy. It was not the presence of death, which after all is what a cemetery is all about. It was the sadness in this neglected building, once so elegant and now so deteriorated. Or perhaps I had brought the sadness with me. I pulled out the list of needed photos from Dr. Flint and completed the job as quickly as possible.

I was happy to return to the brightness and warmth of the outside world. I shivered and sucked in a few deep breaths of fresh air before I struggled to pull the heavy door back in place. A brisk walk back to the cemetery entrance helped to clear my head. A helpful young staffer at the visitors center—I knew she wasn't twelve but she looked it—did find a photo of the dimly seen window in an elegant and expensive book the museum would have to buy for me if they wanted me to have it.

It was not the Biblical or mythological scene I was expecting but a spectacular river view, the Hudson with the cliffs of the Palisades on the western shore. I'd know it anywhere. A shimmering brilliant blue sky reflected in the blues of the water, there were multiple shades of green forest in the foreground and dark storm clouds off in the northern distance. It was a scene from a museum, from the great Hudson River paintings of Cole or Bierstadt, and just as breathtaking in glass, even in the small book illustration.

There were no bridges or cities or even the small villages that hug the riverbanks. There were no Iroquois longhouses either. The sole sign of human life was a small three-masted ship under full sail and heading north, upstream. The tiny flags in the picture were too hard to see, but the text told me it was Henry Hudson's ship, the *Half Moon*, claiming this land and this river for the Netherlands. As a historian I had to be charmed, though it seemed pretty odd for a memorial chapel. It resembled the brilliant but somewhat cloying religious window of the other day in nothing but its art.

The missing window on the side depicted a harbor with tall ships and canoes, and a windmill in the background. I recognized it immediately as New Amsterdam.

The caption in the book explained that "the chapel was built by Cornelius Konick IV. Konick Avenue and Konick Park are named for him. He was a descendent of one of the earliest Dutch families. They owned substantial property in Flatbush and had a country estate near where the Tappan Zee bridge now crosses the Hudson River." Of course. That was Tarrytown, right in the middle of the old Dutch settlements. It was Rip van Winkle's storybook home; Tappan Zee itself is a Dutch name.

I wondered if the thunderclouds were a reminder of Rip van Winkle and the magic game of nine pins that caused the thunder. And then I wondered if I wasn't getting carried away by my imagination.

The book didn't tell me anything else, but with a name and a picture, I could certainly find out more about who he was and what happened to the family. The Dutch theme in the chapel window suggested pride in their ancestry but it seemed that old Mr. Konick's money had not insured that he and his ancestors would be remembered here. I could use the museum library for this. And then maybe Dr. Flint would forget about me for a few days.

My job was important to me for a long list of reasons, but Dr. Flint was not my job, not really, and events in my life were looming much larger right now. I needed some breathing space.

The shop was almost empty but the helpful young girl at the register was being monopolized by a young man who seemed to be annoying her. I dropped off the book she had given me and left, anxious now to get away.

Chapter Four

I pointed myself home. I could scan the photos to Flint from the local copy store and then the plan was crawl into my burrow and catch up on my own work. Chris had after-school plans; I had a good long afternoon. And I did it. I glued my backside to my desk chair and my fingers to the keyboard, and by the time my eyes finally started to blur, I had a good piece of work done. Saved. Backed up. Sent to my adviser.

As I started to stretch, find a snack, warm up a mug of coffee in the microwave, I was free to think a little about my job, the demanding Dr. Flint and smart-but-clueless young Ryan. I still resented the way I had been arbitrarily reassigned to work with them—what was I, a piece of office equipment? But I had to admit it: Our project, the Maude Cooper letters, was going to be interesting.

Not so much, the errand running to Green-Wood Cemetery. So, there had been an accident. Evidently a window had become loose in its frame and removed. Was it broken? Did an accident suggest someone was hurt? As long as I was admitting things to myself, I admitted I was curious. And I did know someone who could maybe explain to me what I had seen there. My friend Joe knew everything about old buildings, old houses, old crafts. He renovated nineteenth-century houses for a living.

I left a message. "Are you free for dinner? I need to pick your brains. I'm buying the pizza." A second later, I had a text.

"I have a free hour around 6:00. Does that work? Mushroom and pepperoni."

Just like that, I had dinner plans.

Joe and I connected originally when I needed some very basic, essential work on my new (old) house. We became biking buddies. He did a large renovation for me years later, when I had come into a bit of money. Chris has adopted him as an uncle, which seemed right. I thought of him as the older brother I never had.

He arrived at my door along with the pizza delivery. He paid and laughed at my protests.

"You still have that problem with your garbage disposal? I'll fix it right now, while you tell me what's on your mind."

While he lay on the floor and took a pipe apart, I described my two recent excursions to Green-Wood. "Weird, isn't it? I live ten minutes away and I've only been there once. Now it's taking over my life. Anyway, here's my question. I would like to know what I was looking at today. If I tell you how the windows looked, would you know what happened?"

"Aha! I've got it now." Two turns of the wrench and he sat up. "Maybe. I've done a little repair work on windows—so many houses around here have stained-glass for trim—but I'm no expert. However, I do someone who is. We'll throw it at her if we have to."

He washed his hands and we attacked the pizza. I put out a couple of wine glasses and cheap, leftover red wine from the refrigerator. He made a face, asked me how long I'd had the wine and helped himself to a beer. He knows my kitchen as well as I do. Maybe better.

When I had described everything, showed him my dim photos, and we'd made serious inroads into the pizza, he shook his head. "Not a clue without seeing it. Maybe not even then, but I think my friend might be around tonight. Eat up and we'll make a visit." He looked at me with scrutiny.

"What else is going on? This didn't make you look so stressed."

I finally poured out the news about Dima. I know my voice shook.

"Damn. Damn, that sucks. I know the guy. Knew him. You introduced me one time. Remember? And then he got me to do some work at the school. Helpful, smart, nice. I like him—liked him—a lot."

"Everybody liked him. Everybody. Except his brother maybe." I told him about my encounter with the apparently evil relative. Poured it all out—my visit to Natalya, Natalya's conviction that he was somehow involved, and then I stopped myself. "I'm sorry, I'm just babbling away."

"Babble anytime." He patted my hand. "That's what friends are for. What are you going to do?"

"Be a friend to Natalya, help Alex any way I can. It's hard enough just to be fifteen. I have so much on my own plate, but hell. I can't possibly not think about them."

"Don't forget I have big shoulders. There's one for you if you need it, while you're sharing one with this Natalya. Is she normally a little crazy?"

"Not at all. But she's sure entitled to crazy right now. Her world just smashed into little pieces. Normally? She's a little sharper than Dima. I don't mean smarter but more prickly. You know. Sarcastic, cynical. But fun."

Joe was smiling at my words, laughing at me.

"What? You think that's what we have in common? What nerve! Okay, maybe. A little. Yes, I appreciate her sarcastic humor. But Dima? He was the kind of person who took care of people. When she was little, he knew Chris didn't have a father. And Chris and Alex were best friends, so he just included her and then thanked her because he didn't get to have a daughter."

I found myself crying, and Joe wrapped me up in a big bear hug.

"Pretty tough, isn't it?"

"Mmm—hmm. And nothing compared to what Natalya and Alex are feeling."

He went on hugging me.

"Thanks. I'm done for now." I moved away. "I guess I needed that, but I can't turn into one of Chris' drama llamas."

"What now? Ready for a quick outing?'

"Okay, yes. And thank you."

A short drive in Joe's van took us to the area around the notorious Gowanus Canal, being cleaned up but only in fits and starts, and the crumbling industrial buildings around it. We went into one, rang a bell and a rickety industrial elevator, probably an antique, took us to the top floor. It opened directly into a huge room with open space and floor-to-ceiling windows. Once it was a place to make anything from paint and ink to concrete to flour. Now it's a place to make art. Stained glass in various stages stood up in frames or lay on big tables, tools I couldn't even name were scattered about, and tucked into a corner, a desk and files made an ad hoc office.

A tall redhead in work clothes came out from behind the cabinets and hugged Joe. "It's a nice surprise to have a friendly face this time of night. Two friendly faces?" She eyed me with curiosity. "What can I do for you?"

Introductions were made, and I explained.

"That is so intriguing. And you have some photos? Let me take a look." She motioned us over to the large lamp attached to one of the work tables. I gave her my phone, apologizing for the poor quality of the photos.

"Yeah, looks like they did something, and obviously took out that window, but no idea what happened. It could be a needed repair, like the framing was working loose. Or, it could be serious damage, like shattering. Yeah, I see the marks on the other window frames. Maybe checking to see if they were still safe?" She leaned back in her chair. She had long legs in dark leggings.

"The funny thing is I haven't heard anything about a big piece of work going on there. So maybe it's not as big as it looks. We're not such a large local crowd—experts in stained-glass restoration—and you know, with something that old and important, they'd have to go to an expert. These hippie hobbyists with pretensions just wouldn't be up to the job. Seems like I might have picked up news." She looked puzzled. "Is this something important to you?"

"Not exactly. It was just a passing thought. I've been loaned to do some work for a real difficult guy, and that's information he'd, uh, let's say, appreciate having. He's a Tiffany expert named Flint."

She grinned. "Dr. Thomas? Oh, yeah. I took a class with him one time, getting a little art history background on glass to go with the craft skills. Flint difficult? Hell, yes. So, you're a friend of Joe's?" She looked back and forth between us. "I could make a few calls tomorrow. See what I can pick up."

"That would be great! How can I say thanks?"

"Spread my name around your museum. They have glass, and I bet people ask them for referrals too. My bread and butter—and rent and manicures—come from restoration work. My own art isn't steady income."

"I'll do my best. Do you have brochures?"

"Sure do, and let me show you around, so you know I know what I'm doing. Over here is my own work." It was dramatic, angular, almost Picasso-like, a long way from Victorian architecture.

She saw my surprise. "Yes, I personally go for modern abstract, but this one over here is a restoration piece. Not my own taste, but bills get paid and it's an interesting puzzle, getting into the original maker's head."

I would have sworn that one came right out of a Victorian church, with its long-haired angels and shafts of sunlight. Then again, what do I know about art, stained glass or otherwise?

We made our good-byes, and thanks again, and Joe whisked me home.

"She's a great girl. I know you'll hear from her."

"It would certainly help my servitude to Dr. Flint, I think, if I did something to show I am capable." I gave him a little jab. "And how do you know this tall and lovely expert?"

I was amused to see him turn a little pink, but he only said, "She worked on a job for me."

I laughed, thanked him again, and went in to find Chris just coming to the front door.

"Did you have company? I see pizza boxes."

"Joe stopped in, and then we went out for a bit."

"I missed him? He should have come in."

"We didn't know you were home."

"And what is this all about, may I ask? Are you finally taking my advice about him?"

"Oh, please. Really. Just because you found that boyfriend at camp last summer, now you think the whole world needs to go two by two."

"He is not 'that boyfriend,'" she said with great dignity. "He has a nice name. Jared, in case you forgot. And I do not think everyone needs to be coupled up. Just you." She giggled at my indignant exclamation, and then said, "Come on, Mom. I just think you need more of a life."

"I have a life. I have school, work, you."

"That's not a life. And Joe is nice and fun and really pretty hot for an old guy. He seems able to get along with you."

"As friends. As a friend. That is all. And I don't take advice from a fifteen-year-old."

"Sure, sure. Friends. Ha." She gave me a hug but I suspected she was laughing at me. "Now I am going to get to work." That brief exchange was enough family closeness for her. "I need to start my family history project."

That truly responsible comment took me a little by surprise.

"Well, good for you. I forgot to dig out my folder on our family—I'm sorry—but I'll do it right now."

She hesitated before saying, "Umm. I decided to do Dad's family."

Her dad's family? When she first talked to me about this assignment, she thought she would research my family, all those Jewish great-grandparents who had come from somewhere in the Russian Empire before World War I. I could have helped. I had the names of the towns, some of the stories, a family tree. I could have helped a lot.

She doesn't remember her father but his picture has been on her bureau every day of her life. His parents, much older than mine, had been dragged out of the old neighborhood, protesting all the way, into a two-family house with their daughter who lived in Buffalo. Chris hardly knew her widowed grandmother.

She was looking away from me when she said, "I called Grandma Donato to ask her some questions."

"You what?"

A relationship with her grandmother was a good thing in theory, but in practice it was hard to maintain. There was too little face time and too many phone calls that included weeping for her lost son.

And today Chris sucked up her courage and called her on her own?

She saw my face. "Yeah, well, I hadn't talked to her in a while. And it seemed like a good idea to do it when I actually had something to talk to her about. She had a lot to say, too. I took notes."

This felt like a minefield to me. Of course with a fifteen-year-old, anything can become a minefield in the blink of an eye. If I didn't ask too many questions, would she tell me what I wanted to know?

"Well," she said. "Well…" She was silent a minute, then added, "I just felt like…I did have a dad…even if I don't remember him…and I wanted to…I don't know…feel like I was connected to him. Alex said last night, his father would always be a part of him, no matter what."

Ah.

"Maybe I'll go see Grandma Donato? Grandpa said he'd drive me to Buffalo when I have a long weekend. What do you think?"

More minefields. "But Chris. When I suggested you do that in the summer, you acted like it would be a punishment. Remember? You said you'd die of boredom and get fat because Grandma would make you eat all the time."

"Oh, yeah, I did, didn't I? She probably will, too. But I can handle it. I am much more mature now."

"Since the summer? Oh, sure. I also don't completely understand this sudden thickness with Grandpa since he moved back from Arizona."

She stared at me. "I missed him and I love having him back. And you should try to get along better with him!"

"What?" The unfairness of that stung. "I do try, but he never stops telling me what to do. And by the way, I missed him, too, when he was away, but it was his idea to go out there, not mine."

"Yeah, yeah, I remember. You were mad at him about it." She stood up. "I have homework to do." She gave me a hug, combined with a pat on the back. "So now that he's back, get over it, okay?"

Then she was gone, leaving me to wonder who this wise young lady was, and what had she done with my real daughter. I wanted to pursue these touchy matters. Then again, I didn't.

The next morning I brought two egg-and-bagel sandwiches to work and claimed to be too full for the second. I offered it to young Ryan who looked underfed and unhealthy, and he wolfed it down as a special favor to me. Yes, whatever else I am, I seem to be a mom at all times. A Jewish mom at that, with Italian in-laws. Feeding children is in my DNA.

I described my excursion to Green-Wood and he said he'd like to come along if there was a next time. Cemeteries got his imagination going, and this was a famous one. He pulled up some disturbingly weird photos a friend had taken there on Halloween last year.

And he was impressed at my idea of sorting out what was really happening with the missing window.

"Dr. Flint loves to be on the inside of everything. He loves it. Even if it turns out there is nothing to be inside of, he'll love you for helping him be in the know." He nodded vigorously. "Smart move."

Properly fueled, we went to work, Ryan scanning art, me reading letters.

Maude Cooper wrote home every week, and sometimes more often. I was now well into her second year in New York. While Ryan researched the other objects in the box, I was seeing and charting the progress of her life.

Maude started taking on small complete projects and promised to send home gifts. She included more sketches, with lovely tulips streaked with flame-like contrasting colors, some watery landscapes, some attempts at designs for forest animals. I could make out a graceful deer, a pheasant, a beaver, or perhaps an otter. I passed the illustrated letters to Ryan to scan and enlarge.

She still loved her work and her life, but the letters had a more mature perspective. Now she expressed surprise that there was occasional pettiness and jealousy in the studio:

> Some of us have become good friends, and chat and giggle over lunch like schoolgirls, but there is one woman who seems to resent anyone who is young. She certainly dislikes me. And my two best companions have warned me that if I have an elegant design idea, not to share it with a certain other person. She has been known to "borrow" them and Miss Driscoll is not aware of that. I thought it would all be good fellowship and helping other women to succeed—there are so few of us here—but it is not always so.

She described her first exciting visit to the Tiffany factory in Queens:

> The men there do not like to work with women, I have been told, but under Mr. T's eyes and Miss Driscoll's, they were most mannerly. They showed me the frames they are creating for the work.

Ah, I thought. Young Maude has discovered office politics. Someone back home must have responded, because in the next letter she wrote:

> I know, I know. Human nature is what it is. I do my best work, treat everyone respectfully, attend church every Sunday, and have faith that I will succeed. In fact, I have been invited to accompany Miss Driscoll and Mr. Tiffany (!!!) to call on a client next week. My role will be to take notes and observe and learn. Miss

Driscoll said I would not say a word, except "How do you do?" when introduced. I promise I will write every detail!

Maude sketched a new spring ensemble, with a lacy bodice and the stylish puffy leg of mutton sleeves, and joked that her own mother would not recognize her on the street, she was now so *au courant*. Then she added that this was French for "in fashion." She thanked her mother for making her learn to sew.

The design is borrowed from the pages of *Harper's Bazaar*, but the creation is a Maude Original. That is the secret of couture on a budget. I wore it to an art exhibit and it was much admired by friends. And when I was unexpectedly introduced to the famous artist William Merritt Chase I was relieved to be well-dressed. It gave me the confidence to converse with him for a few moments. I told him I would be honored to be one of his students at the Art Students League. It felt very bold!

Harper's Bazaar? Really? Way back then? I made a mental note to take a look at one. I had no scholarly reason; I was just curious and amused. William Merritt Chase? The name sounded familiar; I must look him up.

She wrote of her interest in learning how to use a bicycle, the current craze for both men and women. "Truly, Mama, it can be done in a perfectly lady-like fashion."

And then she returned to her visit to a client:

This family has commissioned a major work. I can't tell you a single word more than that, as the client wishes it to be confidential. He seems to want to spring it on his social world as a surprise. I know it seems foolish, as you don't know anyone to tell—and you never would betray me!—but I must respect Miss Driscoll's word on this. They are Society people with a capital *S*. Their home is large and luxurious, but not a thing I saw in it is as beautiful as Mr. Tiffany's decorative work. (Surely I am biased, but their style is dark and heavy, only meant to impress, and entirely lacks the charm of a Tiffany design.) The wife is your age, Mama, most elegant and really rather scary. Here is a sketch of her ensemble. I know you would like to see it.

In the margins there was a matron in rich violet dress, with elaborate pleating and ruffles.

The husband was there as well, and he was—you must immediately forget I wrote this!—quite pompous and proud, very sure of what he wanted and not much interested in Mr. Tiffany's suggestions. Mr. Tiffany took it well; he is accustomed to persons such as these. I myself have only seen them at the opera, dressed in evening clothes and furs, sitting in the boxes, while I proceed to the uppermost balconies.

A younger man, a son, came in while we talked and made a few intelligent comments on the drawings that were being presented. He spoke only to Mr. Tiffany but when his father was being particularly pompous he—standing behind him—winked at me! I was so surprised I almost disgraced myself by giggling.

So that was my excursion into the world of Society. Interesting, but I prefer the livelier and more interesting people of my own world. It was hard to breathe there.

Her mother must have commented critically, because she wrote back in a later letter:

But I am far more excited about bicycles than fashion or gentlemen, in any case! I intend to do this, dear Mama, and you must not worry. I have a friend who will teach me, and I will practice in safe places until

I am truly confident of being on the streets. It is the
most exciting thing and everyone is doing it. I will
send you a picture postcard that shows the masses of
riders in the park on a Sunday.

In our records database I indicated every letter that discussed
the Tiffany studio, because those details were the most important in the scholarly sense, or so Dr. Flint had insisted. To me,
it was all fascinating, a vivid portrait of a vanished world and a
personality I was getting to know and like—my girl Maude, a
New Woman of the brand new twentieth century.

My fascination was certainly slowing my work, but I didn't
care. I couldn't wait to find out if she learned to bicycle, and
who the friend was who taught her. Was there a resolution of
the thief issue at the studio? What was this issue of the men at
the factory? To me, it was better than a novel.

But I would have to wait for now, because the phone was
ringing. It was Natalya's number. I took a deep breath and reluc-
tantly, purposefully, shifted my mind from Manhattan, 1904, to
Brooklyn, here and now. Another deep breath before I answered.

Chapter Five

"Erica, I hate to impose, but please? If you could? Cops will be here soon to ask many questions. I do not know if I can...so soon...maybe my English quits...my poor Alex is not here... could you maybe come?"

Yes, I could. I could hop on the subway and be a block from the beach in half an hour. Yes, she should not lean on Alex. No, I did not want to do this right now, or ever, really, but I would. There was nothing wrong with Natalya's English normally, but what would happen under stress? I noticed the other night that her accent was stronger.

The thing is, I know cops. My dad's bum knee kept him out of the force but I had relatives, neighbors, some of dad's best friends. My late godfather was a retired detective. I would be a good person to hold her hand today. I needed to work, but maybe I could catch up tonight, Chris and me doing our homework together around the kitchen table.

We used to do that when she was younger. Now we'd be in separate rooms.

I hustled along the neighborhood main drag to Natalya's, walking under the elevated subway tracks, past the grocery stores, cafes, and nightclubs with signs in the Cyrillic alphabet, looking for Natalya's corner.

They call it Little Odessa now. It used to be a community of tiny summer bungalows for sweaty city dwellers hoping to catch an ocean breeze or two. Air conditioning ended that. The bungalows have long since been winterized and turned into homes, but the beach is still there, boardwalk and all, and the community had become home to many thousands of Russian Jewish immigrants when the Soviet Union started letting them leave in the 1990s. To them it felt a little like home, like the famous seaside city back in the USSR. Little Odessa.

There was a car in front of Natalya's home, an anonymous American-made vehicle, unmistakably a detective car to anyone who knew. Natalya looked pale and exhausted. Introductions were made, my presence was explained. There was a man and a woman, dressed in business casual, anonymous-looking clothes; I knew the jackets they wore with their tailored slacks covered their guns. Officer Henderson was a medium-sized guy with a firm yet kind voice and nice clothes, and Officer Rooney was a chunky, fortyish woman with an air of suppressed energy and a great haircut.

We sat in the small front room, which was dominated by a wall-size modern entertainment center, as in many Russian homes, and many family photos.

Natalya chose a seat with her back to the photos, but I looked at them from the other side of the room. Alex's birthdays. I remembered some of those. Natalya and Dima's wedding, in Leningrad way back when, looking absurdly young. A family trip with Niagara Falls in the background. I wanted to get up and look more closely. Chris was probably in some of the birthday pictures.

I had missed the beginning of the interview. Rooney was saying, "...so he checked in for his night job but then, very late at night, around two a.m., the card-reader shows he used his access card to open the gate and go out again. Was that normal?"

"No, no, I don't think so. Perhaps—I don't know—he left to get coffee? But I fixed him a thermos when he worked at night."

"They told us the rules are that the watchmen remain on-site for the whole shift. Was your husband someone who would just ignore that? Was he a rule-breaker kind of person?"

Her look was pure hostility. "He was the most responsible man alive. Never would he have walked away from his job."

"Could he have been meeting someone?"

"At two a.m.? Who? Who would he be meeting then? Up to no good at that hour? I should throw you out of my house."

"Mrs. Ostrov, please…" The nice man spoke softly. "We must ask these kinds of questions to do our job. We all have the same goal, right? To find the killer. We truly do not intend to upset you." He saw her angry glare and added quickly, "Or insult your husband's memory."

I moved over to sit next to her and poured her a glass of tea from the pot on the table.

"I am…not myself…" She sipped. "I will try to answer more questions better."

"You won't like this one either, but we must know." The detective smiled apologetically. "Did he have any enemies? Was he in a dispute with anyone? Fight with a neighbor? Any kind of deal gone wrong?"

"Yes." She said it firmly. "I told other cops. One enemy only, his brother, Vladimir Ostrov. Look, just go look in your police records. You will find him there, I think. He is no good, and he fought Dima all the time. You think someone did this? Who else could it be? Look at him." Her voice rose with every word; then, when she stopped, she seemed to shrink back into her chair, exhausted.

"I promise you were are doing that. We will know everything about him, large and small, that can be known. But we can't rule out the idea that this is a message from an experienced criminal, like a gang. It does look like that."

"Like I said," she muttered, "Volodya—no honest bones in his head."

"Volodya?"

"Vladimir. Volodya is the family name, like I am Natalya but Natasha at home. I forget American word." She covered her eyes with her hand.

"Nickname? Mrs. Ostrov, please try to stay with us. We know this is hard, but everything you say will help us find the guilty person."

"I know. I know." She shook her head as if to wake herself up. "Go on."

"So, given that this looks very deliberate, again we ask, what was he involved in?"

"My Dima? Just what he was supposed to be—family, work, home." Her eyes suddenly opened wider. "You think because we are Russian, he must be 'involved' in something?" Her voice added the quotation marks. "All Russian are gangsters? Ex-KGB scum? Like Italians and godfather?" She made an angry gesture. "Oh, please! What…what…Erica, I am so upset, I forget my English. I need a word."

"I think you're doing just fine with your English. Do you mean stereotype?"

"Yes, that is the one. Dima only tried to do right, and make a good life here. Like most of Russians. Like most people. Give me broken leg."

I patted her hand. "I think you mean 'Give me a break.'"

"Yes, that one."

"All right. We'll accept your word on that." In my mind, I heard that the unspoken end of his sentence was "…for now." I wondered if Natalya heard it too.

"Was he okay with your neighbors? Any disagreements, quarrels, bad blood?"

"No! I tell you, again, he was friends with everyone. Shoveled snow, loaned tools. Planted flowers, all neighbors together. Everyone will tell you."

He smiled. "They did tell us. We have people canvassing the street, asking if they saw anything, and asking a few other questions."

She leaned forward, alert.

"Did they? Did someone see something? I never heard anything at all, I sleep like log, my Alex, too, but someone, someone must have. Someone knows."

He almost looked pitying.

"One person said he heard a car, speeding, about three o'clock, but did not get up to look. He said kids speed on this block many nights."

"Are you at dead end? Please tell me no. I need to know why this happened. Even if I know who, I believe that, but not why."

Henderson said, "We can easily tell you it's not a dead end, because it isn't. Not even close. Yes, in a more perfect world, we'd have a plate number, too, but it doesn't end there."

"Mrs. Ostrov," the woman detective smiled at her, "we appreciate your time this afternoon. We will just make sure we have everything we need about the morning when you found him, and then we'll go. We know you were asked before, but one more time?"

"I got up. I went to door to get paper. He was there on lawn. That is all."

"What did you do then?"

"What do you think? I ran to him. I rolled him over to see his face, and there was blood and wound in head. And I screamed. I knew already, as soon as I touched him."

"And then?"

"Neighbors came, and Alex came out. They called 911, but I knew." Her voice shook. "I knew. They took him away, the EMS, and we went into house, Alex and me and some neighbors."

'So did you hear or see anything at all in the night? Think hard. A sound of any kind? Did you have a minute of waking up?"

"Not one thing. I slept all night. Alex, too. I heard him tell other officers."

I thought that the neighbors and the EMS team had probably destroyed any evidence that might have been left on the lawns. Footprints, tire tracks. They looked at each other and nodded. "Can we talk to your son? And then we can go."

"Alex? No, no, no. He is not here now."

They did not respond but exchanged glances. I was pretty sure if they wanted to talk to Alex, they would talk to him.

"Thank you, and again, please accept our condolences."

Natalya seemed lost in her thoughts. I walked them to the door. They turned to me.

"Let's make sure we have your name and information correct, in case we want to follow up. And how long have you known the family?"

"Mmm, at least ten years. Our children were in kindergarten together and they've been friends ever since."

"What do you really know about the victim? Seriously. Is there anything you know his wife doesn't, or won't say to us? Gossip, questionable friends, anything at all?"

I shook my head. "He was a good man. I mean, that's not just the grieving widow speaking."

Detective Rooney gave me a skeptical look. "Everyone has secrets, you know."

"Well, I don't know Dima's."

"What do you know about this Vladimir, the brother?"

"Nothing at all. I met him for the first time the other day. He seemed very, um, hostile, but then Natalya was hostile to him, too."

"What? You've been friends for ten years but you never met the brother?"

"Well, we were friends first because of our children, and we grew to like each other, but we…we had different lives also." I felt defensive, even though I had nothing to defend. "I always thought that for Alex's sake, they made his school life with his friends, and then a separate other life, with the family and the community. I heard about relatives, I mean, I knew they had some, but Natalya mostly didn't combine us. Oh, and also, when the kids were younger, he was still in Russia. I had no idea there was so much bad blood."

Rooney shook her head. "Family feuds. They're the worst, aren't they? I hate getting in the middle of them, but we'll take a hard look into this one. If you think of anything later, contact us."

They both gave me cards and his name registered for the first time.

"Detective?" I spoke to the man. "Your name is familiar. I wonder if I went to school with your younger brother? I knew he had an older brother at the police academy. He used to say…" I smiled, remembering, and went on, "Uh, forget that. Kenny Henderson?"

He broke into a broad smile, the first I had seen. "You know Kenny? My baby brother? You went to Lincoln?"

"I did. Kenny was…"

"Yeah, I know. Kind of a knucklehead in those days. He was a real pain to me about having a brother who was a cop. Believe me, I can sympathize with the victim's younger brother problem. Hard to believe, but he's an accountant now, married, kids, big house in Bethpage. How 'bout yourself?"

"I hate to break up this reunion, but we…" Rooney tapped her wristwatch.

"Very true. So maybe I'll call you sometime and we can catch up? Man, Kenny is gonna laugh. Who were you then?"

"Erica Shapiro. Ask him if he remembers junior year chorus?"

He grinned. "One more crazy Kenny story? I'll ask. I don't know how any of us survived his teens."

I went back in to find Natalya and met Alex coming downstairs. So he was home, and Natalya was lying to the cops. Protecting him, I thought.

Mom-like, I hugged him. "How are you doing, honey? Are you sleeping at all? You look like you've been up for days."

He seemed surprised but he didn't quite step away. "I could sleep, I think, if my mother could, but she is the one who is not sleeping at all. All night, it seems, she is up pacing." His Russian accent broke through under stress. Normally he talked American teen-speak, like every one of his friends. "I hear her feet. Doors open and close. Lights go on and off."

"Does she wake you up on purpose?"

"My mother? No, no, never. She says, 'You are growing boy, you must sleep. I am fine.' But she is not fine and…" He shrugged. "Then she sleeps on sofa during day."

"I get it." I did. I knew. I remembered. "Is she talking to you?"

"No. She is protecting me, I think, but she talks on phone. I hear." He smiled, sadly. "I think maybe she is forgetting I still know Russian. She talks to people, late at night, and she wants… she wants…"

"What does she want? If you tell me, maybe I can help somehow?"

"A lot of it is old times, old stories I know, familiar things. But I know she is not just sad, you know? She is very, very angry. She wants to know what happened."

"Do you?"

He shook his head. "My father is gone. Nothing brings him back. Police will figure it out, I think, and then I will care. For now, my worry is my mother. I am not little school boy, you know? Now I am man of the house, but I don't know how to help her. She only wants answers."

I had a sharp flashback, across all those years, to the time when I believed that knowing exactly what had happened to my husband would somehow make me feel better. When I wanted to see the man at the wheel of the car, and shake him and scream at him. I was sure it would make me feel better. Then I did see him, and he went to jail, and it didn't change a thing. Of course I was looking for a reason, a way to make sense out of something that made no sense.

But Dima had been shot. It was different. Someone was responsible, not just fate or chance or the wrong lineup of the stars. There was a reason and it could be found. Or should be.

"You talk to me whenever you need to. Any time. You got that?"

He nodded, grinned just a little.

"And you tell me if you see a way for me to help, okay?"

Nodded again.

"Now I'll go say good-bye to your mother."

He turned back to the stairs, and I found Natalya in the kitchen staring at a plate of pastries. She gestured at the platter. "People brought them to me. You eat, my dear. I am…" She made a face.

"Thank you. I will. But are you eating at all? You must."

"I know, I know. Everyone says, but I could not care less about food. I need…I need…I don't know what. Not food."

I nodded, chose the largest pastry, cut it in half, and put one half on her plate.

"What do I do now?" Her eyes filled with tears. "He was a lovely man, my Dima. Now I have nothing. Tell me please. Tell me how you go on." She stopped suddenly. "I am so sorry! I know, I always knew you lost your husband. I heard, but you never said, in all these years of friendship, and I did not want to intrude. I am so sorry."

"It's all right. I never talked about it before, because, because…it was back then, in my old life. And I met you in my new life. How do you say 'Oh, by the way, new friend, my husband died at twenty-six.' It was easier to just be a single mom, and no one dared ask about the story."

I took a deep breath. "I have to answer your question with another question." She smiled faintly. "Did I have a choice? I had Chris. And you have Alex."

"Yes, yes, I have my Alex. If not for him, I would be walking right into that ocean over there with heavy stones in my pockets." She paused. "After, that is, I see the right person gets what is coming to him." She sighed, a long shaky breath. "But then, after that, I will have to live for Alex. He is Dima all over, a good man."

"Would it be a comfort to talk to me about Dima? He was so good to Chris and me. Or is it better not talk about him at all?"

She shook her head. "Not talk about him. Not now. Not yet. I will need to cry if I do and I have no tears left. You talk. Tell me about your husband. If you would. If you don't mind."

I didn't mind so much. Now. There was a time I could not talk about him at all.

"He was my high school sweetheart, a neighborhood kid just like me. We got married when he graduated from the fire department academy and I had two years of Brooklyn College. Chris was a honeymoon baby. I was twenty."

"You said that one time. You were so much younger than most of us mothers in their class. We wondered."

I added quickly, "We were thrilled. Too young and dumb to know any better, I guess. Our mothers babysat so I could finish college and start teaching. We planned that we would have more babies while we were still young enough to enjoy them and he would be promoted and I'd be a full-time mom. I never—well—I never thought past that. Never, in those days. We were happy...." My voice faltered. "We were happy. Then..."

"What happened? Was he...was it from a fire?"

"Nope. He was off that day, and got hit by a drunk driver. It was as stupid as that. He was riding his bike in Prospect Park on a beautiful summer day. Just like that, it ended, my life as I knew it."

"Oh, my dear."

"Yeah. Chris was three. After a while, reality kicked in. I would have to support us, so I went back to school. And now here I am, and a long way from the old neighborhood and Chris almost grown."

I looked at her and added gently, "So you see, life has to go on. Not right away, and not the same, and not easily, but I can promise that you won't be right here where you are now forever. I swear."

She blinked hard, held my hand so tightly I thought it would break, then whispered. "I understand with my mind. But, you know, I don't believe it at all, in my heart."

"You don't have to believe it for now. For now you just need to get through each day. No, no, I mean, each minute, just putting one foot in front of the other."

Her fingers released mine and she picked up the pastry I had cut.

"Dima did not like the drama scenes. He would be telling me to get a grip." There was the ghost of a smile. "He loved the American expressions Alex taught us. 'Get a grip' and 'too much information' and 'chill.' And 'dude.' He loved to say that. He was trying to get his English better, so he could pass his licensing exams. He was an engineer, you know. He could do anything technical here but his reading English was not so good."

"Where did you meet him?" She seemed to want to talk about him after all. "Here? Or there?"

"University. In Leningrad. Just kids, like you." She smiled faintly, again. "We had good jobs there but Russia is hard now— different from hard under communism but still hard. A mess. And always no good if you are a Jew, whoever is in charge. I had no family, and his was moving here, bit by bit, and we wanted better chances for Alex. So we came."

Her eyes filled with tears again. "Now I have no one here for me. His mother. His sisters. And his no good brother. That gonif. You know that word? You know Yiddish?"

"A few useful words. Donato was my husband's name. My people were Jews from Poland and Romania. It means thief."

She nodded. "I could say even worse, in Russian, and in Yiddish too. But that will do." She reached for another pastry and ate it, and I thought, I have accomplished one thing here, at least.

Late that night I found Chris on the living room floor, surrounded by photos, boxes of old photos next to her, crammed with the pictures I had never had time to sort or put in albums.

"Honey? I thought you were doing homework."

She just gave me that irritating blank stare.

"Seriously?"

"They asked us to bring in pictures of Dima. So it's still schoolwork." She looked up at me. "It's harder than I thought."

"I'll help."

"I didn't mean finding them. I meant, it's so sad."

"I know. I'll still help."

So we sat together and trolled for photos of us with the Ostrovs, at birthday parties and picnics and outings, a couple, two cute kids, and a single mom, forming a friendship based on our children. I helped Chris figure out where and when the unlabeled photos were taken, mostly by the size of the children.

They were taller when they rode camels at the Bronx Zoo than they were at the Halloween Walk in Prospect Park.

And after, when Chris returned to her homework, I took the boxes, and while my hands automatically sorted the jumbled photos into neat stacks by subject, my mind flew backward, remembering. It was too painful to think of Dima now, but I thought of Natalya. Natalya, then, and Natalya now, as I had last seen her, because I knew her Before. She would never be that person again.

Here was Natalya, pants rolled up, wading into the waves at the beach, holding hands with both children and laughing. Here she was at the children's zoo, pointing to the penguins and clowning, pretending to shiver. The children were the ones laughing in that one. Natalya standing on her head and demonstrating cartwheels at the park, the day we went to a small circus. Chris remembers that day and Natalya teaching her to do a cartwheel too.

Here was the day the children looked around the zoo on their own, always in our sight, while we sat and talked. And Chris and Alex came running up saying, "We saw a skunk! Ew, ew, ew." And then immediately said to each other, with bravado, "Let's go back!"

I think one of the children snapped that wobbly looking photo of us.

That was the day she told me a little about their move from Russia, how she and Dima had not even had long discussions. How it was in the air, and on the very same day, they just looked at each other and said, "No more. No more. Now is the time." That's all she ever told me about it. But that day I saw a toughness come over her face. I knew that was the side of Natalya that brought them here, but she only pointed to Alex, and smiled. "For him." Her smile grew. "For him, it was all worth it." She used to smile a lot.

Chapter Six

Life has to go on. In my mind, I wanted to make fun of myself for thinking in clichés, but yes, really, it does. That is what I had been telling Natalya, and that is the truth. My mind might be fogged with sympathy, and further fogged with my own memories, brought to the surface by Natalya's tragedy, but Chris still needed meals, my advisor still needed me to edit some pages, and my boss still needed me to be nice to Dr. Flint.

My boss had confirmed this was my job for a few weeks. Maude's story was still calling me. Chris was yet another puzzle, as usual. And Flint had dashed off another incomprehensible e-mail.

The question wasn't: Does life go on? The question was: Which puzzle do I work on first? Today it was Dr. Flint's marching orders.

> "At Gwood talk to dr. Reade, use my name. photos no good. MUST HAVE detils. TODAY. Us beter camra. Ryan help. RE ltrs. Getting all about Tf? most crutchel!"

Ryan confirmed this was not a feeble attempt at text speak. It was Dr. Flint's inability to type.

I gave in to the highest power, looked up a phone number, and called Dr. Reade, noting her title was director of art and history. Not exactly the same as assistant to an assistant. I wasn't intimidated, not really, but I did start right off with the biggest gun and explained we worked for Dr. Flint. The voice on the phone said, "Give me one moment," and returned.

"Dr. Reade is extremely busy today, but will make an exception for Dr. Flint's work. She can spare a few minutes for you after lunch. Say, one-thirty?" She explained how to find the office, I took notes, and then I went back to my work. Later, I glanced over at what Ryan was doing, and then looked again.

He was cataloguing and digitizing the fat file of working sketches. Maude had drawn the same object from different angles, and in different colors. Some were pencil; some were watercolors. Most were easily recognized Tiffany designs, the flowers and butterflies and peacocks that said Tiffany anywhere, but today the designs up on the screen were a little different. They seemed to be forest animals. A graceful deer, a wild turkey, something furry that might be an otter or a beaver. It looked as if she wasn't sure and was trying out both. I thought they looked oddly familiar, even though they were not Tiffany's signature designs.

"You wait right here. Leave them up."

I scrambled through the stacks of books on my shared desk to find the one I had used at Green-Wood and borrowed from the museum library. There it was, the Hudson River scene from the Konick chapel. And under leaves on the shore, there was a family of turkeys and deer peeping out.

"Look at this! This is what I saw the other day. Look familiar?"

Ryan's eyes opened up wide and we shared a real smile. I think it was the first smile I'd seen on his face.

"The boss is going to love this. That is freaking cool. You sure it's the same?"

"Ah, no. Not sure. The angles are different, and then this is so small. Are there any dates on the sketch? I'd like to see if we can match it up with anything in the letters."

"No, no dates. She numbered them when they were a series, but that's it. "

"You know what we need to do?"

He nodded. "Field trip. Go see those windows for real, sketches in hand."

"How convenient, we already have to be there later. Let's go do this now. Pack up the sketches and for God's sake, do it carefully."

He gave me the same look Chris would have. The one that says, "Thanks for the advice, cause I'm an idiot who would have done it badly otherwise." He didn't say it though. I'm his boss, sort of, not his mom.

The subway to the cemetery is one of the slower locals. It is slow, but that gave us more time to discuss what we needed to do. Ryan was carefully clutching the envelope of sketches the whole way. Good. An ounce of paranoia prevents a ton of problems. That was an old saying I made up on the spot.

I remembered how to find the Konick chapel, but Ryan couldn't resist a little sightseeing, and we had enough time to make our walk a leisurely one. And I couldn't resist a little sharing.

When I pointed out the elaborate chapel, and told him it was available for weddings, he said, "A wedding at a cemetery? That is so awesome," and he took off, camera phone ready.

Walking briskly I soon found myself walking up Battle Path, which is not a fanciful name. An early battle of the American Revolution had been fought and lost here, the one when Washington famously said, "What brave men I must lose today." I knew some of them were buried right here where they fell, long before it was a cemetery.

And there was Ryan, waiting for me at the foot of the impressive bronze memorial to the fallen soldiers. I touched his arm and pointed. "Look out over there. This is a statue of Minerva and she's saluting her sister, the Statue of Liberty, out in the harbor."

"Minerva, huh? That seems right. It's the Roman name for Athena, the goddess of war and civic life, both."

I must have looked surprised because he flushed and said, "Mythology comes up a lot in the comic-book world."

"Okay. Now move your mind from Mt. Olympus to a Brooklyn factory. This statue was the dream project of Charles Higgins, who made a fortune manufacturing India ink."

"No way! I used that ink a million times. Funny, you never think about if there was a real Higgins. India ink built this goddess? That's kind of…I don't know…"

"Yeah. Incongruous? And how surprised do you think those colonial solders would be, if they could see this great big golden statue built in their memory? They were simple men, mostly—farmers and tradesmen."

We looked around, finding it hard to move on. The view was seriously spectacular. We could see out over a mile or two of city streets, right across to the water and the great harbor. The endless space of the sky and the water brought with it a kind of peace. If there were ghosts—and I don't for a minute believe in them—the colonial solders had quite a view of the city they helped create. They were indeed resting in peace, I hoped. Ryan sighed deeply.

One more bend in the path and a slight walk downhill brought us to the crumbling building I had visited the other day. We went up the front steps, stepped carefully over the broken marble, and looked at the massive closed bronze door. I pushed it, gently at first, and then harder, but it did not budge. When Ryan stepped in behind me, and leaned in, it still didn't move. This time, it was locked up tight.

"I don't get it. It was open the other day. We can't do our job if we can't get in. Damn. We'll take it up with this Dr. Reade, that's what we'll do. Let's see how far Dr. Flint's name really takes us!"

I didn't know if Ryan got the sarcasm but I thought I saw a tiny spark in his eyes.

"I'm exploring anyway, now that we're here." He went around to the other side, where we could see the massive main window, the small side window, and the boarded-up area. Meant to be seen with sunlight coming through, on the outside they were a blur of dull colors and grime.

"If I climbed up that fence, I'd be high enough to look in."

"What? No, you can't do that! The fence doesn't look any too sturdy, you could get hurt or you could damage it. Either way, it would be…"

I should have saved my breath. He was already pulling up to the top of the wrought-iron fence.

"Ya, I can see in."

"Is it useful?"

"Nope, windows are too dark and dirty. Complete waste." He leaped off the fence, landing neatly on his feet with no obvious damage.

I repeated to myself that I was not his mother and there was nothing I should say.

We turned toward the admin building, discussing what we wanted to say to Nancy Reade. And how to say it appropriately. I explained carefully to Ryan that showing the exasperation we both felt would not get us results, no matter how satisfying it would be to express it. Good advice that I gave myself. I needed to be the one setting a good example. Even if I didn't want to.

I led us toward the entrance. As we walked along I pointed out a gravestone to Ryan. "Did you grow up in New York? If you did, you should stop here and say thank you to this ghost."

He looked at the name, and baffled, said out loud, "Frederick Augustus Schwartz?" and then, "Hey, I get it. It's F. A. O. Schwartz?"

"The very one. He brought a lot of joy to a lot of generations of New York kids, including my own. There's another ghost over there, though I guess he was responsible for equal amounts of joy and despair in Brooklyn."

"Carl Ebbets. Ebbets Field? That Ebbets? The Dodgers?"

"Before my time, of course—it's always been the Ebbets Field housing project to me—but my dad used to tell me about it."

And how odd was I becoming anyway, to be sightseeing in a cemetery?

Yet I was not alone. Though I assumed this was an off-hour of an off-day, to my right were a few people laying flowers at a clean new stone, reminding me that this was still a working cemetery as well as a place of history, and to my left a group of young people walked, stopping to take notes, while an older man talked and gestured. A class, obviously.

We were still too early for our appointment so we went into the tiny, crowded shop. Ryan announced he would be back and purchased a map. He blushed when he spoke to the cute young girl at the register. Lord, he was so young. His aggressive style of clothing made me forget that.

I already knew there was nothing there I both needed and could afford, so I merely watched.

Some of the student group were perusing the art history books, discussing Upjohn and LaFarge and neo-Gothic styles. Some of the tourists were looking over the guidebooks, debating which ones offered the best photos. "Bernstein," one older woman said firmly, "I must have one of Leonard Bernstein's grave."

The very young girl at the register looked overwhelmed.

Ryan had gone outside and now a young man was in heated conversation with the salesclerk. He looked like an ordinary young man, medium height and stocky. He had stylishly gelled hair, dark jeans and t-shirt and sneakers neither especially trendy nor especially sloppy. He looked familiar; I thought I had seen him here before. He did not look like a weasel but he sounded like one. I couldn't quite hear the words, but I heard the tone—pushy and wheedling. I could tell he was annoying her, perhaps trying to get a phone number.

I stepped up with an extremely firm, "Excuse me. I need to complete my purchases." It was my look that said, "If you aren't buying, get the hell out of my way, idiot."

He stepped aside and she threw me a grateful smile while she rang up the random postcards I had snatched up. A few of the students were now right behind me, and there was no space in line for someone loitering.

I joined Ryan and we were off to our meeting. The modern administration building was ground-hugging, set into a low-lying spot on the edge of the property, well planned to not intrude into the historic setting. We were greeted by a security guard at the front desk, signed in, and got visitor badges. It seemed like a lot of security for a cemetery. I wondered if they were plagued by terrorists or criminal gangs looking for drugs? I whispered the thought to Ryan, who appeared to appreciate my snarkiness.

Then we were there at the right office, being greeted by the tall blonde I remembered from my visit with Dr. Flint. She was not as welcoming to us, peons that we were, but she seemed more harassed than hostile.

"I do truly only have a few minutes today, and I stole that from more important problems, but Thomas and I go back a long way. Just what is that he sent you to do?"

"He needs photos of some Tiffany windows. Apparently they are crucial for a presentation he is doing."

Her look was incredulous. "He wants that? He is such a fussbudget." Boy, was that the truth.

"I was here with him a few days ago and one of the buildings he wanted to see—the Konick chapel? Or is it mausoleum?—was closed, so we skipped that. When he sent me back I was able to get in and took some photos he finds inadequate."

"As I said, fussbudget." She sighed.

"So now I am back, with Ryan here, who is his assistant. We found the door locked! Dr. Flint told us to talk to you, so we already had this appointment. And thank you for that, by the way."

She was a shade paler when I finished, and a shade more frazzled. Her words were poised but her voice was not.

"Ah, the Konick mausoleum. Yes, there was a…a…badly needed repair for one of the windows. In fact, I am dismayed that you were able to get into the building at all. It has been off-limits all week. Give me the time you were there. I must have security find out how that happened."

She jotted a note on the pad in front of her.

"Was there danger in going inside as I did?" The question was a devious attempt to find out what happened there.

Ryan surprised me by jumping in. "So can we see them or not? I looked at the window from outside but it didn't mean a thing. One window is gone and I couldn't see anything of the other. And Dr. Flint especially wanted me to redo the photos because he thinks I know how he likes things…" Ryan trailed off after that last confusing sentence, then came back with, "If you know what I mean. And yes, he is fussy."

He stopped abruptly, red-faced. It was a long speech for him.

She took a deep breath and said very carefully, "We removed a window because the frame was looking very insecure. We wanted to take care of it before there was real damage to the glass. Or, of course, before someone was hurt. That is all. And no, you cannot have access to it now. We are, um, concerned about the other windows and are testing them for safety." She swallowed hard and ended, "I am sorry not to oblige Thomas, but that is all. No access until the work is done."

"When will that be?"

"We do not know. These kinds of things are unpredictable "

I remembered my visit to the stained-glass studio and had an idea. "That missing window? Is it somewhere we could see it? Is it here? Or a local studio? Even is if is down, we could get a look, see what Dr. Flint needs? It would only take a minute."

She stood up quickly. "That is impossible. And I must ask you to leave now. I already have another meeting scheduled for right now. "

We had no choice but to stand ourselves. Ryan surprised me again. He looked right at her and said, "I still don't see why someone couldn't escort us into the mausoleum. We only need a few minutes." His eyes darted nervously, but he held his ground. I guessed he was more afraid of Flint than of Dr. Reade.

I brought up reinforcements. "We could pass-on your help-fulness to Dr. Flint and he would certainly thank you and any boss you'd care to name." I smiled, I hope reassuringly.

"Impossible to both requests." She was shooing us toward her door. With a final smile as fake as any I have ever seen, her last words were, "I am truly sorry."

We founds ourselves in the corridor, Dr. Reade's door firmly closed behind us. We walked and talked.

"I don't get it. And I don't know what to tell Dr. Flint. He's, uh, kind of used to getting what he wants."

"Very strange. Very. I have no idea what's next. He'll just have to manage his speech without those details. Do you think they were actually that important?"

"Doubt it. He is a fussbudget, just like the lady said." Ryan's voice and expression were equally gloomy. "But he will have a fit."

"Stop." I looked up and saw that we were in a strange corridor, nowhere near the lobby as we had intended to be. "We are lost! There's an exit arrow up ahead."

We turned, followed the sign, realizing that the building was a circle plan around a small garden and we had gone the long way around. We passed offices relating to the cemetery business, and then offices relating to the historic landmark function. Something that looked like an archive, with steel shelves and acid-free storage boxes. I certainly knew those. And another that was filled with metal files, color-coded. A door that said, Chaplain, a sign pointing to Chapel. Another to Maintenance Services. At last we found ourselves pointed toward the lobby.

Chapter Seven

"Hey!"

Someone in the parking lot was calling me. He came closer, talking as he came. I recognized him as the annoying young man in the gift shop.

"I see you going all over here. You went into the admin building, and I saw you the other day with some of the bigwigs. I couldn't get a thing from that kid in the shop, but you must know something."

"I know lots of things." His attitude brought out the smart aleck in me. "I don't know that any would interest you."

I looked around for Ryan. He was absorbed in his cell phone.

"Aw, come on! I'm just trying to find out what happened here, and I bet you do so know. You look very connected. And people have a right to be informed."

Me? Connected? Oh, sure. I almost laughed, but now I was curious myself.

"Oh? How do you think I can help you? "

"Something happened here. They're trying to keep it quiet, but I know there was something late at night. Why don't you just tell me what the story is?"

"You were harassing that nice young woman in the shop, weren't you? I saw you with her the other day, too."

"What, harassing? I was just doing my job, asking questions. I was explaining to her why it was a good idea to talk to me. Quid quo pro—that means one hand washes the other."

"I know what it means."

"I could give her a quote, or a shout out and she could put it on her Facebook page. Tweet. It's in her interest, you know. That's what the press does."

Something about him repelled me. Maybe because the shop girl wasn't much older than Chris. Or then again, maybe it was because it had been such a tough few days and I was spoiling for a fight. With anyone. About anything.

"Your job? Really? Let's see a press card." He thought I was a big shot? I would act like one.

"Press card? Please. That's so old school. I'm a reporter on a news blog, Brownstone Bytes. We cover everything about the brownstone neighborhoods on the 'Net. Like the old *Brooklyn Eagle,* only for the digital age. We're an important news source."

"What nonsense," I said in my best no-nonsense, big shot voice. "I have a friend who actually worked on the *Brooklyn Eagle.* He'll laugh himself silly when I tell him about this. Important? Not bloody likely. More like self-important."

"Aw, come on. You were here that morning. You must have learned something." He put out a hand to take my arm. I shook it off. "What exactly happened? What did you see? And hear? Can I get a photo?" I would have laughed at how dense he was if I had not been so annoyed.

"Am I speaking Hungarian? Go. Away. Now!"

He smiled sheepishly, shrugged, backed away still talking. "Big mistake. Someone will talk to me and it will be someone with no reason to be careful. Believe it." He tossed a card at me and said, "Think it over" as he left.

He was a joke. Really, he was. The only flaw in my analysis was that, yes, he had provoked my curiosity. He was so very sure something newsworthy had happened here. I was told it was an accident. So what beyond that could it be? Always assuming there was anything at all. Someone was hurt? Something valuable was damaged? And how annoyed would Dr. Flint be if we did not get him the inside story? Again, assuming there actually was one.

When Ryan came back to me, phone in hand and looking rather ill, I put it all out of my mind, at least for now.

"There was a message from the boss. He's demanding to know what progress we've made and he's on the warpath. And we are way behind! I feel sick."

So I was not the only person who thought Flint was a little scary. I reminded myself that I was the grown-up here.

I said calmly, "Don't worry. What is the worst he can do?"

"Fire me. Fire you."

"Don't be silly. He doesn't have the power to fire me."

'You don't know how much influence he has!"

"Not that much. Not for the pittance the museum pays me. And why would he fire you? It sounds like he needs your skills as much as you need the job. Maybe even more. You said people kept quitting on him." He brightened up just a fraction and I added softly, "Maybe you need to remember your own value."

He only grunted but it was a more cheerful grunt, if such a thing is possible, and we didn't say another word all the way back to work. He was lost in his thoughts, and I was concentrating on how we could pacify Dr. Flint.

I thought Flint might approve of an interview with Ms. Skye, especially if I actually learned something useful. Should I take Ryan? That preoccupied me the rest of the way back. I didn't intend to exclude him. On the other hand, I didn't want him scaring the already skittish owner of the letters.

Back at the office, we quickly divided the fat envelopes of letters. We went back to our workroom, tidied up, made notes as needed, then he left, I left.

◇◇◇

When I got home later, Alex was sitting on the top step of my front stoop. He looked sad and cold as the fall evening temperature dropped.

"What are you doing, sitting on this cold concrete?"

"No one home." His teeth were chattering. For real, not as an expression. "Needed to see you."

"You get right in here, and I'll have something warm for you in a sec."

Chris not home? Where was she? I couldn't remember. I had to check my calendar. Nothing. Phone? There was a message I had not heard. She would be home after dinner. Stayed at school library to work.

"Mrs. Donato...I..."

I had been Erica to him since he was six years old. He was really rattled.

"Not a word until you warm up. Grab that afghan on the sofa."

I microwaved milk on High, added chocolate syrup and stuck a cup into his hands, probably scorching his fingers. He gulped it down.

"Better? Now talk. What are you doing here?"

"I found something." He struggled to get the words out. I didn't know if he was still freezing, had burned his tongue on the hot milk or if it was the distress I could see so clearly in his eyes. "I came to you—you said I could. Did I do right?"

His sudden look of uncertainty went right to my heart.

"Yes, you did." That was the only possible answer, no matter what he meant. "How can I help?"

As he took his left hand out of his jacket pocket, I realized he had kept it there the whole time. Was he hurt? Was it a weapon?

It was a cell phone.

"Alex?"

"Not mine. My father's."

"And?" Come on, I thought. Maybe I should have given him coffee; he was having trouble even talking.

"Not his usual phone. My mother has that, or maybe the police now. I think...this is a secret. I found it...."

"Alex! Talk!"

He seemed to swallow hard, shake his head, square his shoulders.

"There is a drawer he has, with old photos and an old camera. I was looking there." He turned red. "Not snooping. I thought

Mom might like any pictures left in the camera. I missed him. I am man of house now." The dazed expression came back.

"This I found. Not his usual cell number. Not a dead old phone either. So do I tell my mother? But what if…" He shrugged. "I don't know what, just I think it is secret."

Stall. That's a lesson I had learned over the years, sometimes painfully. Stall and think.

I made him another cup of chocolate milk and added a plate of cookies. They were old, stale, supermarket brand. He powered through half a dozen without even seeming to notice.

Finally, I said, "Don't you think this might be evidence and the detectives need to have it?"

He nodded. "But there is no news from them. Are they doing anything at all? I want…we must…find out about my father. I need that and my mother needs that. So what if they just throw this back in a drawer and do nothing? And my mother? I don't want her upset. What if…?" After a long silence, he went on. "I don't know. What if my father has a reason for a secret? Something my mother should not know?"

"Perhaps this is just a backup phone, with nothing sinister at all."

"I thought that, yes. Maybe yes. I thought I could call some numbers, find out."

"You didn't! Oh, Alex, that was not a good idea."

"Well, so what? I did it. But then I did not know what to say so I hung up again."

I pulled out a napkin, wrapped my hand in it, and opened the phone.

He leaned over my shoulder as I hit Contacts. What popped up was mostly a list of businesses. "Joe Hlavik and Sons, Plumbers." "Lightning Electrical." "Costa, Pete—see Venice Ironwork."

Just what you would expect from a man who worked as a custodian and lived in an old house. At first glance I did not see anything alarming, like women's names or dating services. Alex might be too young to leap to that idea but a secret phone certainly set off alarms in my older, more cynical mind.

"Alex, this has to go to the police. You shouldn't be trying to solve this. What would your mother say if she knew you were meddling even a little?"

He sighed. "You know she would have a fit. Maybe two fits." He sat up a little straighter. "She thinks I am still her baby, but she needs me now. I will deal with this, find the people he listed and find out who they are and what they know. I will do it. You can help me figure out what to say." He picked up paper and pencil and started a list. "I must keep calm. And sound like an adult, my deeper voice. How is this?" He lowered his voice absurdly. "I start with the ones I do not know."

"No." I put out my hand and covered his, pencil and all. "You really can't do this, Alex. I know you want to find out, but no, absolutely not." He raised a blank face to me. "Someone killed your father. Don't you realize you might run across that person? Or a friend of his? It's not a job for a kid."

"But I am man of the house now. My grandmother said." His expression was less certain than his words. "I must."

"Nope." I stepped up, full on, as mom-on-the-spot. *In loco mater* or something like that. "Hand me the phone. "

He curled his fingers up around it.

"I'm not kidding. Hand it over."

"I need to find out. Since I found this, I think, maybe I did not know my father at all."

"And what would happen to your mother if anything happened to you?"

"Oh." He gave it to me.

Alex had given in now, but I had no doubt he'd try again if he believed he needed to. I accepted at that moment that I would be asking questions myself, to make sure he didn't.

"Cookies for the road?" I poured the rest of the box into a plastic sandwich bag. I added a peanut butter sandwich.

"I…thank you. It is, this is…it is a bad time."

"Of course it is. Hugs for your mother. Now head home before it gets any later."

I did a right thing first. I found the card Detective Henderson had given me, and called him. I didn't reach him so I left a detailed message about Alex's discoveries, and asked him what I should do about getting it to him.

Then I did a wrong thing. I opened the phone again, and looked at the short contact list. I wrote down the names and numbers. I don't know why. At the back of my mind I thought Natalya might want them somehow, someday. And I have an instinct also, part of my work, to want information to be recorded and filed.

I looked at the phone. It was a cheap ordinary model, I thought. No buttons for games or photos or fancy apps. It made calls, took messages, texted. I didn't see the icon that said Messages Waiting.

I pushed the button that would give me the greeting. Dima's voice came on, a little scratchy but definitely Dima. "If you are calling about 16 Brighton 4th Street, leave a message."

What? That wasn't Dima's home.

That was it. No "Hi, it's Dima." No "I'm busy but I'll call back." If you didn't know who you were calling, you certainly wouldn't find out when you called. I wondered if that was deliberate, or if Dima was just awkward with the technology. It was very odd, and it suggested to me that I take another look at the names.

Most were as straightforward as they seemed when I first looked with Alex. One was listed simply as V. I wondered if it was Dima's brother, the scary Vladimir. One said Loan. A bank? Without taking the time to think about it, I tapped the button. Instead of a recorded cheery female voice telling me I had reached the desk of So and So at Citibank, it was a man, not at all cheery, saying "I'm not here, I'll call back. Don't leave a message." That was even stranger than Dima's greeting.

My heart was beating a little too fast, and I suddenly realized my curiosity was leading me down a road where I had no business being. I put the phone into a plastic bag and into a kitchen drawer.

What remained out was the list of names and numbers. I put that away in my desk for Natalya or Alex, if they needed it. Or if I did.

Where did that thought come from?

For now, the question was Chris. Exactly where was she and when would she be home? And what responsibility for her well-being did I have tonight? I would not be able to give any further attention to this problem after she was home.

A quick call established the plan that she and Mel would go to Mel's house for dinner, and continue working. Chem exam tomorrow. I was fine with that. More than fine, because I had an idea, and I couldn't follow through if she was home.

I called the person who knows everything about buildings.

"Hi, Joe. I was just wondering if you have a couple of free hours this evening."

"Lucky timing. Someone canceled an appointment. Is this social or do you have a house emergency?"

"Ah, you could say that, sort of, but it's not mine."

"Got it. I'll be there in fifteen."

That secret phone meant something and I wanted to know what. The cops would figure it out, but their priority was not going to be protecting Natalya or Alex. If I knew what was going on, maybe I could prepare them. Or protect them somehow. I knew it was fuzzy logic, but I could not think more clearly until I knew more.

Battling traffic all the way, Joe and I were there at the mystery address in only about twice as long as I expected. Listening to music and chatting about crazy customers and life with a teen, we had a comradely drive.

The location was in Brighton Beach, as I expected, not very near the Ostrovs' home, but not very different, a tired brick house on a tired but well-kept, homey street. The houses were just barely freestanding; they were separated by the width of the shared driveway that led to garages in back. Lights were on in the nearby homes, and there was an occasional passerby on foot or by car. I heard a TV from the house on one side, and voices from the other. A child's voice was complaining "Spaghetti again?"

"This is the mystery house? Right address? Come on, let's take a look. You'll find a flashlight in the glove compartment."

Joe focused it across the official papers pasted on the window and I tried to read by the wavering light. Using the beam as a pointer, he said, "The work license goes to the contractor. See it? And here is the owner? What does it say?"

"It just says Ostrov Construction."

"So Dmitri was doing the work. Does it show this address? It should be the place where the work is being done."

"Yes, address is here."

"The permission should say what he is and isn't allowed to do. Can you see that? No wait. Hold the light a sec. Keep it steady here." He reached into his jacket pocket to take out his phone, and used it to snap a photo of the paper. "Now you don't have to remember it all."

I kept reading, learning that he had permission to convert the house to a three-family dwelling. Three apartments to rent out? I guessed it could be a nice source of extra income. The paper also said what kind of work could not be done. Various kinds of concrete, as much as I could understand it.

"I thought it would tell me who owns it. "

"No, not here, but there are other ways. I'll tell you later." Joe was peering in the window as he spoke. "Come here. See over there? That's new wiring in two walls, and I see supplies for more." He moved the light. "Sheetrock. That would be next. See? Unfortunately for us, he has the house locked up tight, smart if he is storing materials there."

We walked around to the back, following the light along a humped and cracked cement walk. There was a back door with a short flight of metal steps. It was padlocked, but Joe could see in the window.

"They haven't started on this kitchen. If they are going to make apartments, they'll be adding more kitchens, too. Every-thing here is about fifty years old, but I see lines and arrows penciled on the wallpaper—that's about fifty years old, too—that shows where they are planning to install new appliances and cabinets. Damn, I wish we could get in."

He wiggled the padlock and tried the window without luck. "I could do it if I had my lock picks."

"Wait. You can pick locks?"

"Sure. You'd be surprised how often keys have disappeared in old houses." He smiled. "In this case it would probably be completely illegal."

"Probably? *Probably?*"

"Who are you kidding, Miss Nancy Drew? You'd do it if you could, but it's not gonna happen tonight. Now I'm going to fight through that jungle of weeds around to the back of the garage. Looks like there's another window there. Wait here. I'll be right back."

Alone, I jumped at a shockingly loud noise on the quiet street. I whipped around and saw a man on the lawn next-door. He was hammering a sign and I could have touched him across the narrow space. He looked up suddenly.

"What the hell are you doing at the Grossbergs' house?"

"I…I…I'm just looking for…"

"Are you working for that damn Russki?"

"What? No. I'm…"

"Because it's bad enough having his crew here. All day with the pounding and sawing and jabbering away. I'm telling you, I don't plan to put up with it at night."

He was an elderly man. No, an old man, in a sleeveless undershirt and gym shorts and bare feet. Not a pretty sight, and not enhanced by his hostile expression.

"No, no, you can see I'm not working. I just wanted some information. Maybe you can help me?"

He glared at me and I probably glared right back.

"You from city planning? Someone's finally showed up?"

"Umm, not exactly. I said, I'm just looking for some information."

"Yeah? Who are you? Speak up, I don't hear too good. Are you from city planning like they promised?"

"No…"

"I want to make a complaint about that Commie, I got a lot of complaints about him, that guy. The Grossbergs, now they were decent neighbors. Shoveled the sidewalk in winter and kept to themselves. I wish they wouldn't have moved."

"I don't understand."

He tossed his cigarette into the shared driveway. "Russians took over this whole damn neighborhood, ya know. Damn Commies, all of 'em!"

"Well, actually, most of them…" It's a reflex of my work, sharing the facts.

He rode right over my words.

"They killed my old Brighton Beach a long time ago, ya know, and I lived here my whole life. Well, except for the Army. Walk along Brighton Beach Avenue and it's all Russian. Ya go in to a store to buy underwear or a box of cereal or something and they just ignore you and keep up the Russian jabber-jabber. Now they're buying up my own street." He spat over the porch rail, "That one." He pointed, "And that one. And now right next door. Next freakin' door to me. He's gonna fill it up with more Russians. I been having some little confabs with the planning department about all this."

I looked at his sign. "Are you planning to sell, too?"

He moved away from his sign with a grand gesture. It said: Commies Go Home. Not Wanted in All-American Brighton Beach.

"Hell, no! Hell no, never. But I can speak up." He grinned. I did not like that grin, not at all. Actually, I wanted to slap it off his hateful face.

"Ya know, maybe I'll just make it easier and call Immigration. Bet you they'd like to know about this. Never should have let them in the first place."

"Mr.—uh, your name is…?"

His expression suddenly shifted from belligerent to crafty. "I'm not giving my name out without you do likewise. I want to see some kind of ID! How do I know you've got a right to be standing there?"

"So don't tell me. I don't care." I had his address; I knew I could find his name if I wanted it. "But come on, you must know they're here legally. And they for sure do not love Communism. Why would you…?"

"Sez you. Most of them can't even speak English. And rude! They don't belong here. Who needs them, taking over from us Americans?"

I knew—really, I knew—there is no point whatever in arguing with someone who didn't want to be confused by the facts. But I also knew the influx of Russian immigrants had revived a dangerous, dying neighborhood. I was only writing a dissertation on these issues. So I argued. I couldn't resist nailing him to the wall.

I folded my arms and looked hard at him. "Yeah? I'm just wondering, where did your people come from?"

"What? What do you mean, my people? I'm pure American through and through."

"But where did they come from? Every family came from someplace else, sometime. Unless your background is Iroquois and I'm guessing it isn't." I had a pretty good hunch, but I wanted him to say it.

"I was born right here, in my parents' apartment on Neptune Avenue. Spitting distance from where you're standing. And I'm proud of it. Did my share in the war and fly the stars-and-stripes too. "

"And your parents, or grandparents?"

"What's it to you?"

I shrugged and said nothing. I waited.

He threw me a venomous look and finally ground out the words. "Mostly Ukraine. Yeah, part of Russia in those days. Yeah, Russia. But they were different kind of people. They knew they were lucky to be here. Ya know? These new Russians, they think everybody owes them help when they get here. And they still think they're better than us. And as soon as they have a few bucks, boy do they throw it around. Nightclubs. Fur coats. Me, I've never been in a nightclub in my life."

I thought about how hard Dima worked to keep his house meticulously maintained. The carefully painted wood trim, the rose bushes, the new flagstone terrace he laid and the smooth driveway he poured. I looked at this man's home, with the cracks in the walk, the broken window, the missing bricks. I knew who I'd prefer for a neighbor.

The old man was escalating his rant. "I don't know who you are, young lady, but you can take it for a promise. I'm never gonna have them for neighbors. Not never!" He was nodding now. "That guy moves in next to me with all his friends and relatives? He'll be sorry."

He leaned back on his heels, arms folded, glaring right at me. He'd settled the matter to his satisfaction.

"Hey, buddy, did we surprise you? We don't mean any harm." Joe finally came back from his trek through the weeds. He strolled over to the angry man, smiling, and offered his hand. The man looked it over with hostility and then put his out. Only then did I see he had a gun on the other hand, holding it casually, pointing down.

"I'm a builder myself. Here's my card. I heard this property might be on the market soon."

The old man's face changed. There was some skin wrinkling that might have smiled.

"You thinking of buying? You'd be welcomed. No one likes those damn Russians. And you'd be getting a good deal too. I knew the people before. They took good care of it."

That was an obvious lie. Everything about the house was cracking and peeling, the kitchen hadn't been touched in decades and I was betting the bathrooms were just as bad.

"Confidentially..." He leaned down over the rail, looked both ways as if afraid of being overheard, and whispered—"the new owner died. Something messy. I bet the wife would turn it over for way under value, if you moved fast on it. You know, while she's still not thinking straight."

He peered at Joe with a sly look. "I'll give you another tip. Other people have been here, lurking around, just like you. Bet you're not the only buyer."

"Interesting." Joe kept a firm hand on my shoulder while he said it, letting me know I should keep cool and fake indifference, as he was doing. "Maybe you're right about moving fast. Wonder if I know any of those others? Did you get to see them?"

"How the hell would I know about them if I didn't? I'm old but I'm not blind and I keep a watch on the block. Sure I saw them."

"Anything you'd care to share about them?"

"Russians! After I knew that, I lost interest. "

"I bet a sharp guy like you did see something more. Was it a young man? Or was it men?"

He considered that. "Two men. Different times. At my age, everybody looks young. Ya know? So somewhere between my grandson, who's about—oh, hell. He just got out of the Army, so about twenty-three. So, older than him and younger than retirement. That's all I got. Now go on. I want to get inside. Too cold for old bones out here."

"We appreciate your help," Joe said, "but you don't need to stay out here for us."

He stared at us for what seemed like a long time. "Yeah, I do. You're trespassing and I wouldn't leave you or anyone out here sneaking around. So you stay, I stay." His gun was now resting on the porch rail, as if he thought he was defending his ranch against outlaws or a beachhead at Normandy. It wasn't pointed at us. Not exactly.

Joe smiled. "It's been a pleasure to meet you and thanks for the tip. It's time for us to get home anyway." He nudged me gently along, silently overriding my impulse to stay right there and argue.

Back in the car, he laughed while I tried to argue with him instead.

"The look on your face." He was still laughing. "Oh my God, you were funny."

"Funny? No, I'm really mad."

"Erica, you can't argue with a guy like him! And you learned quite a bit already, didn't you? Plus, and not a small thing, there was a gun."

That silenced me for a minute. "I never thought it was even loaded. Do you think he could, or would…?"

"I don't know, but we'd be the crazy ones to count on that. Right? Come on!"

"I hate to say it. I mean I really hate it, but you're right." I thought a little more. "You handled him very smoothly. Nice going." My admiration was real.

"You know only half my job is building? The other half is handling hysterical customers. I've seen crazier people than that old S.O.B."

"So you agree that he's kind of crazy?"

"Certifiable." He hesitated. "Honestly, I think you need to stay away now. If I hadn't been there, what would have happened?"

"What? It's a regular neighborhood, not high-crime, and it's not late at night. People are still out. It wouldn't have been dangerous, even on my own. Really!"

"Hmm." He was looking away from me, so I couldn't see if he was still laughing. "Funny, I'm imagining you arguing with him, telling him off for the idiot he is, and him taking offense. Holding a gun. What could possibly go wrong?" He wasn't laughing now.

He had a point. I didn't say a word.

"Seriously." He turned to look at me. "Why are you so involved? Dima was murdered. Police are not ignoring that. I know, I know. He was your friend and his wife is your friend and his son is Chris' friend, but finding out what happened can't be up to you. What are you doing here?"

His expression was full of—was it concern? It was my turn to look away.

"I don't know exactly. I feel like I can't abandon them. They want my help so I have to give it, and this is what I'm good at, putting little pieces together to get the whole picture."

And then, when I stopped talking, I did know what I was doing. When Jeff died, we had the only fact that mattered. We knew what happened. A middle-aged man had spent the afternoon at a bar instead at of his job. That is the reason Jeff died, plain and simple. I could not then and would not ever be able to answer the *why* because there was no answer. But maybe there was an answer out there for Natalya and Alex. Maybe, even if I would never help myself, I could help them. So I had to. End of story.

I couldn't say it to Joe. Not that he wouldn't listen. He always listens. I just wasn't ready to say it out loud. It was a silent drive, but after a while, he put out one hand and held mine until the next green light.

It did occur to me, though, that I would be telling the story of this encounter to Detective Henderson. He had asked if Dima had any enemies. Turns out, he did.

Chapter Eight

Music broke the silence. It was Joe's phone, ringing with an old rock song. Duran Duran? Anyway, something from before my time.

He glanced at it, pulled over, and stepped out to talk. I couldn't hear what he said, but I heard the tone. It was warm, a little teasing. Definitely not work.

He returned to the car. "Shall I take you home or somewhere else? I was planning to come home with you, but it seems I have a late date." He looked self-conscious but not unhappy. Usually I would tease him, but I wasn't up to it tonight.

"You've met her. The woman at the stained-glass studio?"

Interesting. How come I didn't notice anything the night we met?

"Good for you. Ask her if she's learned anything? And home for me, please."

I huddled back into my silence. I knew that later I would wish I had questioned him further.

So Dima had a few secrets, after all. I was pretty sure his family knew nothing about this house. Did he own it? Why was it a secret? And Dima did have at least one enemy. However, there is a long leap from a crazy old man shooting off his mouth and a murder. Wasn't there? I supposed that depended on how crazy the old man actually was.

Joe could tell me to let the police do their job, but they were not moving too fast. Alex had no news. I pulled my phone from my bag and looked for messages. None. I dialed in to get my phone messages at home. Precisely zero. Damn. When was that detective going to call back?

A phone call to my father was always an easy way to let off some steam, as we usually ended up in an argument. But no, I just didn't have the energy for it tonight.

However, we weren't far from the exit that would take me to Leary's apartment. Leary was my friend, sort of. He was such a prickly personality, it was stretching a point to say he had any friends at all, but he was an excellent source of information, a retired reporter who once covered Brooklyn and knew where all the bodies were buried. I occasionally wondered if that was literal instead of metaphorical. When it came to secrets, I never doubted he had some. More than a few...

I could count on him being home. A collection of ailments, many lifestyle-related, including the loss of a leg to diabetes, left him with almost no mobility. I originally persuaded him to talk to me about old Brooklyn by bribing him with a couple of outings.

Tonight I had something almost as enticing: my conversation with the self-described reporter at Green-Wood. I was sure his reaction would be entertaining, at the very least.

Further, chances were at least fifty-fifty that in the course of a short visit he would say something so outrageous that I could focus my frustration on him instead of on my unwanted new acquaintance in Brighton Beach. At that moment it seemed like a good idea.

So I said to Joe, "Change of plans," and gave him Leary's address. He waited in the car, though I told him there was no need, while I phoned Leary from the decrepit building entryway. "I'm coming to visit, so buzz me in, okay? I have a story for you." There wasn't any point in asking if he wanted a visit; he would say no. Just because he said it, that did not make it true. I'd figured out a long time ago that the sandpaper personality disguised a lonely man.

He responded with, "What? This is not a good..."

"Yeah, yeah, that's what you always say. I'm ringing right now. Ringing! Buzz me in."

He did. I waved Joe off to his date.

The elevator was as neglected as always, but it appeared to be running. When I got to Leary's floor his door was open so I went right in. He was sitting on the sheet-covered sofa, his crutch nearby. Every other surface in the living-dining room, except for two, was covered as always by stacks of magazines, papers, clothes. His once-a-week housekeeper, sent by a social service agency, did not seem to be making much headway.

The first surface that had no papers was the coffee table, covered by an array of Chinese takeout containers. The second was the easy chair next to the sofa, where my father was sitting.

"Come give your old man a hug!" Leary boomed it out, not dad, but dad did stand up.

"What are you doing here? I don't understand!" I was still standing in the doorway.

"Close the door, honey, and come in." I did. "You introduced us at Rick's memorial service, remember?" Of course I did. Rick was a retired NYPD detective, my dad's oldest friend and my adopted uncle. "We get together every so often and talk about things, mostly old-time Brooklyn. Turns out we even knew some of the same people."

Though I had a mix of emotions, the one that stood out was betrayal. These two people were supposed to be in separate pigeonholes of my life. They weren't supposed to mix them up. Childish? Oh, yes, I knew it was even while I was feeling it. But I did feel it.

"Okay. I mean, I guess it's okay."

Leary said, "Better be. Cause you have no say in it." He looked at me shrewdly and said, "Did you eat? Help yourself to the feast over there. We got carried away on the ordering. And what brings you to my palace this evening?"

I filled a paper plate with rice and mixtures I could not identify. It seems I had forgotten about dinner. What had brought me there? I probably could have said to Leary, alone, I wanted someone to fight with. He's always ready to have an argument about anything, or even about nothing at all. I would not say it in front of my dad. In fact, I didn't exactly want my dad to know what I had been doing.

I led with my story about the blogger. Leary was outraged at the nerve but was still able to see the funny side.

"Annoying, was he? Could be he's got some promise as a reporter." He chuckled at my indignation. "And you did good, cutting him off. No need for you to just hand over what you know and do his job for him."

And he was as scornful as I expected, too. "*Brooklyn Eagle*, my fat Irish ass. He's just an amateur. That's not journalism, it's gossip." He paused, and then said, "Still, maybe I should take a look at these blog things sometime. Got to keep up with the times. Next time I'm at your house?"

Oh, sure. Like that would happen. Leary had never been to my house. And he would have had trouble just getting up the front stoop, let alone the steep stairs to my office where the computer lives. He only used his own ancient computer for e-mail, and he only did that because the publisher of his pseudonymous trashy novels had insisted. He still composed on his antique Selectric typewriter, though, and he is not exactly on speaking terms with the Internet.

"I'll make you a deal…" That was Leary being Leary, ever the old reporter. "Seems like I wrote a story or two about Green-Wood way back when. Probably human interest on a slow news day. Jeez, I hated those! But I could look in the files. And you will send me some of this pretentious kid's stories. Good deal? Makes your visit worthwhile?"

His whole apartment might be a pigsty but his office was perfectly organized and pristine. I think he had every story he ever wrote, and though he might have trouble finding a clean shirt, he never had trouble finding a story. Of course I said sure. It might be entirely unrelated to my work but I knew it would be interesting.

"It's a deal, but I really came to tell you a couple of stories. Today seems to be my day for meeting up with real characters." I thought a minute. How could I tell my story without including details that would start my father on a protective kick? Or give Leary more opportunity to make fun of me?

"I had—umm—something to do in Brighton Beach, and I ran into this old guy. He was kind of ranting." I shared a few choice quotes. Leary laughed but my dad, of course, started in.

"I don't like you doing things like that. What the hell is wrong with your judgment? If you have to go asking touchy questions in dicey neighborhoods, at least take me along." Oh, sure. He isn't old, really, but he also isn't the tough kid he claims to have been back in the day. He broke his leg in a car accident last year. He wears glasses now. Years of smoking cigars left him with some breathing problems.

"Dad. Don't start. And it's not a dicey neighborhood. It hasn't been for a long time."

He was ready to argue, but Leary laughed. "Hey, Len, you gotta let the kid make her own mistakes."

"That is the most sensible thing I ever heard you say. Maybe the only sensible thing." I would have hugged him for it, but I was pretty sure he would not like it.

I jumped up. "Look at the time. I've got to go. Chris is home."

Dad stood up with me. "I'll walk you to your car. "

"I was dropped off. I'll take the bus home."

"At this hour? I'll drive you. I'm leaving anyway. Time for us geezers to hit the hay too."

I started clearing the table, but Leary said, "Leave it, leave it. My aide is coming in tomorrow. Or I don't know, maybe day after."

I cringed at the picture his words suggested but said good-bye and left with Dad. As soon as we were in the elevator he said, "Okay. When were you gonna tell me what's really on your mind?"

"What are you talking about?"

"I would have known from your face, anyway, but Chris told me about your friend who got killed."

No way to put him off now. "Dad, it's horrible. It's so…so unjust. He had a son, Chris' friend. His wife is my friend and I don't know what to say to her."

He looked straight ahead, not at me. "Sure you do. We both do."

"Do you miss mom?"

We were at his car by then. "Dumb question. We were together since we were Chris' age." He was gallantly opening the car door.

"Then how…?"

"Hop in, kiddo." He turned the radio on, loud, stopping conversation. I suspected he didn't want to answer the question I hadn't quite asked.

At my house, he turned to me. "Your life sounds pretty full and kind of stressed. Yeah? Like always?"

"Yeah, like always."

"I'm here if you need me. Don't forget that."

He watched until I unlocked my door and was in my house. I didn't turn around to see him, but I could feel his eyes. It was entirely unnecessary and the kind of thing that drives me crazy. I am a grown woman, not a child. It's entirely different when I do it to Chris. Not that Chris would agree with me on that.

Home, where Chris was already in bed, radio playing softly, phone in hand, deep in conversation. She wiggled her fingers in a "hello" to me. I wiggled mine back.

Home, where the house phone told me I'd missed a call from Detective Henderson. Too late to call back now? Yes. Tomorrow.

The phone rang in the night. I was ripped from a deep sleep. Heart racing, I fumbled for it with my eyes barely open.

"I hope I didn't wake you." The voice sounded amused.

"Leary!" Now I was awake. "Damn it, do you know what time it is?" I squinted at the clock.

"You can sleep when you're old. I thought you'd want to know I found those files."

"What files? Green-Wood?"

"Those are the ones. Something kinda interesting. I'd forgotten. Happened decades ago. I'll get the aide to mail them tomorrow."

Oh, Leary, I thought. Learn to fax. Or scan and e-mail. Join this century. What I said was, "What could be so interesting it's worth waking me up?"

"You'll see. And you're welcome." Was he chuckling? "And guess what?"

"Leary, no games. I'm not even awake."

"I found that pretentious kid's website. Myself. The writing's not half bad. Suggest you take a look."

After, I tossed and turned and never really went back to sleep. I gave up finally and got up, meeting Chris coming out of the shower. She was damp and chipper. "Who the heck called in the middle of the night?"

"It woke you too? I'm so sorry."

"I didn't really wake up. Was it a butt dial?"

"Pretty close!" I had to laugh at the expression. "I don't work today and we're both up so early, I'll make you breakfast.

Over eggs, there was a whole story to tell about Dima's other house and his gun-carrying neighbor. Chris was looking pretty shocked by the end of it.

"Mom! Mo-o-om!" She made it three syllables as only a teen can. "What were you thinking? He sounds crazy."

"Nothing started out being crazy. I was just driving down a normal street at a normal time of day."

"Oh, sure, and if it was me?"

"You are fifteen. Different rules apply."

She looked unconvinced and cleverly changed the topic. "Next time you want to do something like that, take me along."

I didn't have time for a discussion about the multiple flaws in her logic. I sidetracked her with an offer to make lunch.

"I saw Grandpa yesterday." She said it while I was rummaging in the refrigerator.

"I saw him last night, very much by accident."

"You did? Did he tell you?"

"Umm, no. Tuna or leftover chicken?"

"Tuna. Lots of mayo. He took me to the Immigration Museum after school."

That jerked my attention away from the refrigerator shelves. "Why in the world….?"

"History assignment. I told you, at least twice." Now she was rummaging in the food cabinet, looking for potato chips, I thought.

And she had. Seven to ten pages of original research on a history topic. She had said something about family history and I took it for granted she would turn to me, her mother the historian, for help getting started. I do teach this to visiting classes at the museum, after all. I even knew people on staff at the amazing Ellis Island Museum of Immigration. In the derelict buildings where twelve million hopeful, anxious, desperate immigrants had been processed, they had created a stunning modern museum dedicated to telling their story. I knew it well, both museum and story. Whereas my dad would not be any help at all, except for chauffeur services and buying souvenirs.

"Grandpa? You went with Grandpa?"

"We were talking and he didn't have anything to do so I asked him to take me. You know, grandkid bonding. Plus, I really needed to get going on this project."

"Well, good for you." I wanted to be encouraging. "And did Grandpa have a lot of useful information to offer? I thought I would be the best person to get you started."

"No, he didn't," she said in that fake patient tone all teenagers use. "But he did do whatever I asked him. Which you wouldn't. And you are so busy and he had nothing to do. So it was a win-win all around." She didn't actually say "Ha!" but she didn't have to.

"So he drove me over to the ferry—you know it would take forever if I had to go by subway and change trains—and he paid for parking and it was a great day for a ferry ride, so sunny out there on the water, and that whole downtown view from the boat. We looked around the museum a little. He was never there before. Did you know that? How come you never took him?"

I put the plates on the table a lot harder than necessary. "Well, Chris…"

"It was a treat for him. So he wandered around some more while I got to work. Did you know they have a whole family research department? All way cool and computerized, documents and even pictures of the ships and everything, and the nicest people to help?"

"Did I know? What exactly do you think I do for a living?"

She put her entire attention to lining up the lettuce and tomatoes perfectly on her sandwich. Then she was gone.

Chapter Nine

That morning, I couldn't wait to get to work. After last night, I had had enough of crazy people. Ryan was eccentric, but he was not full-out crazy. And he was a little afraid of me, which frankly made a nice change from everyone else in my life.

He greeted me with, "There was a message from the boss. He's coming back sooner." He looked even paler than usual. "In fact he'll be back tomorrow and he expects to see great progress. And we are way behind! I feel sick."

We quickly divided the fat envelopes of letters. If we each read half, we hoped we could do a quick summary of all of them by the end of the day. That should assure Flint of our diligence.

We sat in silence and read, and entered data, and read some more. Every once in a while I would pass him something to look at, or he would pass something to me.

I would have liked to read deeply, absorb, think, even daydream, but we could not take the time today. I would have liked to follow up on Leary's cryptic hint, too.

Finally, Ryan left the room and I did a fast jump to the 'Net. Tap, tap, tap the URL in, and up popped a page that resembled a newspaper. In large letters, a column was headed, "Night of crime at landmark cemetery?" Yes, it was cleverly written, but there was a lot of innuendo and a little bit of fact: an anonymous source said police cars were seen driving in early in the morning. A section of the cemetery was closed to visitors. No one was offering any news or information. Ryan came back in and I hurriedly switched back to our work document.

"Ya know," Ryan said finally, "he should be pretty happy with us after all. There's tons of stuff here about Tiffany and we are capturing it all."

So there was. Young Maude was thrilled and fascinated by everything and she wrote all of it. Phones were a brand new invention then and still rare. People wrote letters, and for those so inclined, every thought and bit of news or gossip might go down on paper. How lucky for us, the historians.

Today I had the second half of her story, when the city was not so new to her and she was not so naïve, but had established ongoing friendships and was digging in deeply at the Tiffany studio. And here was a letter that made me sit up and pay attention:

> "Dearest Mama and Katie," she wrote, "I believe my chance has come at last. They have received a commission for a large glass window, and Mr. Tiffany (himself!) told Miss Driscoll I might contribute a design for part of it. I don't know if they will choose mine. But they will, they must! My head is swimming with ideas and my fingers itch to start. I can't tell you any more than that, as the client wishes it to be confidential until it is completed and unveiled. I know it is foolish, as you do not know anyone who would care, and even if you did, you would never betray a secret, but oh! I don't want to do anything that might put a bad spell on this for me."

"You go, girl," I thought. "Good for you."

I read ahead very quickly, not stopping even to take notes. A letter of a few weeks later said:

> "They loved my designs. They will become part of a larger project. Can you believe that? I am so excited I don't know which way to turn. Oh, yes, I do, I shall turn right to my worktable. As soon as I am done with this happy letter, I will begin refining the designs to

make them as perfect as they need to be for a—can
you guess how happy I am to write these words?—a
Tiffany window."

Then I read this set of letters again, very slowly to see if they
really said what I thought they said. I felt flushed with excitement
as I handed them to Ryan, saying, "Drop everything to read this."

When he finished, he said "Holy cow. Holy freakin' cow."
Then he turned to his computer, typed madly without saying
another word, while I walked around and looked over his
shoulder.

He had pulled up a database with Flint's name on it, but
created, I suspected, by him. It seemed to be a comprehensive
list of glass windows produced by the Tiffany studios, sorted by
date for the period of the letters. He hit a few keys and it was
sorted again by location. We read it together, and found nothing
that came close to what we had just read about.

"Is it possible?" He squinted up at me. "A window no one
knows about?"

"Maybe. They do turn up. They found one hidden behind
a closet in a very old Brooklyn high school not long ago." He
looked skeptical. "No, they really did. They built high schools to
be impressive back then. I wonder if Maude's window was ever
made? I'll zip through the rest of the letters to see if I can find out."

Over the next few months she continued to write about
her life in general, the project, how she helped select some of
the glass and how it would be fabricated at a Tiffany plant in
Queens. But the exuberant tone was gone. The letters became
shorter and either she was writing less frequently, or some were
lost. They seemed to trickle away, and then they just stopped.
I felt like I was reading a book that had lost the final chapters.
What happened to her? Then, and after? I wanted to find out,
but at this moment, Ryan was there, waiting expectantly, mind
on our job at hand.

"It looks like it went into production," I said at last, my voice
sounding strange even to me.

Ryan grinned and I realized, even in the midst of my own excitement, that it was the first time I had seen him smile. "The boss is going freak at this. Just freak. It's huge."

He did some more intense typing and said, "You okay with this?"

It was an e-mail to Flint, telling him what we had found. I nodded and he hit "Send" with a decisive punch.

"Okay. Wow." I actually felt a little dazed. "Um, let's get to the rest of these letters, so we'll be finished when he comes in tomorrow. I'm not supposed to work tomorrow, but I'll be here for this. So we can move on to the next phase, whatever that will be."

It only took a few hours for a message came back from him. It must have been after dinner in Italy. "Tomrow will come strait from JKF." He must mean Kennedy airport, JFK. "Must see IN person what fund." Fund? Ah, "found." "You not authoities. So tell no one until I ok." Of course not. Did he take us for fools? Probably the answer to that was yes.

And Detective Henderson called, finally connecting in person. Could he stop at my house in the early evening to get the phone and ask a few questions? Yes. I was tired of playing telephone tag.

"Ryan, I don't think I can handle any more excitement for today."

He stared at me until I added, "That was a joke. A joke! But I do need to go home early." The detective was not making a social call, but that didn't mean I wanted him sitting in my cluttered living room, with my belongings and Chris' scattered all over and dirty dishes stacked in the open kitchen. And going home and saying to his brother, my old friend, "That Erica sure is a slob." As if anyone would care. Really. I thought, "Mom, why are you still here, whispering in my ear?" The housekeeping maven, setting high standards for what was right even from the next world. There was something about my visitor being a piece of my past that made it hard to ignore.

At home, dishes and pots quickly went into the dishwasher. Did I have clean cups and glasses, to offer refreshment? Check.

Assorted random possessions scooped up all over the first floor, into a laundry basket and upstairs to my room? Check. Accumulated mail all over the table tossed into an attractive basket? Check.

Splash of cold water in my face and a tall mug of iced coffee, extra sugar, for me? Double check. I poured the coffee just before the bell rang. He stood on my top step with a tentative smile and a plastic bag of takeout food.

"Do you like sushi? I never had lunch today and when I passed a place after I parked, I made a stop. There's plenty for two."

"What a nice surprise. Lunch is feeling a long time ago."

We settled at my just-cleared dining table, I put out plates and chopsticks, and we munched while we talked.

"Thanks for calling us, Ms. Donato. Of course I have a lot of questions."

"Of course you do. And it's Erica."

I handed him the mysterious phone.

"Tell me about how this came to you." He pointed his chopsticks at the containers on the table. "And I recommend the salmon roll."

I tried to skim over Alex coming to me instead of his mother, and I tried to make Henderson promise to be careful about that. He wasn't altogether sympathetic.

"That kid may have held up this investigation a few days. That's not okay. You know that, don't you?" I nodded. "But does *he* know that? It's important that he understand." He stopped. "Oh, hell. His father was just murdered. And he's only what, fifteen? Never been in any trouble that we have found. Yeah, we checked." He looked straight at me. "Okay, I do get it. I can't make any promises about who will know and all that, but I'll do my best to see that he's not in any real trouble."

"You mean with your guys, or his mother?"

He laughed. "Who's scarier? Okay, both. Both, to the best of my ability. That's all I can do."

"I've gotten sucked into this because they are my friends, and I'd like to help them if I can." I thought for a moment. "Uh, that's not exactly the whole truth. Dima was my friend, too."

Henderson raised his eyebrows when he played Dima's odd greeting. He jotted down a few points as I spoke, until I gulped hard and said, "I have to add something to this." And I told him about my excursion to Dima's property.

"Right next door? With a gun? Why didn't you say so? Did he tell you anything at all?"

"Just that he doesn't like Russians. Otherwise he seemed, I don't know. Cagey. Crazy, maybe, but sly. Does that make any sense?"

"In my line of work? Are you kidding? I meet people in that category on a regular basis. Actually, I've met him."

"You did? But how? How did you know?'

He looked amused. "Well, it's what we do, you know. Mr. Ostrov owned the property and we found some records, so we went to canvass people on the block, just to see what we could dig up. We've got his name in the notes. The old codger refused to talk to us at first. Even when we pointed out it was a murder investigation and that he would talk to us whether he liked it or not, he hardly said anything."

"So you think what I told you is useful?"

"Oh, yeah. We will be having another talk with him right away. It will be real interesting to see if he has a license for that gun. And it is also useful to have the numbers in that phone. I have some special curiosity about the man whose message is 'don't leave a message.' That's an unusual way to do business." We'll be talking to all of them.

"The crazy neighbor…is there any chance at all that he was the one who did it? I mean, it's hard to believe and yet he was so full of rage. And his gun?"

"Oh, we'll be asking to see that gun, that's for sure. In fact, I'm thinking about paying him a visit before I go home tonight. Funny how he didn't happen to mention owning one. There's no way to know, or even guess, about anything until we talk to him some more. You may have heard we need some evidence?" I could tell he was joking. "He seemed a little frail for hauling a body around but who knows what friends he has?" He shrugged. "We'll be digging."

Then he looked over the littered table. "I think you should keep the leftovers. Does your daughter like sushi?" Was he changing the subject?

"So how are you doing, overall? Are you learning anything? Is Natalya right about her brother-in-law? I met him. He seems pretty scary or at least he's got the scary style. Does that make sense?"

"Sure. Sometimes it's only styling, kind of delusions of being Tony Soprano. But sometimes it is the real thing, too."

"So which is it with Vladimir?"

He smiled. "Kenny told me you were an inquisitive kid even in high school."

"What?"

He shrugged and smiled again. "He wouldn't tell me why he said it. Just laughed. He said to ask you."

"I'll have to think about that. High school seems a century ago most of the time."

"A lot of life lived in between, right? Do you want to talk about the old days over dinner sometime?'

I didn't see that coming. He didn't wear a wedding ring, and I'd known him when I was young. Sort of known him. When he added, "It could be fun," I wondered how long it had been since I'd had plain old fun?

"Well, sure. Why not?"

He ran his eyes over his notes, stood and said, "I think I've got it all. I'll call you."

"If you have any questions."

"Yes, and about dinner, too. How's Tuesday? I see you like Japanese?" I probably turned red. I had gobbled down more than my share. He laughed. "It's fun to have dinner with a woman who appreciates the food. How do you feel about Middle Eastern? Or Argentine steak?"

"Funny, isn't it, how sophisticated we have become? We sure didn't have all these choices when we were young."

He laughed. "Oh, yes, that's me, the epitome of sophistication! Yeah, the good old days when it was either spaghetti joints or imitation Chinese, right?" He left and then turned back.

"I can tell you this. We don't believe no one knows why Mr. Ostrov walked out on his job and what happened after. We will find that someone eventually."

After he left, I was hit with disappointment. It would have meant mean a lot to Natalya for me to say, "They are right on top of it. There's great progress." It would have meant something to me to be able to say it but I knew I was being silly. I knew a cop was not going to confide in me. Or gossip with me either. But I wouldn't mind trying again over dinner.

The next day I wasn't scheduled to work but no one needed to tell me I had to be there when Dr. Flint arrived in the afternoon. What to do with my own morning? My own work? Overdue house-cleaning?

Something to pacify Dr. Flint about our failure to find out what happened at Green-Wood? Before I finished breakfast I had a panicky note from Ryan. Was I ever that young and scared? I didn't think so. I was raised to be mouthy and opinionated. Of course my parents were a little shocked when I turned that on them. It's only now, with an adolescent of my own, that I understand their reactions, but I was never a wimp. And Ryan was. Besides, I didn't have the time. By Ryan's age, I was married and maybe had a baby.

I wondered if Dr. Flint would be happy—happier, anyway— if I could add some basic facts to the collection of Maude Cooper, who seemed increasingly like a friend. And it would be a good way to avoid tackling my dissertation chapter.

I knew there were some ways I could research the history of the house. Perhaps I could find the connection myself. It would help to know the name of the last owner—probably Bright Skye's recently deceased mother—and any other owners. Surely with enough digging, we could get the history of Maude's letters.

It was time to make a phone call.

Bright Skye answered in the same soft, tentative voice I remembered from the museum meeting. I explained who I was and told her we were making great progress on her found letters. I almost told her how wonderful they were, but a little voice stopped me. I had a feeling that maybe my superiors at the museum would prefer I not become too confiding. I simply asked if this would be a convenient time to ask a few questions. She said, "I don't know. Umm, you know I really don't know anything about all this?"

"I understood that from the meeting at the museum, but we are hoping you might be able to answer a few questions for background. We are puzzled about the connection between these letters, sent home to Illinois, and your family home in Brooklyn."

"But I said I don't know anything."

"You know," I said, in as friendly a voice as I possessed, "doing research we often find that people know more than they think, they just don't recognize it as being important. Does that kind of make sense?"

"I suppose," she said softly.

"So, could I ask you who was the last owner of the house?"

"That was my mother."

"And you said the house was in your family for a long time. Did she grow up there?"

"Yes. I guess. I don't know much about this house."

This was much harder than I thought it would be.

"Could you tell me her name...?"

"Ginny. It was Ginny Updike."

"I believe you told us that was her family name. Was Ginny her name or a nickname?"

"Yes, her full name was Virginia. And Updike was her father's last name."

Pulling hen's teeth had nothing on this. I made yet another stab at getting something useful.

"Was that her legal name when she passed on?"

"I don't know if it was and I don't care. She had a few. This is not a good time for me. Please leave me alone!"

Before I could get out "I'm sorry. When would be a better time?" she was gone and I was left holding a dead phone.

It annoyed me. My questions were so innocent, and I was hardly prying, considering that she had brought the material to us. What would happen if I just went over there in person? Surprise her, perhaps with a friendly gift in hand? I knew she was there because the phone number was a landline.

The address wasn't far, just a basic you-can't-get-there-from-here situation. Brooklyn started out as a collection of separate towns, and to this day, some of the geography makes no sense at all. Streets don't connect, or they change names when they cross a now-vanished village border. Streets could be the East or South or North version of the same numbers, and not be anywhere near each other, let alone connected. No choice; I would have to drive over. I scooped up my mail, which had just come through the mail slot in my door, grabbed my car keys, and headed out.

◇◇◇

I soon found myself in a neighborhood I had not visited in some time. And I reacted as I did every time, with a "Toto, we're not in Brooklyn anymore." In fact, I had spent my entire childhood in Brooklyn before I ever saw streets that looked just like Lady and the Tramp, or the illustrations in the Betsy-Tacy books. Who knew?

Even to my grown-up self, it looked like the enchanted but not exactly real world that Jack Finney used to describe so persuasively. Or the beginning of E. L. Doctorow's *Ragtime*. A world where houses have wide front porches with rattan furniture and someone is serving lemonade, where the sun is always shining and croquet is set up on the broad front lawn under the oak trees. And I could easily see my girl Maude Cooper walking down these streets, long swaying skirt and big hat, her head full of dreams and ambition.

Of course gritty old Coney Island Avenue was just a few blocks over and the little neighborhood main street was a mix of pizza slice shops, kebab counters, discount cosmetics, and a storefront shop proclaiming "We ship to the Caribbean," all mixed up with a sprinkling of tiny, trendy boutiques and ambitious little restaurants.

A small playground had a sign about the farmer's market every Sunday; an elaborate mural on the side of a building portrayed a multi-racial, multi-costumed crowd of children and proclaimed Peace to All. So, after all, it was a living, breathing part of the twenty-first-century city and not Main Street in Disneyworld.

I parked on Skye's street and walked along checking for house numbers. I saw several gracious old houses that had fallen on hard times, like impoverished dowagers, and others in the throes of renovation. There was one with scaffolding along one side and with a sign on the front lawn that promised Expert Renovation by Rashid Construction, and another with the elegant wood trim meticulously decked out in four different colors. Very charming, very San Francisco, very, very expensive.

Even before I could see the house number, Skye's home stood out for me, and not in a good way. It was the shabbiest house on the block.

Chapter Ten

It had once been a crown jewel. That was obvious. There were brown and cream shingles in an elaborate design, a porch that wrapped around three sides, a round turret at one corner, strips of colored glass bordering the windows. Now the paint was faded and peeling, the spacious porch sagged, the shrubbery and flowerbeds had not been touched in many summers. Skye had said her mother had died recently. Perhaps old age or illness had forced her to let things go.

I went up the front steps with great care; there were boards missing. Where there should have been a doorbell, I found a tangle of naked wires, so I knocked on the door, softly at first and then authoritatively. I waited and then peeked in the window. In the dim light, I could just manage to see a spacious square front parlor, so different from my narrow tall house. There seemed to be wood paneling everywhere and an impressive staircase halfway back.

I knocked again and wondered if perhaps no one was there after all. Finally, a faint light went on inside, and I heard voices. Skye's face peered at me through the badly cracked glass in the front door, and then I heard the clicking of several locks being turned. Finally, the door opened, and Bright Skye was in front of me, looking unkempt and anxious, just as I remembered her from the museum meeting.

And she was standing squarely in the doorway, most definitely not welcoming me in.

"Miss Skye," I said as mildly as I could, "it's Erica Donato. We spoke a little while ago and we met the day you brought your box of materials to the museum?" I ended on a tentative, upward lilt, like a teenager. I felt it might seem reassuring, since she appeared bafflingly afraid of me.

She frowned and nodded. "Yes, but I told you, this is not a good time. I am quite busy."

"I'm sorry if I'm being a nuisance, but I'm just desperate to get some more information before the boss comes back tomorrow." True as far as it went, but by now, I was just plain curious. "And it's later than when we talked, so I hoped this might be a better time and I was in the neighborhood. I brought you a cake to apologize." I handed it to her with a smile.

Her face lit up. It only lit up a little, but it was the most animation I had seen so far. Then the spark died away. "I'm a vegan." She flicked a finger at the bakery label. "I'm pretty sure a commercial bakery uses all kind of products I never touch." She looked somewhat confused as she added, "But thank you, anyway."

This was going nowhere. Be bold. "Why not invite me in? If you are busy, perhaps I can be helpful. Maybe talking here will dig up memories to answer my questions."

She gave a kind of gasp. "Oh, no, no, that is completely unnecessary. I have someone helping me here in the house and we are very busy. There is so much to do. I…I…trust her… can't have any more people confusing things. She—she knows a lot about old things and I don't know anything. She will help protect my interests.…

This was so much not making sense, I was beginning to feel like I was now in another, different country that also was not Brooklyn and more. More like the one you find through the looking glass.

"But I'm from the museum. Surely you are not afraid anyone there wants to cheat you? I mean, all we ever want to do is learn and educate." I hoped, as I said it, that it was true. Museum curators could be pretty avid about a desirable object.

Skye's bulk filled the doorway, but I could just make out movement behind her. A vaguely familiar voice said, "Louise, maybe we should hear her out after all?" Then, to my astonishment, Mrs. Mercer appeared and Skye stepped back a little to make room for her.

"Why don't you come in, Ms. Donato?" She smiled pleasantly, and went on, "We met at Green-Wood the other day. Yes, I see you are surprised. I live next door, and I was a friend of Louise's—that is, Bright's—mother. Also I know antiques. So I am helping clean out the house." She reached out for my cake box and added, "I've just put on the tea kettle so, Brighty, why don't we put this out along with your muffins?"

She led me through the spacious, shabby parlor I had glimpsed from the porch, the dining room behind it, with built-in china cabinets and elaborate wallpaper, now stained and peeling away from the walls, and into a full size, eat-in kitchen equipped with a chrome and plastic dinette set. It looked like a museum: Typical Kitchen, Circa 1935. The refrigerator reached my shoulder, the sink stood on legs, the narrow, mint-green enameled stove looked like something from a Norman Rockwell painting. I was fascinated and had to remind myself that walking around examining every single thing would be rude. More important, it was not likely to encourage Bright, or Louise, to talk to me. But I did want to.

Instead, I said, "What a charming kitchen."

"Oh, pul—leeze. Even I know it's a dump. And I'm not into material things at all. My mom would have said my own place is a dump—thank the goddess she never saw my wood-burning stove!—but she would have liked to update this." I nodded. I'd just been through a kitchen update myself.

"She just never had the money. Or the will. Or the guts. After a while I was gone, and I don't know which it was when she got older."

"I would say," Mrs. Mercer added, gently, "she was just overwhelmed by this house."

"And now I am." Bright looked glum. "Some of this junk might be valuable, which really would be goddess-sent, but I have no idea. Mrs. Mercer is helping…" She turned red, and stopped in mid-sentence.

Did I only imagine rage in Mrs. Mercer's well-bred face before it was gone and she said smoothly, "Yes, there are a few nice pieces of silver and china that might give Bright some much-needed cash. Sorry to say, but there's not much hope of a fortune here. Bit by bit, we are digging out what is not just family junk but so far, nothing worth much." She shrugged. Then she put her teacup down on the table with a firm gesture and stood up, saying, "We must get back to work now."

"But I was hoping to get a little more information about this house and those letters you brought to us. The connection is kind of a mystery, why the letters were here, and whatever we can learn about the person who wrote them. We need to know, just for scholarly purposes. They might turn out to be the real treasure from this house."

Bright gave me a surprisingly shrewd look and said, "Maybe I'll be more interested in talking when I see some money. Maybe there's a private person who would have more to give me than a museum." She shot a proud look at Mercer, and added, "I left home as soon as I could get away and found my perfect other life. Talking about this house won't nourish my inner being by a single crumb. You don't need to know any more."

"But that's just what I've been saying. We do. We do need to know more." It was hard to understand or accept that she was so unwilling to answer my innocent questions. "And with so much history accumulated here, it is just is not possible there is not one thing that would help us. You'd be surprised at what is helpful. Maybe I could work with you for a while? Look over what is here and kind of zoom in on papers from the right period?"

They looked horrified. Mercer was silent but Skye said, "I don't need any help from anyone but Amanda. She's done every-thing for me since I came back, I've known her my whole life,

I know I can trust her. Things are different in Arizona where I live, but I know I can't trust anyone else in New York."

She was holding the front door open by then. "Please just go. Go now."

"Good bye, Ms. Donato," Mercer said with a courtesy that seemed exaggerated. "I think Bright is saying clearly that there is nothing more for you to do here."

I had no choice but to walk through the door. Mrs. Mercer followed and whispered quickly, "You have to forgive her. Poor child, she is just overwhelmed by her mother's death and all this work. I know she doesn't mean to be difficult. Please believe we have no problem with the museum. She is just letting off her anxiety, poor child."

She gave me a wavering smile and then she was gone. The tantrum I felt like throwing would have been entirely inappropriate. Worse, I was sure it would be unproductive.

And then I stopped, still on the porch, because voices were coming from the other side of that door. I guessed they didn't realize how easily sounds came through the porch window with the broken glass.

"You almost gave it all away. Have you forgotten every single thing we talked about? Do you want them looking for a donation of every antique here?"

"I know, I know. I forget this is Brooklyn. Where I live people help each other out."

"Well, don't do it again! You went to the museum before you talked to me. What were you thinking? They don't care about you; trust me, I know all about how they operate. Just because they don't buy and sell like dealers doesn't mean they wouldn't rob you blind."

What? Had Mrs. Mercer just said two completely contradictory things in as many minutes? She looked like a sweet, eccentric old lady but it seemed she was playing one of us for a fool? But which one? And why in the world would she do that? None of it made any sense for now, but it would, I promised myself.

I would not forget this puzzle, but it was time to head to the museum. Flint would be in soon.

The moment I arrived, before I even had my jacket off, Ryan pounced. "He said to meet at the cemetery. He is fuming."

"What? I could have gone there straight from home."

"Listen." He held phone up and hit a button.

"You and Ms. Donato meet me at Green-Wood entrance. I should be there in thirty minutes. I plan to give Nancy Reade a piece of my mind. My presentation was incomplete because of her foolishness. After that you will share your findings with me."

"Why does he need us at Green-Wood for this?"

Ryan shrugged. "Reinforcements? Showing off? We're his posse?"

When he looked at me, we both started laughing and could barely stop. Dr. Flint and posse in the same sentence was a funny thought.

Dr. Flint was standing right at the entrance, looking tall, dapper, and irritated. He got into my car and without a word of greeting, pointed toward the administration building.

"Drive me over there. I have been up for many, many hours and I am not willing to lose a moment. We will surprise Nancy in her office."

The security officer we had met previously was not about to allow us to waltz right in, but Flint made a call and handed the phone over to him. He nodded, wrote something down and pointed along the corridor.

"Turn right, third door on the left."

Dr. Reade was standing up, smiling, hand out to Dr. Flint.

"Thomas, so nice to see you."

Ryan and I stood behind Dr. Flint and exchanged glances. She could not possibly be sincere but I was fascinated by her smoothness under pressure. I could learn by watching a pro in action.

Perhaps I was kidding myself when I thought I saw uneasiness in her eyes. Nevertheless, they shook hands before Flint started. "Nancy, I have a bone to pick with you."

"Now Thomas, you know you get too upset. What could possibly be such a big problem you came in with no…" I thought for sure she would say warning, but she said "appointment."

"Did we have a meeting I have forgotten about?" she continued. "I think not."

"Nancy, Nancy. After all this time and our history, you should know you can't tell me a tall tale. I needed something from you, something very simple, and yet you couldn't come through." He was not smiling. "How in the world can you explain this?"

"Ah. Well, Thomas. I don't know that I have to explain anything. I have always been happy to accommodate you but right now it is just not possible." The smile was slipping. "I had direction from my own bosses."

"But you don't have a boss…"

"Of course I do. I report to the trustees."

"That high up?" He had a gleam in his eyes. Then he looked right back at her and tried another approach. Clearly this was a man who did not accept no. "I'm the reason you have this job. My recommendation and my introduction to the right people…"

"Oh, nonsense. Yes, it helped, I suppose, but I earned this! I'd like you to leave. I have an important meeting, a genuinely important one, about five minutes ago."

Flint folded his arms. "You can't keep secrets in a large organization. In fact, there is already gossip out there on these Google places."

I turned to Ryan and mouthed the words, "He knows about Google?" I was even more surprised when Ryan turned red.

"How do you know that?" Her smile was completely gone now, and her poised shell was cracking.

"Someone showed it to me, of course. Ryan, that phone blog. Show her."

That explained a few things.

She glanced at it. "Oh, that annoying young man. Yes, he has been sniffing around, but if you had read it you would know he has nothing say. It's all out of thin air." Her confident words did not match her pale face and grim expression but she said, briskly, "I have to say good-bye for now." She was ushering us to the door. "Thomas, I'm sorry I could not be more helpful. I'll certainly let you know when we are back to normal and you'll be more than welcome then."

"Was there a robbery here?" I don't know who was most surprised when those words came out of my mouth. It might have been me.

Three people were staring at me now. I felt like a zoo animal in a cage. Dr. Reade was white. Dr. Flint looked astonished but also calculating. Ryan was just confused.

I reached in my bag, my hands shaking, and pulled out Leary's stories.

"A friend, a former reporter, sent me these. I glanced at them while we were waiting at the reception desk." My voice hardened. "It was a long time ago, but there were windows stolen here and at other old cemeteries. You said there was an accident but I asked. I asked around." I turned to Dr. Flint. "I tried to find out if there was a big window-repair job from here. There isn't even a whisper of one. And it is a Tiffany window, it must have some market value...." My voice trailed off.

It took a minute to see that Dr. Flint was not angry. He wasn't quite smiling, but he had a kind of gleam in his eye.

"Well, Nancy? What made you think you could play me off?" As if he had come up with the answer instead of me.

Her poise, already cracking, had crumbled away completely. She sat down in her desk chair with an inelegant thud, and covered her face with her hand. Then she looked up with a facing-the-firing-squad expression. "So you know. Lucky guess. We have been doing our best to keep this hidden, thinking we would eventually hear from the thief. We originally thought it would be a blackmail situation. Now, we're not so sure, but we are still doing our best to keep a lid on it."

I wasn't following her reasoning, but Flint must have been.

"How many other Tiffany windows do you have here?"

She smiled at that, though sadly. "You know perfectly well."

"And a few LaFarges too?"

She nodded.

"And plenty of statues?"

She sighed, nodded again.

"Well of course you are keeping it quiet. You're worried about someone else getting ideas."

"Of course we are. What do you think? Those old incidents…?" She gestured to me. "Way before my time, but our board has not forgotten. There was some copycatting then."

"Yes, there was." I jumped in. "Someone stole a window from a chapel at Woodlawn and then other…"

Flint gave me a look that said "shut up." So I did.

"So now we know that big secret that got in the way of my work. How long are you planning to keep this hidden? I believe it has to be reported before you can claim insurance."

"Insurance is the least of it." He looked at her skeptically. "I mean we're sort of underfunded, as much as any cultural organization, but the family has died out, the memorial is neglected, in short…"

"There is no one to sue you. So you could wait a little on reporting."

She nodded.

"You're worried about a scandal? Criticism? Report it anyway. You can't hide it forever. I mean, my God, every employee must know by now and that's already a substantial number. Make it public. That's my advice, and you should take it. After all, I was once your official advisor." He looked pleased by his small quip. Dr. Reade managed a ghostly smile. "If it would help, I'll talk to anyone you want. Buck up, woman. It's a terrible thing, a crime in a sacred place like this, but you have to deal with it."

"Thank you, Thomas. You are saying just what I've been thinking." She sighed. "Expect to see us on the morning news tomorrow, but for crying out loud, no one tells that nasty little toad from that website!"

Chapter Eleven

We barely spoke to each other on the ride back. Flint never got off his phone and Ryan and I just tried to stay out of his way.

When we were back at the museum, Flint looked at his watch and said, "I have a lunch date with Kip. You look puzzled." His sympathetic expression was mocking. "Kip to me is the museum director to you. Go nourish yourselves, children, and we will reconvene at 1:30 sharp. We have much to discuss. Come ready to work."

We scattered. I had my lunch with me and gratefully sank into my office chair, wishing my cubicle had a door so I could close out the world. It had been a full day already and it was only lunchtime.

Rummaging in my bag for my sandwich, I also pulled out the articles from Leary. They were important enough for him to wake me up with a call. Unless, of course, he just did that to be irritating.

I'd only glanced at them earlier. Now, I tore into my peanut butter and jelly, and began reading.

Was the man telepathic, along with his other mysterious skills? The articles described a long-ago series of art thefts from cemeteries and neglected old churches. Decidedly wrong and decidedly spooky, but it's true that they would be prime targets. Old cemeteries have the Tiffany glass of Flint's obsessions, and other valuable stained glass by other famous artists. They have sculptures. They have bas-relief plaques in both stone and bronze.

In those days they built them beautiful on purpose and spared no expense. I myself know where there are two lovely LaFarge windows, and I am not even knowledgeable in this field.

I found a highlighter on my desk and began the process of marking the papers while I ate.

Quite a long time ago—let's see, I was in fourth grade then—over a period of several years, items were stolen from Green-Wood and other historic cemeteries, and also from a few once-wealthy but now almost forgotten churches. So much for building for eternity.

Well, that explained a lot. Dr. Nancy Reade was terrified to have the news get out; that was obvious before we even knew what the news was. If it had happened in the past, perhaps they should then have put better security in place. True, the old churches, with their large and wealthy congregations had now shrunk to a handful of parishioners and were struggling to keep their buildings standing, but Green-Wood is different. At least that's what people would say. And then it dawned on me that publicity might give another thief an idea, too.

I read on, silently thanking Leary for his precise reporting. It turned out that the actual thief was a former employee. That made sense, too, in a warped way. Of course it had to be an inside job. And then I read that he was working with one of the foremost experts in the field of Victorian stained glass. Good lord. One of his scholarly works was right there in the stack I had borrowed from the museum library. His name was not Thomas Flint though. Flint would have been maybe still in college at that time. It certainly would be interesting to see how he reacted if I mentioned the name, though.

Like any good citizen, or good historian, I was horrified as I read the details of this elaborate scheme. Does it make me a bad person if I also laughed at the audacity of the whole thing? Their defense pointed out that they carefully chose only monuments that were neglected, where there was no family left to feel violated. And the thief testified that he meant no harm; he loved the neglected art and wanted to rescue it. The famous expert denied everything right up until he went to jail.

Of course in the end they had been caught, so they weren't actually very good at it after all. A lot of the stolen material was found in a shed on the thief's property. One Tiffany window had been sold to an overseas collector for a lot of money. A huge lot of money. I kind of gasped. That was two decades ago. What would the missing Konick window be worth now?

◇◇◇

Ryan and I were in a museum meeting room, files in front of us, looking at each other anxiously. Professor Flint's voice was moving down the hall, giving his very definitive opinion on something to someone. We could not hear the details but there was no mistaking the attitude.

We heard a final burst of laughter and the voice of Dr. Rhodes, our museum director. Then Flint blew into the room, his tailored suit and perfect silver hair only making the shabby workroom seem shabbier.

"Now. Lunch is over. Time to get to work. Start."

"Dr. Flint, before we get involved, I thought you might want these." He threw me an impatient look.

"There were other robberies at Green-Wood, decades ago, stained glass and other artwork."

He raised an eyebrow. "So there were. And to think I had forgotten." He held out a demanding hand. "I will deal with these items, and this whole issue from now on. You don't need to do anything else. It's not even related to your work responsibilities."

He must have forgotten I only had to print more copies if I wanted to. I didn't remind him.

"It seems there was a famous art historian involved." I kept my voice as neutral as possible. "He knew just what would be valuable and nobody questioned his roaming around the old cemeteries and churches."

"I do know that, Ms. Donato. Actually…" He paused. "Actually, he was one of my thesis advisors, a great historian who somehow lost his mind. Yes, I see you are shocked. So were we, at the time. You can be sure of that. Now, enough frivolity. Let's get to work. Report your findings."

Ryan looked white with nervousness, so I plunged in, fearlessly.

Okay, I was not actually fearless, but I was senior to Ryan so it was up to me. And why should Flint scare me anyway? Maybe the playground bullies I grew up with were not so suave—okay, they were definitely not suave—but I knew a bully when I saw one. And besides that, however much of an expert he was, I now knew some things he did not. So I began.

"The carton of material that dropped into our laps appears to be quite a find. They are letters, with some other material such as sketchbooks, all written by one of the female designers in the Tiffany studio from 1900 and a few years after. This is similar to the Clara Driscoll letters that created such a stir a few years ago, but at a slightly later date."

Flint was nodding, not smiling, his eyes locked on to me.

"Ryan and I have done basic archival cataloguing, and noted where some physical preservation is needed. Ryan created the template for the catalogue and everything is properly saved to both your computer and here in the museum."

"I took it for granted young Ryan would take care of all these mundane details. Go on to the important news. Was he correct about what he sent me?"

I took a deep breath. And had to smile. Even Ryan looked less scared and almost happy. "Oh, yes. That first part was just the housekeeping." Another deep breath. "We found a few letters that seemed to us to be a true find but we are looking to your expertise to confirm that. Here are the originals, in these folders, with working copies to minimize the need for handling."

I passed the folders to him, and then we had to wait, as he looked them over. I had the pleasure of seeing the color in his face change, and his hands start to shake a little. Ha. When he looked up at last, those cold blue eyes were lit up like street lights.

"Extraordinary. This is everything Ryan suggested and more. It's hard to believe…a young woman hitherto unknown to history, even to me." I grinned, wickedly but invisibly. How much fun it was, to see him hit with the fact that he does not, actually, know everything.

"It's almost shocking that she could have designed some windows on her own and yet remained unknown. There may actually be some undiscovered Tiffany windows out there. I admit I am stunned. Extraordinary, if true." He paused, tapped his fingers on the desk. "We don't know yet if it exists but at least she does discuss her design going into production. A good beginning." He looked at us, sternly.

"You must go over every letter again. Extract every mention, every clue...No! I will do that. You might miss something." He leaned forward, fixing us both with an intense gaze. "Please tell me you had the good sense not to gossip about this all over the city?"

Ryan looked horrified, turned red, and shook his head vehemently. "No, no, we were just working away and waiting for you to come back. And we don't know anyone to tell, anyway. At least," he whispered, "I don't."

I wanted to shake some backbone into him. Or maybe just give him a hug.

"I'm gratified that you showed such good sense. Yes, I think it's the real thing, but of course—of course!—I must study all of this in detail before I make any kind of announcement. If it's what we think...." He shook his head as if to clear it, then said briskly, "If it is, that announcement will be a moment to remember. Reputations will be on the line, not least my own. We must be very, very sure."

He stood up suddenly. "Pack it up. It goes home with me right now. I need to compare the information to items in my collection at home."

Ryan immediately got to work, but I was not so quick to jump.

"You can't do that!" The words just popped out. "We have copies for you, and can make extras, but I'm sure the originals are never supposed to leave here. There are policies. I certainly don't have the authority to give special permission. I mean, what if something happened to them?"

I knew I was right. I didn't falter until he turned his steel gaze on me.

"Are you saying you are worried that I might spill coffee on them? Laughable." However, he was not laughing. "Copies? No, indeed. There is information for me just in handling the originals. Furthermore, all you need to know," Flint said, "is that I went to Yale with Dr. Rhodes, your director. He's been Kip to me our entire adult life. I was in his wedding." He raised an eyebrow. "I applaud your exaggerated sense of responsibility, but I do rather think that covers the issue."

This wasn't a Brooklyn playground and I was being out-maneuvered. Short of a football tackle—appealing but not practical—I didn't see how I, one step up from an intern, could stop him. While I was defiantly trying to call my boss, they just walked out, taking the large cartons with them.

Maybe they'd stop him cold at security. I was momentarily comforted by that picture. I hoped handcuffs would be involved.

My boss did not respond but I left him a message. By the time I reached the security desk at the door, it was too late. They were gone.

I collected the folders of copies and returned to my office, not at all sure what to do next. Hiding out for a few minutes seemed like a comforting idea and hiding out by strolling the information superhighway seemed like an even better idea.

I wanted to see what I could find about the Green-Wood Cemetery event.

I found precisely nothing. And maybe I despised that annoying young reporter—self-styled reporter—but now I was disappointed that he had not learned any more about the events at the cemetery and put it up for all of us to see. The irony was obvious even to me. I could contact him directly—he'd be happy to hear from me—but no way was I going to give him the satisfaction. Instead, I punched in Leary's phone number.

I was pleased that he sounded groggy. "Did I wake you from a nap? Consider it payback for last night."

He chuckled. "Did I disturb your beauty sleep? Just thought you'd want to know about that right away."

"Well, I want to know more and I can't find anything at all. Not a word."

"So you're turning to the pro?"

I thought of telling him about Dima and Natalya and Alex, but I didn't think that would increase his interest. He does have a soft spot—really, he does—but it is buried deep and he seldom admits to it. Flattery, on the other hand, is often quite effective.

"Why, yes I am, you old newshound. Evidently that creepy kid I told you about could not get anything more, but I bet you can."

"Bet you're right. And you can cut out the flattery crap. I do know a couple of people who might know someone. What's it worth to you?"

"What is worth to you?"

"Homemade manicotti," he said immediately. "Garlic bread. Chianti. Cheesecake. I'm sick of these damn healthy meals they bring me, those social services do-gooders. And don't even think of telling me why I shouldn't drink."

"I wouldn't waste my breath, and yes, manicotti I can do. I learned some useful things from my Italian mother-in-law. When you deliver the goods, okay?"

"Start grocery shopping." He hung up.

Before I could figure that out, a message flashed on my screen. "In my office. Now." It was from my boss.

Deep breaths, I told myself.

Eliot looked as disturbed as a normally good-natured guy can look. Bern Dixon, the head of museum security was sitting there, too, and he looked even more disturbed, and way less good-natured. In fact, he looked just like what he was, a very large, very unhappy ex-cop.

He launched right in. "You have no authority whatever to allow museum property off the premises."

"I know that! I would never..."

"I just had a very disturbing report about a Professor Flint, who was carrying out material without any authorization and then had the nerve to give my man on the desk a hard time. And he said you knew all about it."

"I did know all about it, but I did not say it was okay!" The injustice of that made my voice squeak. Another deep breath and an attempt to moderate my voice to office appropriate levels. "I told him…" I turned to my boss. "Really, I did tell him. I said he shouldn't do it and I couldn't okay it and there would be some problem at security. He said, 'I went to Yale with Dr. Rhodes. I was in his wedding, I call him Kip. I applaud your exaggerated sense of responsibility, but I do rather think that covers the issue.' Kip, for crying out loud!"

My boss gasped and then he started to laugh. "He didn't! Did he? He didn't say that!"

Dixon did not see the humor. "I was out of the building. Apparently he handed my desk man a note from the director asking all staff to give him every consideration."

"And?" Eliot said it; I was keeping quiet.

He admitted, "And he walked out. I ripped him apart, my man. He's new but he still should've had more sense. Then again," he looked at me in a way I did not like, "you're not new and you should have had more sense, too."

Eliot said. "I can see you felt outgunned but you should have called me…"

"Or me," Dixon said. "It was a huge lapse in judgment. Huge. If I had a heads up I would have handled it very differently."

"But I tried to…"

Dixon held up his hand to stop me. "If anything happens to that stuff, we are all in trouble. Is that clear enough or do I have to make a speech?" Then he left.

I said, "Eliot, I am so sorry. I feel so stupid. And responsible, too. Just tell me, how bad is this, really?"

He shrugged. "The boss should have known Flint might take advantage and not been so accommodating. Maybe it will all work out. We just have to wait and see." He turned to papers on his desk, and I could see I was dismissed.

I did not find any of this very reassuring.

"Remember," he said as I was leaving, "I said your involvement with these Tiffany letters could be a very nice boost to your career? That's a good reason to be careful." He added, "However that boost has to come with some kind of price tag. Make more of an effort to charm the difficult Thomas Flint. I'm sure you can figure out how."

Yeah, yeah, I thought. One, charm is not my strong suit; I'm more of a straight-to-the-point person. Two, he seemed immune in any case. Three, I didn't want to charm him, even if I could.

But, yes, I certainly did want to remain on this project now. Maude Cooper was beginning to charm me.

I took a short walk to clear my head. Hell, I wasn't even supposed to be working that day; no one could tell me I shouldn't leave my desk. They'd better not. Maybe fresh air would chase away the knots in my stomach this whole discussion had caused.

I couldn't seem to get a fix on how badly I had screwed up. I'd been at the museum long enough to know that the genteel behavior in a scholarly organization only covered up all the usual undercurrents of jealousy, ambition, and just plain old bitchiness. Some people were wonderful; some would gladly step on your hands as they climbed over you on the ladder. However, I still had trouble, sometimes, reading the signals through that fog of gentility.

I needed this job. The flexible, part-time hours made it possible for me to work on my dissertation. The pittance of a salary helped me augment my patchwork financial life of fellowships and insurance. The practical experience helped me gain credentials for a real job.

My eyes began to prick, even as I ordered myself not to even think of crying in a public place. I walked faster, no longer noticing the lovely surroundings. I just needed to keep moving. And maybe find a cupcake or two.

An hour later, I had a plan to rescue myself.

"Ryan?" When I called, I used my best mom-not-to-be-messed with voice. "I need to double check some details on those documents your boss took. It can't wait. I'll come look at them tonight, wherever they are.

If I didn't tell him what I really wanted he had no opportunity to say no or to discuss it with Flint. Face to face, I hoped I could persuade them to hand over the boxes. This time I would be grounded in sure knowledge that I had been right, and I would be fueled by Dixon's scary words.

"Uh, okay, they're here at Dr. Flint's house. I'll be here too, all evening, working on them. I guess it's okay for you to come over."

"Sure it is. We're all working together, after all."

"I can't ask him anyway. He's out for the whole night, some fundraiser in Connecticut. I'm working and house-sitting."

Yes! Perfect. In Flint's absence, I was sure I could persuade Ryan—okay, bully him—to hand it all over to me. I would have it all back where it belonged first thing in the morning.

Chapter Twelve

I drove slowly through the quiet back streets of Greenwich Village, looking for the address Ryan had given me. In the busy heart of the Village, you would not think there were any quiet back streets left. The sidewalks always seem to be thronged with NYU students and suburban tourists looking for adventure, and any block might offer a tattoo and piercing shop, a multi-starred restaurant, and one of the few remaining jazz clubs—reminders of an earlier age—or the entire block might be pizza shops, cheap shoes, and cell-phone stores.

Yet, the quiet spots remain. These blocks are lined with exquisitely preserved brick row-houses, much older than those in my neighborhood. There are gracious trees, and well-dressed adults walking sleek dogs. Yes, I could see Dr. Flint here.

Until I found the address, I hadn't realized I was not looking for one of the grand old apartment buildings that anchor some of the corners. I imagined him there in Edith Wharton-ish splendor, but in fact, it was one of the brick townhouses, in the restrained Federal style, with none of the Gilded Age embellishments of my neighborhood. Elegant planters with clipped boxwood lined the stairs. Sleek black painted shutters. And, yes, there was a smartly polished brass plaque next to the door. It said 1823.

I ran up the short flight of front steps, rang the doorbell, waited, and rang again. I was anxious to get the unpleasant errand done.

True, Ryan was a bit flaky but we had just talked, so where was he? I was beginning to be annoyed. Perhaps I should have gone to the old tradesman's entrance under the stairs. I rang the bell down there, peered through the wrought-iron security gate and even rattled it, looking for a sign of life.

I dug my phone out and called, and when there was no answer, left a message: "I am right outside. Answer the damn doorbell!"

I returned to the main door, determined to pound on it until I had his attention. All of the neighbors', too, if necessary. With the first smack of my fist, it gave and I realize it was not quite locked. Okay, I would go in and wake him from his nap, or his video game-induced stupor or whatever it was. Perhaps it was a substance-induced funk. He seemed to be too anxious about his job to try that during working hours, but what did I really know?

I stepped into a dark narrow hall, papered in an elaborate antique-looking design. There seemed to be a parlor off to the right. Though I would normally have been full of curiosity about this elegant old house, I was too annoyed to do more now than take it in, in passing. It seemed surprisingly messy.

I walked to the kitchen in the back, calling Ryan's name, but the room was empty. I looked out the French doors, into a tiny, well-lit garden, to see if he was out there.

There was another room, a kind of study I guessed, as I saw rows of bookcases beyond the half opened door. That looked like the right place for Ryan to be hiding out. It was even messier than the parlor.

And there he was, slumped over a huge old wooden desk, in front of a huge modern computer, sound asleep.

"Ryan!" It was my exasperated mother voice, my "Chris, out of bed right now" voice, inappropriate for a work situation. I didn't care. "Ryan, damn it!" When I put my hand on his shoulder to shake him awake, just as I would Chris, he moved, stiffly and then I saw the wound on the side of his head. He had hit something or been hit. There was blood.

I guess I screamed.

The next thing I knew, I was in the kitchen, as far from Ryan's lifeless body as I could get, dialing 911, giving the necessary information and being told to stay right there. I sat down, shaking and wondering if I would throw up.

Then I called Chris, leaving messages at home and on her cell, that I was delayed, no idea how long. She should do her homework. No going out. And she could call me if she needed to.

My voice sounded weird, even to me, and I wondered how long it would take her to call and demand to know what was going on.

Then I sat in the parlor, on an antique sofa, unable to move or even think, until the police came. I sat there for what seemed like a long time and I could not even have said later what color the sofa was.

The next hour was a blur. Some officers talked to me, asked me a lot of questions about who I was, why I was there, when I arrived, where I had been earlier, when I had talked to him. I could easily establish when I'd left work. I told them I understood this to be Dr. Flint's home, but had no idea where he was or how to reach him; someone in uniform was examining his phone for information. Someone else was dusting the computer for fingerprints, and then began to wrap it up. Someone else asked me if I could see if anything valuable had been taken, and I said I could see items all over the house that I suspected might valuable, but I had never been there before so I could not know what might be missing. I realized the mess might have been made by burglars. If only I had been there earlier.

It didn't come to me until later that if I had been there earlier, I too might have been lying facedown on the table.

Something else hit me first.

"Officer." My voice went all weird. "I told you I came to pick up some historical documents? They were in boxes…I didn't see them there…in the study…"

"And they would be valuable? Papers of some kind?"

I nodded. "And they really should not have been removed from the museum at all. I mean, they are not valuable in dollars like—um, that silver bowl over there…but they can't be replaced."

"Describe the boxes." He motioned to one of the crime scene team. "Can you take her in there? Just to look around? Listen to what she says about the boxes, look all over the room, then someone take her upstairs too, if they're not in there. And could the contents be out and like, scattered around?"

I nodded again.

"Don't touch anything, not one thing, but speak up if you see something like what you're looking for. Got that? You can get started in just a minute."

I nodded again. I stood up and saw some people going into the study with what I was sure was a body bag.

It felt like a bitter clear moment in the midst of all the activity.

"I…before…" I swallowed. "I knew him. Can I see him… before you take him away…?"

They stopped and one said, "Yeah, sure, but quick."

I went back into the study for the first time since I found Ryan. He was ready to go now I could see his face, still as a mask, eyes closed. I had wanted to say good-bye, somehow, but now I did not know how to do it. This was not the smart, goofy kid I had liked and who had exasperated me. That person was gone from this body, but I stayed while they moved what was left behind into the bag and took it away. It seemed the least I could do.

An hour later, we had established that the boxes of documents were not there, and the individual documents did not seem to be lying around anywhere. Not on the shelves in the study or on the floor under the desk or in the credenza. It turned out there was a safe in the study, hidden behind an engraving, but it was unlocked and empty. There was nowhere in the exquisite parlor to stash anything, and nothing was hidden in the kitchen cabinets either.

Later, they would do a full search—every dresser drawer upstairs, every closet, in the basement if there was one. I gave them as detailed a description of the papers as I could. In fact, I would scan and send a few of the copies from the office in the morning so they would know exactly what to look for, but I had no hope.

They had been in Flint's possession for only a few hours, and Ryan had told me he would be working on them tonight. They should have been right there on the desk and he should have been right there, too, conscientiously making notes and frowning with anxiety.

They told me I could leave at last, and I walked to my car with tears running down my face.

It was late now. In the surreal atmosphere at Flint's house, I had lost all track of time. The main avenues were still clogged with traffic—this is the city that never sleeps, after all—but as I approached home, only an occasional car drifted down the small streets and no human was out and about on the sidewalks. Parking spaces were all taken, and I had to circle for several minutes, park two blocks away and drag myself to my house, while I longed desperately for home and warmth.

My house was quiet too, and dark. There was a note from Chris: "Mom, WTH, where were you? Ate leftovers, did home-work like a good little girl, and went to bed." I wandered around the first floor looking for mail, checked for dirty dishes lying around the kitchen, checked for phone messages. Finally I gave in to my need to see my own child, even if she was asleep. I knew nothing about Ryan's family, but he was someone's child and he died tonight.

I wanted to wake Chris and hold her tightly in my arms. Just hold her. If I did, she would be either angry or annoyed at me. Choose one. And she needed her sleep. Her alarm clock would wake her for school in just a few hours.

I stood in her doorway and looked at her by the light from the hall. On this chilly night, she was wrapped in the stylish comforter she picked out for her fourteenth birthday, but I could see the ears of her old stuffed bunny peeking out over the edge. Tousled hair, clothes dumped onto the floor. She was breathing.

I was in shock, I suspected, but my own world was intact.

◇◇◇

I woke up with bright sunlight in my eyes. I had forgotten to close the shutters last night, and it was now nine o'clock. How could it be so late? The house was silent. Chris had left for school and I had slept right through it. I never did that except when I was up all night writing a paper. I was not scheduled to work today, thank heaven.

I put my head under my pillow, trying to find my way back to oblivion, but the doorbell rang. And kept ringing. I finally gave in, got up, fumbled for a robe and fumbled my way downstairs, eyes half-closed, brain more than half-closed, and completely resentful.

It was my father.

"Ohmigod, Dad. What the hell?"

I was standing there in the open doorway, unable to move, but the morning chill was starting to shock me awake.

"Are you going to let me in?"

Trapped, I sighed and stepped away from the door.

"What's going on?" he said. "Chris was real worried about you last night, and she called me this morning."

"She sent you over here?" I could not believe she would do that.

"Why does that matter?" He stopped, then said, "You know, you really scared her. She said you sounded very weird on the phone, and you wouldn't wake up this morning. If you're in trouble, let me help you both, okay?"

"Oh, sure. That's just what I need to do." He hadn't been helping much in the last few years.

He looked back without blinking. "I'm right here now. "

Then I burst into tears.

By the time I was able to blurt out "young person" and "old friend" and "killed," plus "nightmare'" and "falling apart" and "Natalya" and "too much sadness" we were sitting on the sofa and my sobbing was taking place on my father's shoulder. He was mopping my face with a large plaid handkerchief and I wondered how many years it had been since I cried on his shoulder.

"Oh, Dad. It's just...I don't understand...so much is happening...."

"I know, honey." He kept his arm around my shoulders, and held me a little tighter. "Life is just throwing too damn much at you, right? Are you ready to tell me about it?"

I was, finally. He shook his head at the deaths, patted my hand and stopped me at one point to pour coffee and make me some toast.

When I said, "But what am I going to do? I feel all involved with Ryan—he was just a kid!—but I don't know what I can do. And Chris and Natalya. I don't have the energy or time to be involved. And I don't even know how I could be. And I'm in trouble at work, maybe big trouble."

The words came pouring out before I realized I was saying them. And to my father. I had spent so many years establishing that he could not tell me what to do. Ever.

"Honey, I'm here to help, any way I can, including talking about it, but you need to figure this out yourself."

Who was this sane creature and what had he done with my real parent, the protective, overbearing one?

And was there a faint twinkle in his eye when he said it? He went on, "Maybe I can start by making you some breakfast. Got any bacon? Have you eaten lately? Hard to think clearly on an empty stomach."

I shook my head. I was pretty sure I had skipped dinner last night.

He pulled me to my feet, pointed me to the stairs, and said, "Shower now. Plenty of hot water. Food will be on the table by the time you are done."

As I moved away, I mumbled, "No bacon for me. I just keep it for flavoring a salad. And use the lowfat cheese."

"No chance. Right now you need calories, not health food crap."

That sounded more like my dad and I was too exhausted to argue.

A few gallons of hot water, three eggs, a pile of cheddar and four strips of bacon later, I felt a little less shaky. That was a good thing, because the phone rang and it was my boss, telling me I needed to come in, day off or not, and how soon could I be there?

When I put the phone down, I took a few deep breaths.

"Those suited-up bastards. Do you want me to come in with you? "

"What? NO. I am not in kindergarten, for crying out loud. I will handle it, I can handle it, myself, like a grown-up. Which I am." I hoped saying it made it true.

"Well, I'll drive you there. You don't need the stress of waiting around for a bus or subway. And I'll stay to take you home, too."

"No, Dad. Thanks, but no. Don't wait." If I was getting fired, I did not want to have to deal with him right after. Then I caved a little and said, "But I'll take the ride there. Thanks."

I dressed in my most professional clothes that were clean and ironed. I put on full makeup. It was all armor. Look like a person with lots of confidence, and that was who I would be. I hoped.

We didn't say a word in the car, but when he dropped me off, he said again, "Any help you need, I'm on it. You and Chris are everything to me. You need to talk, figure things out some more? I'm here. If someone is treating you bad and you need him to get straightened out, I can do it. You need money, I've got some saved, too. You just gotta tell me, okay?"

"Don't, Dad. Thank you but just don't. We'll be fine." My momentary breakdown was over.

I was already getting out of the car, and I didn't look back, but I heard his voices behind me, saying "Honey, don't let the bastards grind you down."

I'd been told to come to the conference room, and there they all were, my boss, Eliot; his boss; Dixon from security; and Dr. Rhodes, our director. Some other big shots. Plus Thomas Flint. Flint looked as bad as I felt and maybe a little worse. His face was ashen and his eyes looked as if he'd been up all night. Even his sleek hair looked rumpled. When I saw them all, waiting, I paused at the doorway, took a deep breath and told myself to be calm. Then I went in. Ready or not.

"Erica, have a seat," my boss said, genially enough. "We are in crisis mode here, and we need information from you to help us get out of it."

Dr. Rhodes, the big boss, leaned forward to address me directly. I was surprised he knew who I am.

"Ms. Donato, we need to talk to you about the situation regarding Flint's unfortunate young assistant."

"Ryan?"

"Yes, I understand that's his name. For us, as people, we must acknowledge the tragedy, but right now we are here as museum employees, with responsibility and loyalty to our institution."

I told myself to be quiet, to wait, to let him talk. Not exactly my natural style.

"Dr. Flint informs us that the valuable documents you allowed to leave yesterday have disappeared."

I gulped. Then I looked directly at Dixon and said with entirely faked calm authority, "I want it on record that I did not allow them to leave. I protested to Dr. Flint but had no authority to stop him. He seemed to believe that permission had come from higher up." I kept my voice calm. It took some effort to do it.

Dr. Rhodes paled but said, with visible effort, "Dr. Flint presumed too much. I have to take responsibility for that."

Flint added, in a shaky voice, "As do I. I was so excited about this extraordinary find, I got carried away. I could not get back here for a few days and I wanted to begin work immediately, first thing this morning. Now I am paying a heavy price. I don't know how I will complete any of my work without young Ryan's help."

Was I the only person at the able who thought Ryan had paid the heaviest price? Eliot at least looked appalled and a few others looked away in embarrassment at Flint's words. At least I hoped it was embarrassment.

One of the other suits at the table said, "The issue is not who is responsible, but how in the world the museum handles this.

The documents are gone. We had responsibility to safeguard them. The owner has grounds for legal action."

Dr. Rhodes turned a little paler, but said with authority, "We are getting ahead of ourselves. Ms. Donato, let's go over yesterday's events briefly and then please tell us about last night. Dr. Flint has already informed us of your presence at his home."

I would not lose my temper. I explained how the documents had left the building, treading carefully, sticking to facts but putting everyone's actions in the best possible light. I tried to convey that it was all a series of misunderstandings instead of the display of arrogance and bullying behavior I knew it actually was.

Their questions were mild and I believed they bought it.

Then I had to tell them about my visit to Flint's home last night. It was hard—even harder than I expected—but they were less interested in my discovery of Ryan's body and more interested in the search for the documents. Their expressions became steadily more depressed as they realized that nothing I said was helpful. Not only was I confirming that the papers had vanished, I could not give them the smallest clue about Ryan's life or contacts or anything else that might point to how someone could possibly have known about what he was doing that night.

Neither could Flint. When asked, he hemmed and hawed and finally said, "We had a proper working relationship. We never discussed personal matters at all."

Dixon, the former cop, said, "Never? You don't know anything, after he worked for you for a year?"

"I will not accept being badgered by you. He's a student at Pratt. I assume some people there knew him more personally. I did not."

Dixon went on. "You did know your home, though. Was anything else taken? I mean, could this have been an ordinary burglary?"

"Some items were taken, but with a home full of quite valuable antiques, they took only a few and also some of no value whatever, just objects meaningful to me. And then the papers.

How could they know they were important? Or did they just make a guess because Ryan had them out?"

"Perhaps they got a clue on that if he tried to protect them." Dixon's voice had an edge of hostility, though his face remained emotionless. "Or perhaps they were there on purpose and just trying to make it look like an ordinary burglary."

Flint looked around the table, and shook his head. "I believe this is all aimed at me. MY home invaded, MY papers were taken, MY valuable assistant. Even the robbery at Green-Wood was related to MY life work."

Everyone at the table snapped around to stare at Flint, while I held my breath waiting to hear more, and Dr. Rhodes said, "Tom? What in blazes are you talking about?"

"You haven't heard? There was a robbery at Green-Wood Cemetery. A Tiffany window was stolen in the night, lifted right out of a chapel. My last scholarly article was on Tiffany's work in cemeteries." He looked around the table. "Now do you see what I mean? That this must all be directed at me somehow?"

"Tom," Rhodes said, "you must have been up all night with police, right? You're exhausted, old friend. I'm going to ask Shawna here to take you up to my office, give you a cup of herbal tea, and let you rest for a bit on my couch. Doesn't that sound like a good plan? Then you're going home. Is your housekeeper there? Shawna, please show Dr. Flint where he can rest."

As soon as Flint was gone he turned to all of us. "I think we can end this ineffective meeting now, except for the PR team. You stay—we need to plan. The rest of you—nothing on this, and I do mean nothing, to anyone, ever. All questions go through my office."

Bern Dixon said, "I still have friends at Police Plaza. Want me to see what I can find out?"

"Certainly. And I will be contacting all our board members—the ones who haven't already contacted me—to see what pressure we can exert to make this a high priority." He stopped, as if hearing his own words, and added, "Of course I know they will give this murder their attention, as they should, but I can't let our special problem get lost."

As we all got up to leave, Rhodes looked my way and said, "Ms. Donato? You should hope that we somehow retrieve those papers because your lack of judgment remains a serious issue. If there are major consequences for us, there will be for you. You are not free of that."

I felt myself turning red, and was ready to respond, vehemently, but saw Eliot, behind him, shaking his head slightly.

I stopped myself, and only stared at Dr. Rhodes as he said, "Not free at all."

Chapter Thirteen

I went straight to my cubicle, wishing I had a door to slam. I felt like ripping pages out of a book. Or throwing a phone. I also felt physically ill. Lack of sleep can do that, but most of it was my frustration was over Dr. Rhodes' last words. And my fear. Let's not forget that.

I was so tempted to follow him to his own office, and demand that he tell me what he meant. Then sanity reasserted itself. A little voice—perhaps my mother's ghost—was urging me to make better choices.

I could turn to Eliot, who was a great mentor, but that might put him in a difficult position. Another mistake I've finally learned not to make: Never put your boss in a difficult position.

I admitted to myself that I could not talk to anyone right now without sounding needy, unsure, and even whiny. Any mother who's been on the receiving end knows what kind of results whining produces. Negative ones. So I would buckle down and think hard and keep my mouth shut until I had something profoundly useful to say.

I wondered if there was anything in the work Ryan had been doing that was a piece of this sad puzzle. I had all his files right here, both the copies of the papers and his computer files. It might be a long shot—I admitted to myself that it probably was—but at least it was a place to start. And if his death was in fact related to the theft of the documents, perhaps it would turn out to be the best place to start. I could hope.

I turned the office computer on and started roaming through the work he had been doing, but I was sidetracked by the ping that told me I had an incoming e-mail. Chris.

"Mom. WTH is going on? It would be nice if you told me. Like,—AHEM!—you expect me to tell you. 2 night??? Where are you now? I'll call you at lunch."

I steeled myself for her lunchtime call, and tried to focus on the files in front of me, but it was late. She called before I had accomplished anything much.

She began with a cascade of questions and comments. "Where were you last night? Your phone call told me precisely nothing. And I had a killer math test and I was freaking about it. Alex was all weird and no one knows what to do. And where were you last night, anyway?"

I had to stop it, not with the verbal smack I felt like, but with a measured and calm, "Chris? Chris! Slow down and let me give a coherent answer."

Dead silence and then "Okay, mom. Go."

"Something happened last night and I am very shaken, so just listen and don't push me, okay?"

And then I told her.

This time the silence went on so long I was not sure she was still there.

"How can that be?" It was a little tiny voice. "He was there in your office. I talked to him…"

"I know, hon. I'm feeling the same way. How can this be real? It was terrible; I won't tell you how bad. "

"Do they know what…what happened? Or why? I mean, he seemed so…uh…harmless. And clueless."

"They didn't tell me anything. Probably they didn't even know yet. It was literally the start of their work, but I'm sure…."

"Well, did you tell them everything you know about him?" The voice was still tiny but my smart daughter was coming back. "Did you?"

"The sad thing—one of the sad things—is that I don't know anything to tell. We only worked together for a few days, and we mostly talked about work. He was an art student. He liked graphic novels. That about all I know. "

"That's pathetic. And awful." Her voice was rising with each sentence. "I don't understand grown-ups. If it was me, we would have exchanged life stories in the first hour. Don't you care?"

I gasped. "How can you say that? May I remind you I found him? How could I possibly not care? But I'm sure the detectives will start with his classmates…"

"Mom! Geez! I know you live in the past but please. Look for him on Facebook. Duh."

"Facebook? He did not seem like the kind of guy…"

"Oh, please! There is not a Facebook kind of guy. It's everyone." She sighed a martyred teenage sigh. "You do still have the Facebook account I set up for you, don't you? Do I have to come by after school and walk you through it? You need to know about him."

Humbled, I said thank you but that I could handle it. Who knows? Maybe she was right. I had an account but was far too busy to ever look at it. I thought I was up to the simple task of finding someone. I'd get to it as soon as I finished Ryan's notes.

Just on the unlikely chance that the missing papers were stolen on purpose, could there be something in them that was important? Not just important to a select circle of history and art nerds but important in the bigger world? The one most people would call the real world? I wasn't sure Flint or Ryan were well-acquainted with that world, but I was, so I was the one to do this searching.

So. Back to the computer. Open the files Ryan was working on to see what he had done. We had split reading the letters. Now I would look over his half as carefully as I had read mine.

Meticulous Ryan had set up a meticulous table to organize all the details found in Maude's letters. I still needed to fill it in for my half, refreshing my memory as I went.

I was discouraged to see that I had not overlooked a single detail about the exciting possibility of an unknown window.

I had been hoping, against all odds, to make a discovery that would answer all the questions.

I did enjoy being back in Maude's world, though. I'm far too much of a historian to really believe life was better in the "the good old days." There were no good old days. It was just that right now Maude's life looked a lot better than mine.

I attacked Ryan's half of the letters first. He had noted every theme in his chart: Tiffany—sub-headed into studio, art, people—life in NY, and Maude's personal comments. Precise to the nth degree, but not too personal, so I went back to the letters themselves.

This time around, doing more than my initial skimming, my attention was caught by the way she wrote some letters to "Dear Mama and Katie" and others to just Katie.

She confided only to Katie that a theater party included a young man with a handsome blond mustache and twinkling eyes. She told them both that she loved the speed and sense of freedom her bicycle gave her, but only told Katie about the dashing man who rode with her. And when she assured her mother she was faithfully attending Madison Square Presbyterian church, only Katie knew the same companion carried her prayer book.

Hmm, I thought. This was a theme we had not picked up earlier.

I returned to my own stack of letters. Had I been so excited about the Tiffany details that I had missed something else? Oh, yes.

She wrote Katie that she had dinner alone in a respectable restaurant with "my friend" and explained that this was not as daring as it would be at home. She told only Katie she had been to see Loie Fuller, the avant-garde dancer and was mesmerized by her delicate butterfly costume. "She is a client of Miss Driscoll, you know, but I would not have gone if my friend had not escorted me."

Even as the letters began to trail off, and focus on her work almost entirely, there were brief references to a picnic in a secluded park and dining in quaint restaurants in obscure

German and Italian neighborhoods. She did not write any more about outings with a group of friends, and she never named the companion who was taking up so much of her time, but she did say, once, "No, Katie, I do not know where this may lead, but do not worry about me. I am not unhappy."

"Oh, Maude," I thought. "It seems you had a few secrets. You are not that naïve young thing from the Midwest anymore, are you? But you are certainly not giving me one new thing to help understand what happened to Ryan."

Maybe it was just a robbery after all. I put my head down on the worktable. Someone knew Flint had a house full of valuables, and it was just Ryan's tragic luck to be there. I had come to a dead end on this.

I sat up, refusing to let Maude's story dead end, too. I had been wondering what became of the mysterious companion, of Maude herself, even of Katie. I smacked myself, because I did know where to look for answers. If I found some, maybe I could start redeeming myself here at work.

Here was the name of Maude's hometown in Illinois, River Bend. A quick web search gave me the name of the local newspaper, *River Bend Daily*, and—aha!—it still existed. It had a website. Its electronic records only went back a few decades, but there was an e-mail address for a librarian. I shot off a note with Maude's and Katie's full names and asked how I could learn if there was ever anything about them in the paper, anything at all. I hit "Send" just as Chris looked in the door.

I stood up and embraced her in a long hug. At that moment, it did not matter to me at all if she wanted one. After the death of a young person, I needed to hold tight to my own child. She stiffened at first and then hugged me back.

She broke first and said, "What did you find out about Ryan? I came because I know you won't do Facebook without my help."

"Yes I will! I'm sure I can do a simple name search, but I had to do my own work, so I don't lose my job. You know, that pays your phone bills and puts food on the table?"

She gave me an exasperated look, sat herself at my computer and said, "Now pay attention. First you need to do this."

Ryan's page was up there in seconds.

"About time!"

"Chris, please cut it out."

"No, I won't. I'm really mad at you. Okay, I know—I know—last night was awful for you. But you never called back. Two people I know died this week. That's crazy. And then you stay out till all hours and I don't know what is happening to you and I get scared. How would you like it if I did that?"

"Chris…"

"I thought you would help more with Alex and his mom. Because…you know. He is only my oldest friend and I want to help him and I don't know how. He worries about Natalya. He said today that when Dima left for Green-Wood that night…"

"What did you just say? Say that again!"

Bewildered, she stopped the torrent of words and said, very slowly, "He worries about his mother…

"No! The part about Green-Wood."

"Oh. That's where he worked a couple of nights a week. Night watchman." She looked bewildered. "You must have known. He used to joke that he liked it because none of his customers could talk. "

"I had no idea." My mind was spinning now. I jotted down a few notes, thinking about what connected.

"Mom? You're zoning out again. Which was my point. Okay, just forget about it. I'm going home."

She was down the hall before I could even answer.

I wanted to reason with her. Smack her. Apologize to her. Cry. Chase her and drag her back. She wasn't making sense, and yet she was.

I wanted to call my friend Darcy who has raised three teens and cry on her shoulder. She would be at work now, so I poured out my heart in an e-mail and knew she would call me tonight. I even knew what she would say: Let her calm down and get calm yourself before you try to talk it out.

Easier said than done. I couldn't obsess about Chris and still have my breathing and heart rate returned to normal. There was Ryan's Facebook page. Now I would concentrate on exploring it.

I learned that Ryan, mild-mannered and meek in person, could be quite snarky online. I learned he only had a few friends, but they seemed to be involved in an intense, endlessly looping conversation about girls, comic books, and the meaning of life. And dumb jokes.

I looked at what he wrote his last few days, even while I flinched at the thought that they were his last few days. Headed to his "artpeeps":

> Unfuckingbelievable day at work. We're going through these old letters I told about and it looks like we found something BIG for real—a Tiffany window no one even knew exists. Yeah for real. As good as finding an original Superman #1 comic book? (ha, ha) Nah. (But then what would be?) But good enough to make Dr. Flint my SOB boss happy? Yeah. Good enough to get my name on a paper he will most likely write about it? Yeah. Good enough to get me to graduate with honors. Yeah, maybe. Today we did the slave work—made back up copies, made notes, sent him an e-mail. His mind will be blown when he gets back. Yahoo!"

I stopped breathing for a minute. Oh, Ryan, I thought. You dope. No wonder you turned red when Dr. Flint said keep it a secret. You had already failed at that. So other people did know what we found and not just your friends, either. Even I know there are no secrets if it's out there in cyberspace. Did someone come to Flint's house looking for more details and find you instead?

Chapter Fourteen

My computer gave that annoying little ping, reminding me of something. What? I was busy thinking about Ryan. Oh, dinner tonight with Detective Henderson. No. I couldn't go somewhere and look okay and talk like a normal person. Not tonight.

He never answered and when his message system came on, I hung up. I should go after all. I would look a mess and be completely unable to make light conversation. It would be nobody's great first date, but he was a cop. He was on Dima's case. He could help me find my way through the random but startling information I seemed to be collecting. He might even have heard something about Ryan.

I checked my clothes. They'd do if I tided up a bit. Undo my long, curly hair, and pin up again in a nice twist. Sponge a spot off my blouse. Switch shoes to the better pair I keep in my desk for unexpected meetings. Oh, lipstick. I would do. I'd have to.

Fortunately we were meeting at a seafood place a ten-minute walk from my job. I walked along a street crowded with Manhattan-quality restaurants at—almost!—Brooklyn prices, a change of the past few years. I'd been to a few for coworkers' celebratory events. Here it was.

I stepped into a loud buzz mixed with loud music. It was party time here. Friday night and the drinking had already started. Henderson stepped in a minute after. He had to shout when he said, "Do you like this? I'll stay but it's noisy for my tastes."

I pointed to the door. The street noises were much quieter, and we both laughed.

"Thank you! It's been a crazy couple of days. I wasn't in the mood for a fraternity party."

"I got it. I know a nice place just down the street. You like Thai?"

We turned into a storefront with a spacious, almost empty room in the back and enticing odors of garlic and ginger.

"Better?"

"Perfect."

"Wait till you taste the food if you want to say perfect. Would you like a drink?"

I had an Asian beer, appetizers turned up without ordering and I felt the tight coils in every muscle start to unwind.

"I may not be the best companion tonight. In fact, I'm sure I can't be. A young man I know…I worked with him…was murdered last night."

His expression changed completely. "I get that. It's happened twice in my career. Maybe I'm a good person to be out with tonight? Do you want to tell it all? I'll listen. Or completely leave it alone?"

"I have no clue." I smiled, shakily. "You tell me. How do you deal?"

"It's a little different in the cop world, but I'd say, for you, talk and then change the subject. Make sense?"

It did, so I told him.

"You knew that kid? I heard about it and it's out in the news world, already. Surprised? It's not two drug dealers having it out, it's a crime that is news in a bunch of ways—young student, upscale neighborhood, house full of valuables. But I must be slipping. I should have connected it to you myself."

"There's more. I was there." Under his gentle questioning, I told him all about it and he was right. It helped. At the end I said, "Do you know anything about what they've found?"

"It's not my case, so not much more than you could hear on tonight's news. If it was a professional robbery, something stopped them before they finished the job, that's for sure. Of course the other possibility is that the victim left a door open, and it was a crime of opportunity. Real nice house, easy access, probably has some things worth snatching. They went in, were grabbing whatever they found and he stumbled into it."

"That makes me want to cry." I had to stop and get calm. "Did you know they apparently snatched up some valuable papers that are mine? Uh, not really mine, the museum's. Why would anyone do that?"

He shrugged. "Panic. Stupidity. Evidence, like blood on it. Lots of reasons. What do you mean by valuable? Worth real money, like…"

"Like an original Declaration of Independence? Or, oh, Jackie Robinson's autograph on a baseball? No, they only have historical value. Plus they weren't even the museum's. They were on loan. I am in big trouble for letting them leave the building."

"I see. Did you do it? Let them leave?"

"Hell, no, I'm not a complete idiot. I just couldn't stop them."

"Cheer up." He poured the last of my beer into my glass. "Another? Or food?"

"Both, please. You know this place, you order. I can' t even focus on the menu."

I was soon making inroads on my second beer. "Maybe I can help you, too. Did you know, that night that Dima was killed, he was working at Green-Wood Cemetery? "

He looked surprised. "Of course."

"How come everyone knew but me?" The beer was starting to hit me. "I guess it wasn't one of the things Dima and I talked about. No overlap. It was not as important as what we shared, like school and kids and fixing houses. Just his other job to pick up some extra bucks. Hmm. Probably used it to buy that other house. There was a robbery there that night at Green-Wood. I suppose you know that, too?"

"Yes. But remember, Ostrov left the job in the middle of the night. He used his card to open the gate. We can't rule out that someone else used the card, but that, plus the way they left his body, makes our best guess that he wasn't killed there and it's not about the robbery. Not that we aren't looking at that, too."

"The cemetery honchos sure didn't want anyone to know about the robbery."

He looked a little grim. "Damn right. They didn't even tell us at first. Not telling us is borderline concealing evidence. Idiots, but it probably doesn't matter." He smiled at me. "You're looking a little spacey. Here." He slid his plate across the table. "Eat up the rest of my appetizers. And here's the food, too."

A big drink of water and scarfing down some rice soaked up some of the alcohol. Two beers didn't used to do this to me. Probably it was the exhaustion. And not eating much today. Surely it was not age creeping up.

"So what are you focusing on? With Dima?" I asked the big question. "Was it his brother? Or that nutcase guy on his other block? I know, I know, the way they did it, the way they left him, looks like something professional."

"Yes, well, everyone knows that these days, thanks to cop shows on TV. It doesn't help us do our job, believe me. What jurors think about the magic powers of DNA you wouldn't believe." He shook his head. "The short answer is, we are taking a very good look at the brother. He certainly has some history. And we are taking a very good look at the neighbor, because he is one loose cannon altogether. And we are taking a very good look at every piece of Ostrov's life, not to miss some crucial connection. He had one secret, about that house. There may be others. And that's all I am going to say."

"Shucks. And here I thought I'd charm you into telling me absolutely everything and then I'd go out and solve it all."

He laughed. "I suggest you watch fewer crime shows ."

"I don't have time to watch any. I haven't been to a movie since the days I had to take my daughter. Now she prefers her friends. And I don't watch crime shows. I grew up around cops."

He asked how I grew up around cops and I told about my dad's best friend and where we lived and my mother's cop cousins. He kind of laughed and said he got it.

That led naturally to high school and which teachers we had in common and some of his brother's exploits. I claimed not to have been involved in any of them, and he said that wasn't what he heard from Kenny, and I, on my third beer, started laughing, too, claiming I had to deny it all. I had a high school daughter who needed a good role model.

Third beer and the last of the curry, Thai salad, shrimp in coconut milk. Mango sticky rice and fried bananas for dessert to share. And espresso before I went home to Chris.

Against all odds, we were having fun. At my door, he kissed me, just like his brother Kenny would have, like an old friend, but said, "Next Saturday night? Fish and chips?" It sounded good to me.

I came home to Chris pacing the floor and snapping out at me, "Where have you been?" before I even had my jacket off.

"What are you talking about? You were out, so I had dinner with a—with a friend."

"Until 10:30? Did you forget you have a child at home? You're the one who sets my school night curfew."

"Chris. Listen to me. You. Were. Out." It had been too hard a day for this.

"You weren't here when I got home. And I needed you."

The headache was starting again, right behind my eyes.

"Okay, Chris. What is going on that is so important?"

"Everything. My life sucks. All of it. "

Oh, lord. It was an extension of the argument we had in my office.

"Uh, could you be more specific? I can't deal with 'everything.' And maybe we need cocoa for this."

"Mom! Am I a baby? Cocoa??? I have grown up problems here. A chem test I am bound to fail. Guidance class assignment is a sample college essay. How—how?—am I supposed to do that without help? I'm not ready. Oh, yes, one more little thing. I know two people who were just killed. That's not normal for my age! I'm just like Alex—who is getting weirder by the day, by the way—I only have one parent. But I don't even seem to have that lately."

Her voice rose with each sentence.

"Chris." I took a deep breath. "You can't just dump all of these things on me at once. Be reasonable. I have grown-up problems. Yours are different." I saw her expression and quickly added, "Not that they don't feel big to you, I know they do, but give me a break here. It's been a tough day." I took another deep breath. "If you're failing chemistry—which I don't even believe—I'll scrape up the money for tutoring, okay? Ask around at school for a name. I'd love to hear about Alex but not right now. I'll help with the essay over the weekend. Okay? Anything else?"

I was so tired I was swaying and sat down quickly.

"Is that it? That's it? Like, we just had a meeting?" She started to cry. "You don't get it. You don't understand. My life sucks. It's all a mess, all of it. I need…" She was sobbing now. "I need…" She gulped and finally said, "On top of everything else, I haven't heard from Jared in three days."

"That is what this drama is all about? You haven't heard from this…this teenage twerp? I can't do this, Chris. I have very real, very serious problems on all sides of me that you can't even imagine, and I am so exhausted I am shaking. It's not that I don't care, but not now. The problems will still be there to talk about tomorrow. "

She stopped in mid-sob and looked at me with an expression I could not read. Not then.

"You think my life isn't serious like yours is? Well, it's serious to me. You just don't get it. Not one thing. Even if you are a PhD candidate."

She turned without another word and walked away toward the stairs. I tried to say, "Oh, Chris, I didn't mean…" Then I heard the door to her room slam, and right then, I just didn't care. I couldn't. As I said, the problems would still be there for solving in the morning.

I slept and slept and woke up and rolled over and slept some more. I was recovering from this extraordinarily stressful week.

It was not a workday and it felt like a gift not to have to deal with anyone there. Or like an answered prayer.

Chris' door was closed when I finally got up. I knocked and called her name, just making sure she had gotten up and to school on her own. Getting up on time is not a key skill for any teen.

No answer but I could see from upstairs that her backpack and jacket were gone from the coat stand. Good. I concluded she had gotten up and out on her own. I left her door closed and reveled in the prospect of a quiet morning with no drama.

Food and caffeine started to work their magic. I hit the speed dial for Darcy but she didn't answer; it was the middle of her busy working day. My buddy Joe apparently had a new girlfriend. I didn't want to talk to my always-stressed out grad school classmates. I especially didn't want to talk to my dad. Maybe I'd go see the one person I knew who might have some practical advice. Leary. He would be distracting company. And he knew an awful lot about crime.

I picked up a rotisserie chicken at one of the many delis, added some sides and was ringing Leary's lobby bell in precisely twenty-seven minutes.

Someone with a key went in and I just followed. Not real smart of the key holder, but he probably figured someone who had a shopping bag smelling of roasted chicken was not dangerous.

"Leary!" I pounded his door and shouted and pounded some more, and finally I heard the multiple locks clicking open.

"Well?"

"Try to pretend you're glad to see me. I need advice and I brought lunch."

His expression changed from annoyed to interested. "There wouldn't happen to be a slice of fudge cake in there?"

"Oh, sure. A six-pack, too."

"Don't torment an old man. But come in, I guess. A man's got to eat, even if it's healthy crap."

He didn't fool me. I knew he was glad to see me.

I cleared a mountain of mail off his only table, rummaged in his kitchen and tableware, and said, "Was your aide here recently? I'm finding clean dishes."

By the time we had demolished the chicken and the pasta, he had stopped grousing about the lack of alcohol, and said, "So, Miss Meals on Wheels, what's on your mind?"

I blurted it all out. Ryan. My work issues. Dima's murder. My questions about the stolen window. My worries about the stolen papers.

"Whoa. You're flipping all over the place. And I don't deal with feelings, anyway. Or office politics. I wasn't good at it when I had some and you wouldn't want my advice. Now crime, that's another matter altogether. So let's break it down."

I nodded.

"You got all these weird events, right? Maybe just coincidences? Nothing to do with you, anyhow. But you want to know if they are connected? Yeah? That's all it is?"

"I guess. Yes." His cold water actually did seem to make it less of a muddle. "At least, it's a start."

"Hmm. Back when dinosaurs roamed Prospect Park and I was a hot reporter, we started with Churchy Lafam."

"What? Who the hell…"

"Churchy Lafam, cookie. Find the girl." He looked smugly amused. "You never heard that expression? And you a doctoral student?"

The fog cleared. "Oh, for God's sakes. You mean *cherchez la femme*. Very funny."

"Well," he said mildly, "we used to think it was."

"Doesn't apply here. There are femmes all over the place. Natalya. Chris. Bright Skye. Dr. Reade."

"Go home and make a list with notes. Put in all the names, no matter how unimportant. Sometimes your typing hands know what your brain hasn't figured out. Know what I mean? And, no, you can't do it here. No one but me touches my keyboard. Then the other old saying is 'Cui bono.'"

"Leary!!! Dammit. I came for help, not mind games."

"Okay, okay. In courtroom English, 'Who benefits?' or, translated to Brooklyn English, 'Follow the dough.'"

"That might make more sense, or it might if I had any answers." I checked them off on my fingers. "Dima—no one benefits…"

"That you know about…"

"As I was about to say, maybe his scary brother, if Natalya is right. Ryan, whoever broke in? Window theft, the thieves. Duh. I feel like I am the place where it all connects." I got up and paced his cluttered living room. "I knew Dima. I have had dealings at Green-Wood about a Tiffany window. The Tiffany letters were in my possession. And if there is a mystery about Maude, it's my job to solve it. But I'm totally useless. I can't make any sense of any of it. "

"Nah. You just need to noodle it some more. Start with what you know most about, those letters. Or tackle your most solvable personal problem and get it out of the way. Or," he said, with unusual gentleness, "you could just let it go. It used to be my job but it ain't yours."

I thought it over, ignoring his last sentence.

"The window is just a theft. Probably. It's appalling, but yeah, it is not personal. I only really, deeply care if it has something to do with the rest. Do you think it does?"

He shrugged. "Not thinking anything, because we don't have enough to go on. Ever hear of facts first, then theory?"

"And Dima—that's for the police. Totally their job. I do know that. But people I care about care about that. A lot. Natalya. And Alex, who I know is in pain. I've known him since he could barely walk. Even Chris."

"And this kid? Ryan, is it?"

"I don't think I can forget about him either."

"Ha. I wouldn't know about this, personally—thank God!— but sounds like a mom kind of feeling in there? Yeah?"

"Maybe. Yes. "

"Well, get rid of it! It's not helping you. Jesus, Mary, and Joseph, have I taught you nothing? You need to think, not feel."

I considered smacking him, but after silently staring away for a long minute, I decided to make better use of him.

"You've been around a long time. What do you know about Russian crime in Brooklyn?"

"Not a damn thing." He didn't hesitate for a second. "After my time. In my day, Russian crime meant spies, cloak-and-dagger stuff. All I know is that when the USSR opened up immigration, not all of them were bleeding-heart-worthy refugees. Sure, there's a mob, maybe more than one. Why should they be different from any other Americans?"

"That is not helpful. I was thinking about Natalya's brother-in-law."

"Sorry. Like I said, after my time. When they came in, I wasn't covering Brooklyn anymore and then I wasn't working anymore at all."

He grinned. "You just got to keeping pulling on those threads until it starts unraveling. Start with the one thing most likely to get you results. And okay, I do know who might know something. I already got my phone calls in. I might have an answer as soon as tomorrow."

"And you'll tell me as soon as soon as you have something?"

"Maybe." He saw my face and laughed. "Yeah, you little persistent mosquito, I will. See, I always said you have the makings of a reporter."

"You know, Leary, if we went online…."

"Ha. Even I thought of that, but not everything is out there, ya know? And what you maybe don't know is that not everything reporters learn gets into print. I've still got a few sources so I'll do it the old school way—we'll talk."

I left feeling better all around. Surprising—no, incomprehensible—that a visit with a grouch like Leary had helped lighten my mood.

I walked the block to my car, quickly, purposefully, and with a posture that tried to say, "Mess me with me and I'll rip your eyes out." Attitudes can be armor. I hoped. And I hoped the guy in that doorway across from my car was just waiting for a friend. Or someone to mug that looked more vulnerable than I do. And that he was not looking at me. Or for me.

Chapter Fifteen

I thought some extra time at work would give me the chance to pull on some of those threads.

Then the chance came to me. Dr. Flint was at my doorway, just in time to interfere with my need to find some giant cookies. Stress eating was kicking in full force and I did not care.

Even in my present distracted state I could see he did not look well. The perfect hair was sticking out oddly, the elegant clothes were mismatched and rumpled.

"I am going to have things out with you. No more nonsense." He stepped in without being invited. His eyes were like marbles and his tone was belligerent. I gave him a glassy cold stare in return. Country clubs are not the only place to learn how to stare people down. Not even the best place.

"Really? Just what is it you have to say to me? Let me rephrase: just what is it you *think* you have to say to me? And why should I listen?"

He checked, perhaps surprised, and then seemed to reboot. "You made a fool of me in front of my colleagues. I am not having a little snip like you demeaning my reputation…and my professional integrity…."

I folded my arms, and said, "I could not have made a fool of you without your abundant help. I didn't force you to steal—yes, steal!—those documents. I tried to stop you. And if that's all you have to say, get the hell of my office."

I dimly knew this might be a career-damaging moment. I no longer cared.

"Your job is to assist me! I am doing this for the museum as a favor, at nothing like my usual fee. You were assigned to work for me. Who are you to question my judgment, a little student with no experience? You overstepped…"

His words felt like shouting but his voice was a sinister whisper.

At that moment, I knew had some choices. I could collapse, as he obviously expected. Or I could start shouting for real, as I deeply, sincerely wanted.

With fierce calm, I said, "I so did not overstep. In fact, I got into trouble for not stepping further. I work for the museum. Their needs, not yours, are my job. Do I look that stupid? You are not here as a great culture vulture do-gooder. Whatever you find here will feed into your glorious reputation. Ryan told me that, as if I could not have figured it out for myself."

He face went from sickly pale, to red, and back again.

"Now you can leave my workspace and let me get on with my true job."

And then, all of a sudden he seemed to collapse into his clothes and onto my single office chair. He put his head in his hands.

"Everyone knows. I don't know how it all got out. I am being criticized everywhere. Attacked. If I lose my reputation—probably it's already lost—I have nothing. No career, no standing professionally or socially. My whole life is being destroyed."

"And I am to blame for this?"

His head, still buried in his hands, went from side to side. Was that a no?

Then what was he doing in my office?

"Dr. Flint? Do you have a reason for being here? I have work to do. "

He seemed to shake his head again and whispered something.

"What is it that you think I can do for you?"

His head was still buried in his hands but this time I could hear him. "That poor boy."

"Ryan?"

He did not look up.

"Dr. Flint!" I still had not an atom of sympathy but I had a wisp of curiosity.

"He was an odd young man," Flint whispered. "A lost soul. Clueless is the word he used himself. Not part of my vocabulary but it is descriptive. And classless. Not my usual type of assistant but he did the job brilliantly. And I never told him—never said a word—but he was hugely gifted in his art. There, he had that spark…"

"All this—this emotion—is about Ryan? Really?"

Flint finally looked up. He looked like a ghost. "Perhaps." He took a deep breath. "Perhaps. I am not a complete monster. I live my life as I have chosen, no regrets, but I know that if Ryan had not been at my house…I've spent my life studying artists, but he was a real artist. Do you see the distinction? And I've never been wrong about that. Now that promise…it's all lost… because of me…I was too eager…those papers…"

"Dr. Flint? Perhaps we should go out for a walk?" He didn't move. "When did you last eat? You come with me and have a coffee, at least."

He stood up and turned toward the hall, without actually looking at me. I led the way out, and over to the farmers market on the courthouse plaza. He followed. I didn't care what he needed, but I needed fresh air at that moment, and I couldn't leave him sitting in a stupor in my office. I also needed a fresh-picked apple. Or maybe a cider doughnut. Or maybe a whole bag of them. I bought him a ham and cheese sandwich, too.

I didn't ask him. I sat him on a plaza bench, thrust a sandwich half into his hand and set the cups of hot coffee, heavy on the sugar, on the bench between us.

"Now eat," I ordered. "Start with the doughnut."

He looked mildly surprised at that and mildly surprised at his surroundings.

But he picked it up and ate.

Between my personal high stress and the overall weirdness of the situation, the food had no flavor. I chewed and it helped somehow. The coffee seemed to have no flavor and no aroma, but it was hot. That was enough.

When Flint's sandwich had disappeared, and I was sufficiently fueled, I finally turned to him. "You tell me what is going on right now. And no more verbal abuse, or I will leave you right here to have a nervous breakdown all alone, in public."

"My life is over." He said it clearly enough, though he still could not look at me. "I spent my whole life…created my whole life from nothing…nothing…and now I am…nothing again. Calls and calls from the professional journals…and my colleagues…all oozing sympathy but smiling behind my back…I don't use all those online things…Ryan did it for me…but I'm sure they are buzzing. I made a misjudgment…they don't understand it was from good motives!…and someone died. That harmless young fool." He stopped suddenly, then added, "Does that explain it enough?"

"Not even close. I had a second when I thought it was about Ryan. Now I'm back to thinking you are just embarrassed."

He turned even whiter. "Is that how it seems? Have I lost all my social skills? It's not at all…well, maybe some of it is…but there is more.…"

I waited. And then I kept waiting. And then I stood up, and said, "I am going back to work. We're done." I turned and walked away.

He caught up with me at the first stoplight, and kept pace with me back to the building and into my office. Again. Before I could start protesting, he said softly, "I will never have children. Never wanted them. I never even wanted to mentor young people. I wasn't good at it when it was forced on me. I used interns occasionally only if they were thrust on me by a patron, or I was desperate for help. I preferred ambitious debutantes with art history majors. The world was already their oyster, they were useful enough and they didn't need anything from me."

He stopped talking.

"And this matters to me—why?"

"Ryan was different. I did need him. He solved problems for me and then he got to me. In my own, not-very-warm-hearted way, I tried to help him. To become a person who could belong somewhere in the world. Now I am…"

"You are sad." An emotion I knew too well.

"Sad? No, not possible. I have not been sad about any personal thing for…forever. Professional disappointment—the rare occasions!—certainly. And I did not after all know him well. He was not important to me as a person."

He still had not apologized to me. He still was barely looking at me. And he still was not leaving. I had an inspiration.

"Dr. Flint, how about doing some work today? We have copies of all the original documents. Why don't we spread them out in the workroom and you can look them over again for anything I might have missed? Ryan and I might have missed?"

I did not think we had missed a thing, but it would get him out of my office. I set him up with a computer, pulled my notes and Ryan's, showed him how to navigate and then he seemed so confused, I went and printed it all for him.

I couldn't settle back into productivity because something was nagging at me. Finally I went into the workroom and said, "Stop what you're doing. I want to show you something."

He accepted my bossiness and stood up right away. It must have been a measure of how shaken he was.

I had Ryan's Facebook page up on my screen. "Do you know what this is? It's a network. People write about their lives and other people—anyone they give permission to—can read it. Some people have hundreds of Facebook friends. Maybe even thousands." I pointed. "Read this."

It was Ryan's foolish musing about this project.

"He wrote about it? After I told him to keep it quiet? How could this have happened?"

I shrugged. "Before you told him. And they forget. Young people just forget that nothing on the Internet is private, even if it feels like a dormitory bull session. And then word can spread from Facebook friends to, well, everyone. But do you see? Other people knew about this. Give yourself a break."

I knew I had given him that break. I wasn't sure he deserved it, but still.

Some color came back into his face. "Maybe it wasn't me. I can…"

He looked right at me for the first time that day. "Who do I seem to be, to you?"

"What?"

"Yes, who do I seem to be?" He ticked off on his fingers. "Supremely well-educated. Brilliant at my work. I do everything with style, refined yet suave. Right? Would you assume I came out of a prep school background? Old money? The world of Edith Wharton and Louis Auchincloss? Because believe me, that world still exists."

I was so taken by surprise by this train of thought, I barely nodded. It was all true. That is exactly what I thought.

"Behold Pygmalion. And Galatea. Or Eliza and Higgins. Shaw knew. I created my own new self from the son of a dairy farmer in overalls with manure on his work boots. No one knows that." He shook his head, surprised, perhaps, that he was talking about it now.

"The right Ivy degrees, the right tailored clothes, the right ways of speaking. Do it well enough and you have the perfect disguise. Ryan was doing it, too. That's why I even made some efforts—not so large, but large for me—to give him guidance. He was wearing a disguise, too. His was an ugly one." He shuddered. "But he mistakenly thought it to be edgy. In any case, it prevented people from seeing who he really was—a kid off an alfalfa farm in one of those rectangular Midwestern states. Chemical fertilizer on *his* work boots." He rubbed his eyes. "I'm going home now. I am better. And I will deny everything I have just said, so I wouldn't repeat it if I were you. Who will they believe, you or me?"

He left and then turned back. "You and Ryan did a fine job on the Maude Cooper papers. Who would have expected it from a Brooklyn guttersnipe and a farm boy? But you missed the underlying story. She's hiding something, too."

"Oh? I had that feeling, too."

"She's hiding something, just like me and just like Ryan. I have no idea what, but I know she is. I can feel it."

He was gone and I was left trying to take in everything he had said, my mind really too full to absorb one more new idea.

I went to the workroom and put away all the document copies Flint had left out. Then, mindful of Leary's words, I tackled one more doable task. I wanted to talk to Natalya about Dima and his job.

"Ah, Erica, you have read my mind," she said when I called. "I was wondering if you had some time tomorrow. I could use help, Alex and me. We are meeting with police. Is there…could you…I am nervous to ask. Is there any chance you could come with us? They scare me. Just going to their building scares me. "

"But Natalya? You did battle with the Soviet bureaucracy. What are New York cops compared to that?"

"I know." She sighed. "It's true. They are little baby chickens beside what I dealt with back then, but also I was young and stupid so I could be fearless. And I could talk my ways through in Russian. With cursing, if needed. Or flirting or humor, whatever it took. Now I am not fearless. And you would help, in case that I do not understand all their English?"

I was pretty sure that Natalya's English comprehension was way more than adequate, but I guessed she needed to know someone had her back.

"Do you know who you are meeting with?"

"Ah, yes, that Detective Henderson."

That clinched it for me. Whatever else I might have done would wait.

"I'll be there for sure. Now I have a question for you. Did Dima work at night at Green-Wood Cemetery?"

"Yes, of course he did. He was a night watchman a few nights a week. I worried, having him work all week and also nights. He started last year. But you knew this?"

"Strangely, I didn't. How did I not know?"

"Ah, it started when you were so upset last year, so many problems, your grant, your father. And then I suppose it just didn't come up."

That made sense at last. It had been one of those times when life was throwing one thing after another and I was just barely getting through my days. We didn't talk much then.

"So that's the job he was at, that night, and left during the night."

"They say. That's what they say, he unlocked the gate with his card in the middle of the night. The people there, oh, they are so sympathetic but they want him really to not be killed there, it is bad for them, for their name. And it changes their insurance, too, I think." She sighed, a sigh from her toes all the way up. "The police say it, too. You see why I am upset to talk to them?"

"Oh, sure." I said it absently; I was not sure I understood but I would be there tomorrow. I hadn't talked to Natalya for a few days so if she needed me now, I was there.

I knew daily calls would only drive her crazy. How many ways are there to say "I am lonely today and my heart is broken"?

For a day I wasn't even supposed to be at work, I certainly had put in some real effort there. Now it was time to go home and straighten things out with my daughter.

For a guy who claimed he could not give life advice Leary has given me something helpful. Knock off one question at a time, easy ones first; work my way through the list. Not that Chris would be easy.

She was not yet home. Did she have after-school plans? I checked my calendar. Then I checked my phone for a message. She was allowed to make spur of the moment plans but I needed to know what they were.

No messages. None on the house phone. None on my e-mail. I called into my work phone, just in case we had missed each other there. Nothing. Was there a chance she actually was home, in her room, napping?

Her door was still closed, just as it had been in the morning. I knocked softly, then hard. Really hard. No response, so I went in. By then my stomach might have been jumping around a little.

Her bed was made, her room perfectly tidy, unprecedented on a busy school day. No books lying around, no schoolwork, no discarded clothes. No earring tree on her dresser. No art supplies. No plush gray bunny that had lived on her bed since her second birthday.

The piece of paper in the middle of her smooth comforter said, "I am going to go stay with Grandpa. He has time for me."

Chapter Sixteen

It took me long, measurable minutes to comprehend those two simple lines. She had run away from home? And not even to her friends, but to my dad? That guy, who couldn't be in the same room with me, in my own teen years, without turning it into a battlefield? Who deserted Chris and me, and went off to Arizona because the new woman in his life insisted, and then came back when she left him? Who tried to make amends now by constant meddling? That guy? And she thought he would be a better parent than me?

I didn't know whether to laugh or cry, or perhaps hurl some of her personal possessions at a wall in her room. So I did all three, but stuck to the old stuffed animals for the throwing.

When I was done I was sitting on her floor, back against her bed, breathing hard. Only the fact that there was no phone in her room kept me from calling my father and yelling at him. Getting up and walking into my own room, finding my own phone, going back to Chris' room to tidy up the mess I had made and get rid of the evidence that I had lost my mind…well, by the time I had done all those things, I was ready to have a somewhat more sane talk with my dad. I hoped.

"It's your daughter," I said. "Remember? The sole parent of your only grandchild?" I was in no mood for niceties.

There was a long silence. I knew he was still there because I heard him breathing.

Finally he said, stuttering slightly, "Nice to hear from you. What's up?"

That's when I lost it again. "You have kidnapped my child. I'm coming to get her."

"Now, Erica. You know I could not have kidnapped her. Do you think I drugged her and carried her out of your house? Come on."

"Why should I listen to you? Let me talk to her. Right now. Immediately, if not sooner."

"She's at school. Now think. Couldn't it be normal for a teen to need a little break from her parents? Think about it. I remember a time when you did the same."

And, somehow, I was able to let a memory come through the red fog in my brain. Tenth grade. My favorite possessions and a change of underwear, in a pink backpack, at my best friend's. Her indulgent mother let me stay for two nights before sending me home for clean clothes. And I could not even remember what it was about.

"That was different," I said. Maybe my voice did not have as much conviction as I would have liked, because Dad replied, "Really?"

"Okay, Dad, let's quit playing around. You tell me exactly what the hell is going on."

"Not much to tell. She called and said she needed a change, and could she bunk in with me for a while? She promised she wouldn't be any trouble and she would even take care of dinner for me."

"She said what? She can't cook."

"I think she meant she would take over ordering out. And I said she had to get to school every day, do her homework—I would be checking—and all regular rules apply."

"Yeah? Like no TV on school nights?'

"What?"

"That was your rule for me."

"Well, I…times change…"

"Ha. Just as I thought. The real rules were only for me. You've always spoiled her. Do you know that? She doesn't know it. But why? Why did she do it? Surely not because you would let her get away with murder? I'm not that godawful strict."

"She said you would know and I should not tell you a word about it. It's an easy promise to keep, because she didn't tell me anything."

"I'll pick her up after school and get this straightened out. " He sighed. "She did say one thing, loud and clear."

He waited so long I had to say, "Come on, Dad. Give it up!"

"She'd like to not talk to you for a while."

I slammed the phone down.

I could go over to my dad's and drag her home. Perhaps in handcuffs. No.

I could go for a walk. I thought of Joe, who believed exercise was the cure for most ills. It was late afternoon on a crystal clear fall day. Maybe the sun and crisp air and moving my chair-anchored body would provide—what? I didn't even know what I needed. Energy? Clarity? Cheer? Probably none of the above.

I seemed to have conjured up the devil because there was Joe headed my way.

"Playing hooky? I am. It's such a great day, I couldn't resist stealing some time to get out."

"Leaving frantic customers having breakdowns?"

"Who knows? Who cares? Isn't that what playing hooky is all about? I was checking on some work and have a little time now. Going to the park? Care for some company?"

I was going to the park. Where we live, that means Prospect Park, the great Olmstead and Vaux masterpiece, a refuge for all seasons. There was a while, after Jeff, that I couldn't bear to even walk through the gates, but then I came to feel the opposite. I liked it because it was the last place he was on this Earth. However, I know the exact spot where the car hit him, and I never go near it.

I didn't exactly say yes to Joe. I wasn't so sure I wanted company, wasn't at all sure I wanted cheerful company, and was very sure I would not be pleasant company myself, but I did not say no, either. Then we were there, walking through the panther-topped stone gates.

"How are you? You don't seem your usual chipper self."

"How long do you have? Because my life seems to be falling apart in all directions."

"Not in love with another upper-class sociopath, are you?" I didn't care for his tone and I did not want to be reminded of that recent misadventure.

"Oh, give it a rest! That wasn't love—infatuation, maybe—and he wasn't a sociopath, just a…"

"Whatever. So that's one problem that isn't happening. What else?"

"Oh, work is…. I don't even…"

"Uh-uh. Work doesn't do this to you. "

"You have no idea."

"About your work? True. I'm just an ignorant blue-collar guy." He was laughing at me. He isn't, and I know it. And he knows I know it.

"I'm in no mood for teasing. "

"So what has Chris done?"

I just stared at him for a moment. "Ouch. You put your finger right on the sore spot. She ran away."

He didn't express appropriate shock. He just waited.

"She went to my dad and left me a note."

"You call that running away?"

"It feels like it to me." I sighed. "I don't know what to do. She is angry at me all the time. You know? She's stuck in a teenage… some kind of vortex. The real Chris has disappeared."

"An *Invasion of the Body Snatchers* situation?"

"That's it exactly. That writer must have had teenagers."

By then, with Joe leading the way, we had reached a playground. The park has many of them, but this was the adventure playground I used to frequent with Chris when she was little. She loved the climbing structures shaped like animals and a fort with ladders and doors and ropes and slides.

We took a bench. "You know the real Chris has not disappeared, don't you?"

"No, I most definitely do not."

He smiled at me. Or he was laughing at me.

"Oh, okay, I know it, but I just don't actually believe it. She sure doesn't seem to be around, my old daughter. Even when she is not moving somewhere that is not home."

"What were you like at fifteen?"

"Made my bed. Did my homework. Babysat. I was…I was a good kid."

"Oh, sure you were. Sure."

"Yes, I was." I thought back. "Well, okay, not exactly. I thought my parents were idiots. My mom's clothes embarrassed me. My dad's jokes embarrassed me. I wanted…what did I want? Everything to be different, I guess, especially me. And of course just the same, too."

"Is there an echo going on here?"

"Damn it, Joe. Don't play that wise older brother with me." He laughed.

"We didn't end up here by accident. Look around you."

I watched the very small children as they ran and laughed and hollered under the watchful eyes of sitters and parents. Snacks and sippy cups were distributed, scraped knees band-aided, a hair-pulling incident resolved. A barely walking boy was forcibly removed from the highest level of the fort before he took a tumble. A little girl with bows in her hair insisted she could go on a slide "all by myself" and giggled maniacally all the way down. A little boy in a baseball jacket sobbed as if his heart was breaking, saying, "No, no, no" as his mother tried to console him.

"All right," I said at last. "I get it."

"Ah, you're a smart girl. I figured you would."

"Calling me a girl is very annoying." I said it without rancor. "This is a devious plan to remind me of the good times with my kid, right?"

"And?"

"And even though her brain might have been taken over by aliens, it's not more permanent than—well, that." I pointed to the tiny sobbing boy, now fast asleep on his mother's shoulder.

"Mmm."

"I hate it when you're right."

"I'll take that for a thank you."

"I suppose this means I have to make up with her? If she'll talk to me?"

"One of you has to be the grown-up here. You seem most qualified."

"I'm scared. You know? I don't know how to do this."

"Make up?"

"No. Be a mom now. I used to be able to muddle through and it seemed to work out. Now…" I shook my head and looked away, just in case the wetness in my eyes might be visible.

"Try not to be stupid. You're doing fine. She's a great kid. You think that's an accident? You turned out okay, so your folks must have muddled through, right?"

He had a point. And it was true that I gave them some shaky moments. I didn't see it then—not any more than Chris would—but I could see it now.

"Okay," I muttered, then said it again with a little conviction. "Okay. I'll deal with it, doing my best impersonation of a grown-up." I stood up quickly. It was time to end this discussion.

"Yeah," he said, "I have to get going now, too. "

"Another appointment?"

"I have a date tonight. I've got to get home and clean up."

"Anyone I know? That cute redhead from the glass studio?"

"That's her." He didn't seem to want to say any more, which was not like him, and I wasn't up to thinking about what that might mean. If it meant anything. Probably it didn't.

I changed the subject.

"You knew, didn't you? About Chris? You knew! You came to find me on purpose? Wait." I grabbed his arm. "Did you know before she left, and didn't tell me?"

"Of course not. If I knew, I would have talked her out of it. No, she called me from your dad's."

"She called you?"

"We do talk sometimes. Come on, you knew that. We kind of bonded when she worked for me last summer."

"She talks to everyone but me!"

He said, very slowly, "It sounds to me like she needs something at the moment, and maybe it isn't her mom. It's always been the two of you and she's reaching for something to—not to replace you—but to fill in a space in her life. You're smart. You can probably figure out what it is."

I could, but I wasn't ready to talk about it. Not then, not there, not with him.

"How'd you get so smart about other people's kids?"

"You know how many nieces and nephews I have? Thirteen. They come to me when their parents are driving them crazy and vice versa. They let off steam and then I send 'em home."

We had walked all the way back. Joe gave me a quick, friendly hug. "Relax! I can feel the knots through your clothes. It will be all right."

"Thanks for listening, Uncle Joe."

I managed to say it jokingly, in spite of my own mood, and I didn't realize until later that he didn't laugh.

I planned an evening of eating all the random leftovers in the refrigerator, and going to bed. I wondered where Joe was going tonight.

Chapter Seventeen

I snapped awake. Was it morning? I squinted at my clock. 6:30? How could that be? I closed my eyes again, but had to squeeze them tight to keep them shut. Chris used to call it "squinching." I had to face it. I was up for the day.

And so I resolved that I could and would make good use of this unwanted early morning. Somehow, during my day of worrying and my night of restless, anxiety-dream-filled sleep, I had made a decision. I wanted to see her face-to-face. A confrontation? Oh, I didn't know. Maybe. Maybe just a talk.

If I scrambled, I could be waiting in front of her school before she arrived for her first class.

So I scrambled. I stood there in the early morning chill, wrapped in the too-light jacket I had grabbed on my way out. The block was crowded with high school students, arriving on their own, mostly, and milling about, socializing. There were parents' cars, parked every which way, creating traffic nightmares, dropping off the ones who lived furthest, or arriving early for middle-school, which would start a little later. And there it was, my dad's car, stopping up at the corner, wisely avoiding the scrum. Chris was just getting out and walking briskly toward her pack of friends.

My baby. My big girl who was so angry at me. I took a deep breath and moved to waylay her before she went too far. Making a scene right in front of her school, in front of her friends, would be a good way to make sure I was not heard. When she spotted me, she turned pale and faltered. I had caught her off-guard. Perfect.

I was shaking inside, but I had given myself a pep talk all the way. I was determined to impersonate a calm, rational adult. As Joe had said, one of us had to.

I took her arm, gently, but firmly, I hoped, and said, "Come off the street. We are going to talk and you don't want to do it right here." She looked panicked, tried to pull away, then stopped and went with me. She saw she would not be able to avoid it without making a scene. Smart girl, my daughter.

We turned into a quiet side street. I said, as calmly as possible but still holding her arm, "Now tell me what is going on! You can't just stop speaking to me. You cannot."

Her chin jutted out in the same stubborn expression she had as a two-year-old. I shook her arm, gently, and I said, "C'mon, Chris! You aren't a two-year-old."

She pulled her arm out of my hand, but didn't run away. Instead, she folded her arms across her chest. Protecting herself? That thought hurt.

Finally, she said, through gritted teeth, "I needed at least one parent. You don't have time to be mine, and Grandpa does."

No, I would not lose my temper. Not happening. I said, ever so calmly, "That is ridiculous."

She turned and glared at me. "It. Is. Not. You are running here and there and all over. You work, you study, you run around for your job. You work in a museum, for crying out loud! It's supposed to be boring! Instead, I never know what you're doing. You come home late and don't tell me and you forget that I might worry. Bad things happen. And you're never around when I need you anymore. You are busy everywhere but with me."

"But, Chris, you know why I do all of this."

"Do you think I don't need a parent anymore?" She charged right ahead with her argument. "I've always had to make do with only one, but lately I feel like I only have maybe half. Or even none. Grandpa is really there for me, whenever I need him."

My calm snapped and shattered. "Oh, yeah? Wait until he's there all the time, when you don't want him at all. Cause believe you me, he hovers."

"That would make a nice change! I wouldn't have to get arrested or be in an accident—or die—to get some attention. My own dad has always been gone. Now my substitute, my good friend's dad is gone, too. And his mother is all over him, but mine? Mine is nowhere to be found."

She turned and walked way before I could even form a reply, let alone get it out of my mouth. She was gone, just like that.

My heart was beating fast and I had to blink a lot of times to get my eyes to focus. It's not that we had never had a fight. Two strong-willed women in the same house? Of course we had. But she had never been this angry, this resentful. I had never felt she was going for the kill.

I fought down the panic that this was our whole future together, that it would just get worse and worse.

I walked away from where I stood, directionless. I could move my body, but my mind seemed paralyzed. When I turned the corner, I saw a familiar old car standing next to a hydrant, flashers on. My dad was leaning over to open the passenger door.

He said, "Get in. For God's sake, just once don't argue with me."

I walked past the car, not even turning my head, but then I turned back. Why not? Nothing he said could possibly make this day worse than it already was. Maybe having a full-on fight with him would actually cheer me up. I was ready for a fight with someone.

"Are you following me? How dare you! You…" I started while I was still sliding into the seat.

"Chris did a number on you? Oh, yeah, I saw her stalking away. Can't imagine where she got that mouth." He reached over to help with the seat belt and left his hand on my shoulder. He was looking at me and was a lot calmer than I was.

"What do you mean by that? I never talk to her like that. She has never—ever—heard me talk to anyone…"

"Going out on a limb here, but you think it might be in the genes?"

I sulked as long as I could stand it, then found myself saying, in a voice so small I almost couldn't hear myself, "Dad, what am I going to do?"

"Don't do anything for a few days, is my advice."

I sat up in instant protest, but he said softly, "Take it easy and listen, would you? I think she just needs a break and a chance to figure some things out. Give her the space to miss you. "

"No. Okay, yes, maybe. I sort of get it, as a—as a strategy. But I don't understand what's going on."

"Are you sure about that?"

"Yes! I'm sure. She has lost her mind.…"

I saw him shaking his head, and I stopped then and thought about her actual words. I had a glimmer.

"Is it because her friend's father died? She's feeling…"

"Could be."

"She feels scared? Dad, that makes no sense at all. Has she gone crazy? Dima was a tragedy but it's completely, totally unrelated to her life."

"She's fifteen, kiddo. Everything is related to her life."

"Then in the name of all…why hasn't she said that was it? She's just dramatizing instead of really talking. We used to be able to talk about everything."

"I repeat. She's fifteen. My guess is that she doesn't know how to say it."

"She ran away from home, Dad. How can that be? I can't lose her. Nothing else would matter in my life…"

"Uh, yeah, and who's over-dramatizing now?" He was patting my shoulder. "She sure didn't run very far. She just needs a little breathing room. I do know how you feel." He cupped my chin and that forced me to look right at him. "I do. Guess how? And she will be fine. She's smart. She knows you love her. Let her work it out. She's safe with me."

I closed my eyes. I couldn't look at him anymore. "But I can't just sit back and not do anything!"

"Not your style, is it? Well, yeah! It is hard. You thought it's all a walk in the park, raising kids?"

I did look at him then. "You never used to be this calm. Never. You were the one who did all the yelling. Did you get smarter behind my back?'

"Ya think?" He started the car. "Traffic cop is coming down the block. I've got to move. Where can I drop you?"

"I'll walk." I opened the door but after I slid out I popped my head back in to say, "Dad? Take care of my baby?"

"Goes without saying."

Talking to my father had actually helped clear my head. That was a surprise. I was just a little less disturbed about Chris. It was a phase, right? And she would get over it, right? I could stop panicking.

In any case, I had to stop, because it was time to meet Natalya at the precinct, and now I'd have to hustle to get there on time.

I spotted her from a long block away, apparently in heated discussion with someone I could not quite see. She gestured dramatically, walked away in apparent anger, then turned back and held out her hands.

As I got closer, I was surprised to see that it was Alex. He stood hunched over, head turned away, not responding to his mother, but finally, as I reached their end of the block, I saw him step up and wrap his arms around her. He let go suddenly when I called out, and Natalya turned to me with a social, completely unconvincing smile.

"My dear, I thank you for coming. As you see, I have Alex out of school today, he will look at police photos, too."

Alex looked grim and gave the briefest possible nod to acknowledge my presence.

"Come. It is time." She tapped her watch and looked meaningfully at her son.

We were whisked in to a bare room with a table. Henderson came in.

"I have brought my friend, Erica Donato, she will help with English. And my son, to look at the faces you have for me. Erica, this is Detective Henderson, in charge of finding out truth of what happened to my Dima."

"Yes, we met before, at your house."

He nodded and smiled at me from behind her back. "I remember. Do you have anything to add? I would love to move this case along faster, and I know the family would appreciate that, too."

I told him I could not help him, much as I'd like to, and he went on, explaining the process. "Miss Donato, I gather you are here for moral support, so you won't have anything to do, really. I want Mrs. Ostrov and her son to examine these photos to see if they recognize anyone, in any context, and particularly as relating to Dmitri Ostrov."

I said, "These are people you have some reason to suspect?"

He smiled and said, "We have our reasons to ask about them. Let's leave it at that. There is an officer right out there who will get me if needed, and I'll be back in a little while. Are you all comfortable? Would you like coffee, or a soda?"

Alex asked for a Coke, but his mother immediately said, "Have you lost your common sense? Not soda in the morning! Juice or tea only is not bad for you." Then she turned to the detective.

"But," she protested, "but—you cannot go. I have things to discuss, information I wrote out. We need to talk."

"And we will when I return. I promise."

He was gone, and she said, "You see?" She looked from Alex to me and back again. "You see? The brush-off? Isn't that the word? Always the brush-off"

Silently, not even looking at each other, she and Alex began turning page after page. Alex went in search of tea for both of them and returned. I read the newspaper I had shoved in to my bag and wondered why I was there.

Then Alex suddenly put his hand down on a page. "Him." He pointed, and said, "I have seen him with Papa, one time, drinking tea."

Natalya stared.

"He is no one to me. Were you with Papa then?"

"No, no, I was on the street and I saw them through a café window, and I knew him because—because I had seen him before, just you know, around the neighborhood. You know how you never see some people and then others everywhere?"

"But who is he?"

Alex shrugged.

"We must get Detective Henderson back in here."

"He said to look at all of them."

"All right, all right. I mark this page and we go on."

Soon after that the detective returned, and Natalya excitedly showed him the page she had marked. The detective only said "Hmm," but he noted the photograph and turned to Alex, gently asking him more about where and when he had seen the man. I watched and listened as Alex insisted he could not remember more and said he had no idea who he was.

Henderson said, "Hmmm" again and then asked to talk with Alex alone.

"No. I do not leave my son alone and unprotected in a police station. No way."

Henderson smiled just a little and said, "I swear we won't hurt him. We don't use rubber hoses anymore. Seriously. But sometimes young people—ah, remember things better without a parent around."

"Not my son. Whatever he knows, whatever he needs to say, he can say with me. We have no secrets."

Any parent who believes that is in for some great big surprises, I thought.

Alex again looked as if he wished he would slide into a hole under the floor.

"Mrs. Ostrov, this is a murder investigation." The smile was still on his face, but his voice was significantly less cordial. "Have you forgotten what we are trying to do? We have the same goals. Please allow us to do our job."

Natalya glared at him but said only one word. "No."

Henderson considered that and then turned back to Alex. "All right, son. This is someone we would like to know more about. It matters so let's not waste anymore time. Think hard. Where did you see him with your father?"

"I think it was through the window of the Caspian Tea Room. It's on Brighton 5th Street."

"And you don't know when exactly?"

"Not exactly, but after school, a few weeks ago, I think."

"And you are sure it was him? Sure? Because you have seen him before? So where was that, where you had seen him before? Your neighborhood is pretty busy and crowded, yet you remember him." Henderson sounded skeptical. "Did you ever have a run-in with him anywhere?"

"What? What do you mean? No, never."

Natalya put a hand out to rest on his arm. "Alex is a good boy. He does not have run-ins."

"Come on, Alex. I think there's more. Remember, this is about your father."

Alex shot a glance at his mother. It seemed nervous to me, or fearful, and then perhaps defiant.

"I've seen him with Uncle Volodya."

Natalya made a gasping sound.

"And you did not tell me? Me, your mother? Knowing how I feel about him, that snake?

Detective Henderson said, "Mrs. Ostrov, please sit down. Now." Polite words but commanding tone of voice. "Please! This may be very interesting and helpful for us." He turned to Alex. "Do you mean your uncle, Vladimir Ostrov?"

Alex nodded.

Natalya said, "Who is he, this guy? Some thug, if he is a friend of my brother-in-law. I have here a list—I wanted to bring to you and discuss…a list of all wrong things and suspicious things he has done." She smacked her hand on the table for emphasis. "Is very important you know this!"

"I don't have time to discuss it right now, but I will add it to the file and read it later." He held out his hand for it. "Now,

Alex, tell me, did you talk to him or have any contact when you saw him with your uncle?"

"No, no, nothing. Only, it was more than one time."

Henderson looked ready to ask more questions, but Alex added on his own, "I don't know where or when—just, you know, walking or something. I noticed because it was my uncle. It was a couple of times. They were talking. That's all. I never heard what they said or anything."

Henderson nodded. "And you, and Mrs. Ostrov, you are both sure you saw no one else that you know, in those pictures?

Alex said softly, "I saw faces I have seen, just around, but no one I know and no one with connection to my family."

Natalya nodded. "The same for me."

"Ms.—um—Donato, do you have anything to add to this?"

"No, not a thing."

"Then thanks to all of you. You can go now."

Natalya shook his hand and then laid her finger on his sleeve. "And we will be in touch? You will look into Volodya? Is so important, we must know, what really happened. We need— Erica, what word I need?"

"Is it closure?" I noted her English got weaker when she was more emotional.

"Ah, yes, that is the one! Please, you will keep in touch?"

"Yes, ma'am, I will." Behind her back, he smiled at me and mouthed, "Friday night?" I nodded.

Alex edged toward the door. "Mom, I have to go. I need to get to chem class. Now."

He was halfway down the stairs, gone, before she was able to get a word out. Her expression of surprise was almost comical. "I wasn't done talking to him! Always, he runs. We do not talk lately. He is out on a planet, somewhere."

I said, "Oh, brother, do I ever hear you. Chris, too. You know, it must be the age, plus…" I faltered.

"Plus this has been hard time? I know, I know, but oh, Erica, I feel like I am losing him, and myself, too. I was not always this crazy woman, was I?"

"No, of course not. You were a lot of fun, but right now…"

"Yes! I used to be fun, and Alex and I, we had laughs together, too. And if I do not stop, with all this crazy feeling, what becomes of Alex?"

"You are allowed to be crazy for a while." I hugged her. "It's okay, for now. You know, my friend Joe always says to exercise when you are sad. Even if it doesn't help, after, you are too tired to think." I smiled, hoping she would smile back.

Instead, she said something Russian. From her voice and face, I guessed it meant "Don't bother me with that nonsense." Then she said in English, "And tell me, does it ever work for you? Did it, when you lost your husband?"

"No. I mean, I didn't know Joe then, but no, it wouldn't have. Not so soon. What really works is time. Really."

"Oh, very good." She had a sardonic smile, more like the old Natalya I remembered. "What am I supposed to do until I get there?"

We had reached her subway station. We hugged good-bye. I was saved from trying to answer that question.

I needed to make a few stops before heading home myself. I found myself pointed toward Chris' school. And it was just about dismissal time.

Was this a good idea? No. But there I was anyway, feeling like a stalker, standing across the street and behind a van.

The upper-school students came pouring out. The younger boys were jumping around, leaping down the steps and tossing books, punching each other's shoulders, while the girls made fun of them. Some of the older boys and girls were slinking away to the corner and lighting up cigarettes as soon as they were off school property. Or maybe they weren't cigarettes.

On the narrow street, cars honked repeatedly, signaling parents double-parked for pick-up that they needed to move pronto. The block was complete chaos.

Here was a pack of Chris' girlfriends, chattering away, stopping to fix each other's scarves in the sharp breeze. Where was she? What day was it? Oh, damn, Tuesday. Basketball practice. She would not be out for two hours.

I needed to leave before someone spotted me.

Then I spotted someone myself: Alex, across the street, walking up to a man in a black leather jacket. They turned toward me, still across the street, but I could see them clearly, the man with his arm casually slung across Alex's shoulders as they walked. They were deep in conversation and Alex did not look unhappy. Or coerced. Or uncomfortable in any way.

The man was his Uncle Volodya.

Chapter Eighteen

They walked down the block having a lively conversation. Was that Alex laughing? They looked perfectly normal together. In other words, the exact opposite of everything I had seen, heard or would have expected. I was completely baffled.

They turned toward downtown Brooklyn and it wasn't hard to follow discreetly on these heavily trafficked sidewalks. They went into the large chain bookstore; I followed, just a few shoppers behind them.

When they entered the crowded bookstore café, I finally had the sense to stop and ask myself what I thought I was doing. Before I had a good answer, and before I had time to duck behind the nearest book display, Volodya was walking in my direction. He looked large and angry. As usual.

"I know you." He spoke in a whisper, not attracting attention, but it was a whisper with the force of a shout. "You just accidentally turned up? I don't think so. What do you want?" For emphasis, he grabbed my shoulder in a tight, painful hold and gave it a shake.

I tried to step back but couldn't break his hold. I forced myself to look right at him and say, with completely phony calm, "You are mistaken. And you need to let me go."

His grip only loosened slightly while he said, "No. I am not mistaken and you should not mess with me. You tell me now. I do not accept being spied upon."

Alex came up behind him, red-faced and upset. He put a hand on his uncle's arm, the one holding me, and said, "Uncle, she is the mother of my friend. Please. Let go."

He gripped me tighter for a moment, then gave a disgusted shake of his head, and let go. He said to Alex, "You call me!" and walked away.

"Please. Please do not tell Mama. I must go now, too." As he turned away, I grabbed his sleeve.

"Oh, no. You tell me what is going on. Why are you seeing that man? And looking all friendly?" I fixed him with my best terrifying mom look and he started to crumble. The anxiety in his face went up the scale, and his voice followed.

"It's not what you think, well, maybe it is, I don't know what you think, but it's not something bad. But my mama would not like it. But…"

"Slow down and take a breath. We are going over to a table, and sit and talk. Got it?"

He took a few deep, gasping breaths, as if he were hyperventilating, and finally was able to say, "Mama hates him. And yes, okay, he is kind of a tough guy, yes, but he's not so bad, not really. Ever since Dad…" He had to stop there and get himself under control. "Ever since, he has been keeping in touch with me. It helps me, to talk to him man-to-man. We can talk about my father. It upsets my mother, to talk like that, so I am glad to have uncle. I am glad. Glad!" Then he looked away from me, stood up, walked away and came back.

Oh, my poor boy, I thought. When he came back and sat down again, he was calm, though his face was red.

"I understand, at least I think I do, but do you think it's all right to deceive your mother?" Coming from me at that moment, it was not a neutral question.

"I don't know. No, I guess not, but what choice? He's my uncle. My dad loved him in spite of everything. I can't cut him out and I can't talk to her about it. She has reasons. I guess. I think, no, I'm pretty sure, Volodya messes around." He looked down and then back up at me. "Makes money in bad ways, you know?"

"Can't you see why she doesn't like him?"

"Yeah. Yes. I said. But if my dad still saw him? He used to keep dad company sometimes, at the cemetery, when he was working there. Nights were long and boring. They would talk and walk. Dad told me this himself. So he was doing it, too, seeing Uncle Volodya without my mother knowing."

"I bet she's worried you will want to be like him. Any mother would be."

He looked just like Chris when he gave me one of those special teen have-you-lost-your-mind? looks.

"Not in a million years! She should know me better. If I did, Dad would. Dad's ghost would. I would never. Besides…"

"Hmm?"

"Look," he said with grave, almost adult seriousness, "can I trust you? I mean, really, really trust you? If I tell you something?"

"Yes, sure. No, wait. Let me think about it." He was a kid, after all. I was his mother's friend, after all. "As long as it is not something dangerous for you, I can keep a secret."

"He thinks he knows something about how my dad died. Or he can find out. He's working on it. He knows people."

"He says. Do you believe him?"

"Yes, I do. Or I want to. I don't know!"

"And if he knows something, why isn't he taking it to the police?"

He gave me a look that was way beyond his years, and said, "Uh, maybe he has his own reasons for not wanting to discuss anything with police-type people?'

"Oh, Alex, be careful."

He shook his head, "No matter what my mother says, he would never hurt me. He doesn't like Mama any more than she likes him, but he cared about my dad. He did. Truly. And me."

He looked so lost and confused, so like a much younger child, I wanted to hug him—which I knew would embarrass him completely. Then he jumped up and said, "Look at the time! I have to meet my mom and I am way late." He shouldered his pack and was gone, leaving me with a lot to think about. Too much.

Was Volodya just a neighborhood bully or was he actually a criminal? Was there any way for me to find out? I had as much as promised not to tell Natalya about any of this, but did I maybe have an obligation to push Alex to tell her? Maybe. Probably.

I took care of some errands and headed home at last, getting a seat on the train. My feeling of being on automatic was sliding into sleepwalking and my thoughts were harder to control.

I would be all alone tonight. Not that this has never happened before—sleepovers, camp last summer, a school trip. Visit to the Nona in Buffalo. I've been a single parent for twelve of her fifteen years; usually I relished some time alone, it is so rare.

This time was different. This time I was being deserted. As I dozed off, my mind was a jumble of my dad ("how could he?"), and Alex's words about missing his father, and something Joe once said about a teen girl needing a father-figure.

I woke up with a start, two stops past my own. I swore, gathered my belongings and got off. I trudged up the stairs, crossed and then trudged down, to the other side of the platform, to get the train back. I'd get home even later, but what did it matter, since no one was there waiting for me? I could have chocolate-frosted doughnuts for supper. Or no supper at all. Or a six pack. Watch *Friends* re-runs all night, or turn on a shopping network or MTV. No one to set a good example for.

But in my little catnap, I had a glimmer of an idea about what was going on with Chris. Aside from her just being mad at me, of course.

It was still bright sunshine outdoors, but with later-afternoon lengthening shadows. In my house all was dark. No lights left on all over, telling me Chris was back. It felt lonely. I flipped a light on in the foyer and then in the living room, hung my jacket on a hook, dropped my purse and keys and the mail on the table next to the door, checked the usual places for messages. No e-mail, no voice mail, no text, no snail mail that wasn't trying to sell me something. A hundred ways to keep in touch and my daughter wasn't using any of them.

Then I heard footsteps upstairs. It's an old house. The floor-boards creaked.

Chris? Before I called up to her, I stopped myself. Not one item of her belongings was scattered in the living room. No jacket, backpack, books, papers, snacks.

It occurred to me that I should just leave. Go over to a neighbor's. Call 911. I slid my feet toward the door, silently as I could, and silently lifted my purse, and moved to the still unlocked door.

Footsteps were coming down the stairs. I didn't have time to get out the door so I hide behind it, hoping he could not hear my heavy breathing.

Next thing I knew he was trying to charge through the door himself.

I screamed. He jumped back and shouted.

It was Volodya, and he looked as frightened as I was. He grabbed me by the shoulders and I kicked him. He let me go, screaming "Ow! Ow! What are you doing?"

"What am *I* doing? What the freaking hell are you doing in my house?" I was panting. "You keep away from me. I have neighbors, I have a phone, I can scream."

He stepped back, his hands up defensively.

"No, no. No! You have it all wrong. I am not…bad guy. I am not here to hurt you. Crazy lady, believe…"

He ran his hands through his hair, put one out again, con-ciliating. "Because…because…I can help you."

"You stay far away from me. Go sit—over there—and talk fast. I have 911 on speed dial. Phone is in my other hand, in my pocket. No tricks."

He sat on the sofa, looking surprisingly meek. He said, "Please, could I have glass of water?"

"Hell, no! Do you think this is a social visit? You broke into my house. You better tell me why. Right now."

He swore softly in Russian—at least, it sounded like swear-ing—and finally said in English, "Is big mess, but please believe, I am not doing harm." I glared at him. He took a deep breath and said, "Dima. My brother. Who I loved, no matter what Natasha thinks."

"Yes?"

"I know what happened to him."

"Say that again. I don't believe what I think I heard."

"Is true." He looked at the floor, shoulders hunched, hands gripping his knees. He looked up at me, finally, pain in his eyes and face. "Is true. I know about that night. I was not there. If only I had been. But I know about what happened."

"Are you talking about the cemetery?"

He did not answer, but slowly, he nodded his head.

"How is that even possible?"

"I helped someone. I helped them to do something. I knew what to do because Dima worked there. And it all went wrong. Wrong guys. Did not follow my plan."

"Then what the hell are you doing here?" My voice rose with each word. "Here, snooping around in my house? What do you want here? And why aren't you taking it right to the police so they can do their job? This is...."

"As to what I am doing here, that I cannot tell you. Is confidential, but you must believe it, it is part of my new plan. To trap someone. I need to know what they will do next. I was only looking for information here." He squared his shoulders, "And police? We don't discuss things with them."

"We who? We, bullies and thugs? We, gang members?" He didn't look so frightening, and speaking my mind seemed to make sense at that moment. Not so much, when I thought about it later.

"You have it all wrong, because you listen too much to my sister-in-law!" he said with resentment. "She does not know truth from—from gossip. I am not some punk in a gang. I am—I am a businessman."

"Businessmen behave lawfully. Like citizens. And they go to police with crimes."

"Not Russians. At least, not smart ones. You Americans are such children. You believe what they say in kindergarten 'nice policeman is your friend,' yadda, yadda, No. No policeman is a friend. No, forever nyet."

I knew not all Russians believed that—there are Russian-American cops!—but of course it provided a convenient excuse.

"You know that word? *Nyet*? Dima was my only brother. I will handle this. Me. The guilty ones will get what they deserve." He folded his arms across his chest and his eyes became harder with each word. "You must not, must not call police. Please. It would mess up all my plans."

He stood up and said, simply, "I go now. You keep quiet about this. You will. You must. Because, you know? I could come back." He almost smiled, and then I was definitely scared. "And then I would be less polite."

And then he walked right out my front door. Just as if he was a regular person. A visitor. A friend.

And then my knees gave out as the adrenaline receded and the reality of what just happened hit me. Someone had broken into my home, I had talked to him, he kind of, sort of, half told me something important. Or at least, implied it. And then he just walked out. Poof.

I had a flash of being profoundly glad that Chris had run off to her grandfather. If I was going to attract this kind of craziness, I did not want her to be anywhere near. And I knew that my dad was a tough old guy. True, no longer the scrapper he claims to have been in his youth, but still, tough. Anyone who messed with Chris on his watch would regret it for a long time.

So I only had to worry about my own safety, not hers; the security of my house; my job-related mystery and with it, my job security. Oh, yes, and the murders of two people I knew. That's all. And however much I wanted to creep up under a quilt and sleep for a week—preferably snuggled up with a stuffed bunny—I had a job to do. Volodya had let himself in somehow and I had damn well better find out how.

I worked my way from the top floor down.

I checked the old skylight, original to the house, high above the stairwell. It locked from the inside. The lock was probably as useful as a safety pin, but I could see that it had not been disturbed. The dust of decades was in place.

There was a ladder to the roof, a scary wooden thing that went up a narrow chute and ended in a trapdoor to the roof. The trapdoor locked from the inside of the house. No one could open it from the roof without breaking down the door.

The windows at the back of the house open on to the enclosed space of adjoining gardens. There was no possible way for him to get to the back windows without being seen by a neighbor. Right?

The back door to my deck was still locked from the inside. It was a heavy padlock, not simple to remove or tamper with. I thought.

The windows at the front. Yeah, right, he had come down from the roof on a rope, on a public street in broad daylight. The lower windows had steel security gates. No way he got through those without power tools. I thought. I hoped.

Well, damn! Had he just walked in my own front door?

I got a hammer and banged with all my stress energy on the rusted old dead bolt on the front door. It has not been used in decades, but it would, by God, work now. Finally it budged and satisfyingly inched its way closed. Ha. He would not be able to break in again while I was inside.

Before I was done panting from the effort, the phone rang. It was from Illinois. Who the hell could that be? If it was a fund-raising call, I did not have the patience right now. Or the money. Just before it was too late I remembered that I did know someone in Illinois.

"Ms. Donato! I am so pleased to be talking to you! First, let me thank you for sending me on a hunt. It made quite a change from my usual requests. I had to dig right into the storage area. I mean that literally as we don't have the paper digitized that far back. In fact, I can hardly remember the last time I was asked for something that old. Really, it was such an exciting challenge."

Her excitement was encouraging but I had to stop the flow of words.

"Does this mean you found something?"

"I most certainly did. It isn't much but it should be very useful, if I correctly understand what you are trying to do. Now, what is the best way to send it to you? I could fax it, or we could send by express service, but you would have to pay for that. It's not a big package."

"Would it be possible to just scan and send to my e-mail?"

"I honestly don't have the time to do that today. Our equipment is so antiquated it would take forever. Tell you what? Why don't I just describe what I have, and then you can decide for yourself?"

"Yes, that would be great." Let's just get going, I thought, but did not say. The speed of business is not the same outside of New York, I reminded myself. She's doing me a favor, I reminded myself.

"Well, what makes it slow to scan is that there are many separate items. It's a series from the paper called "Our Hometown Gal in the Big City." They were letters Maude Cooper wrote about her experiences. It was quite unusual, you know, for a young lady to move from a small town like this to New York, and local folks were all agog to read about her adventures. At least, those are the responses they printed. If anyone disapproved, the *Daily* was kind enough not to print those comments. And there are twenty columns over a year or so, plus local responses. Then they stop, just like that, and the paper never said why."

"Nothing like a farewell or announcement that she was moving on? Nothing at all?"

"Not a blessed word that I could find, and I did look. Strange, isn't t?"

"I'll say. That's kind of the mystery I am trying to solve."

"Well, there was not another word from her, or news about her either, except that her mother died a few years later, and then, soon after, there was an announcement of a house sale with all contents, and that her sister was relocating to Chicago. And that's it."

I thought fast. The letters probably were similar to what I already had. Maybe they were exactly what I had.

"Probably you could mail it all to me. Maybe fax the obituary and the other item? I'll give you the number at my job." Faxed to work meant I would not see it until tomorrow. "You have been so helpful, I hate to take more of your time, but I am anxious. Could I ask you to just tell me what is in those two items?"

"My dear, of course! I understand perfectly and they are very short anyway. Now just hold on. Yes, here they are. Now, her mother's name was Edith Cooper, maiden name Hart. Here goes…"

The usual details were there. Date of death. Viewing hours. Location of the funeral. Some description of the family in the town's history. Then the gentle voice said, "Mrs. Cooper is survived by her daughters, Miss Katherine Cooper of River Bend, and Mrs. Gerard Konick IV, nee Maude Cooper, of Brooklyn, New York."

When I could breath again, I asked her to read it one more time. Maude was married to a Konick? The Konicks of Konick Park? And Konick Avenue?

And more importantly, the Gerardus Konick III who built the neglected mausoleum with the Tiffany window? There was a connection between Maude and that family? Is this—could it possibly be—where her window designs come in?

"Ms. Donato? Are you still there?"

"Yes, I'm sorry, I am just—just trying to process this. "

"So that was helpful?"

"I can hardly explain. It is—it is a big surprise." I took another deep breath. "In fact, I can hardly talk."

She laughed. "How exciting. Tell you what. I will make time to scan everything and get it to you today! And in return, when you put all the pieces together, will you share it with me? I do love a good puzzle."

"Yes, yes I will. Of course. Thank you. Thank you!"

We thanked each other back and forth a few times, and then at last I was free to move on. I had access from home to some of the history sources I used at work. Now that I knew what to look for, I had it in minutes. There it was on the screen: a 1910 census record for Mr. Gerard Konick, IV, age 35, and spouse Maude, 30. They had two daughters. They lived on Gramercy Park. So he had modernized his name to Gerard. And in the 1920 census they lived at Bright Skye's address.

That seemed pretty clear, but I immediately sent off a request to the city clerk's office for a copy of their marriage license. Then I checked every source I could think of for a newspaper wedding story, but there was not a trace of one.

That was odd. The Konicks were society folks, the kind of people whose weddings were covered in detail, including the gowns and the refreshments. Debutante parties and private balls, too. I had many examples right in front of me on the screen, from old newspapers, but not the one I wanted. That told me something, right there, I thought. No big wedding at a Gothic revival, pipe-organed, impress-with-splendidness society church like St. Thomas on Fifth Avenue.

I continued to scan for any mention of Konicks around the time of Maude's letters, any clue at all. I looked until my eyes felt like sandpaper, and found only one item that mattered:

> "An engagement has been announced between Lucy Beekman of New York and Southampton, and Gerardus Konick IV, of New York and Saratoga. Nuptials are planned for August at the bride's parents' estate in Southampton. The announcement was made at an elegant reception held at the Beekman home on Madison Avenue. The bride-to-be was glowing in jonquil satin."

The item was dated a year before Maude's last letter home.

Well, Maude, I said to myself. No wonder you were so secretive. You were having a romance with an engaged man who was also the son of a Tiffany client. Did you meet him while working on that chapel for his father? Was there a scandal around the broken engagement? Or did you just run off together? How did his family react? Not well, I was sure. Maude Cooper, however charming, could never have competed with a Beekman.

I pictured a wedding at a city office, Maude in a walking suit, perhaps with a fashionably narrow skirt and certainly an elaborate, swooping hat. Did it have feathers? Gerard would have been in business attire from Brooks Brothers. Did he carry a fashionably dashing cane? Did she at least have a lovely bouquet? Did he give her a wedding ring? Perhaps it came from Tiffany.

I went right back to my copies of Maude's letters and here it was, her first reference to the son. And a chilling description of the parents.

If the design she was creating was for the Konick mausoleum—and that seemed the most likely way for her to meet Gerardus, as she certainly did not travel in his social circles—then I knew just where there might be a few more clues.

I would have to go back to Green-Wood, look at paper records, and look again—hard—at the Konick chapel. But not now. It was too late and I was too tired by this endless and endlessly strange day.

Ha. Take that, Dr. Flint and your buddy, the museum director. I am still the Research Goddess. Chris used to call me that sometimes. Today I was earning it.

And then my e-mail did ping. It was Darcy who wrote "At airport. Heading home at last. I am bringing you dinner tomorrow and a great bottle of Washington State wine. And stories about my kids when they were horrid—HORRID!—teens. Everything will work out. Seriously. Say it out loud. Rinse and repeat as often as necessary. Hugs."

The voice of sanity. I smiled for a second, and stretched out on the sofa with a cozy afghan. I would watch the news, all those disasters that had absolutely nothing to do with me. I suspected I would never make it upstairs to my bed tonight.

Chapter Nineteen

I woke up on autopilot, brain still half-asleep. My body ached everywhere from sleeping on the sofa.

"Chris? Are you up? Breakfast in ten." In my fog, I shouted it upstairs before I remembered she was not there.

Somehow I was also thinking about my desk. What? Why? Yesterday was coming back to me. Volodya.

My desk. I forced my eyes open enough to go upstairs. Last night I was so preoccupied by locks to keep him out I never thought to ask myself why he had broken in. I couldn't be just for the fun of scaring me. He was not the usual burglar and I was pretty sure, even in my fog, that he could not be interested in my ten-year-old television or my outdated computer. But I remembered only now that when I confronted him the noise of the printer at work was coming from upstairs.

My docs about Maude were up on the screen, easy to find and open. And some of them were opened. They weren't protected. Why should I use a password? Nobody was interested in stealing my work, no bank accounts were involved, I had no important secrets. The information meant nothing to anyone outside of a small group of academics and art historians.

Did I have that all wrong?

There were papers scattered on the floor. My crappy ancient printer had jammed up, it seemed, as he was trying to print documents.

So that's what he wanted? Information almost a hundred years old? The more I looked, the less sense it made. I was sure Volodya did not share my obsession with learning Maude's secrets. Why would he even know about her? More than ever, everything I knew seemed like a collection of pieces from a few different jigsaw puzzles. I was trying to use bits of the Grand Canyon to complete a picture of the Grand Canal.

I would go back to Green-Wood today. The heck with my dissertation. This was more important. I had an e-mail from my advisor, scheduling a meeting. I responded to say that I would be there if I was recovered from the nasty stomach virus I had. I would never tell Chris any of this, but I didn't even feel guilty about the lie. It would cover my recent lack of productive work.

Back to Green-Wood Cemetery. I could find it with my eyes closed by now. I trudged right up the hill to the sad Konick mausoleum. I was so excited I forgot it might be closed and locked, and it was, but there were cemetery workmen nearby and when I presented my museum ID, they were persuaded there was no reason not to let me in. The NYPD warnings were gone.

This time I was not studying the magnificent window, the spooky atmosphere, or the crumbling architecture. I half-remembered something and there it was, a plaque to the memory of Mr. and Mrs. Gerardus Konick III. It was deeply carved into a marble panel and painted in gold: her maiden name, their parents' names, and a mention of the Gerardus Konick who first traveled from the old Amsterdam to the new one, in the year of our Lord 1663. Gerardus III listed out all his children and grandchildren. There were five children, and an odd, smeary patch at the beginning of the list, where presumably the oldest, the father's namesake, the son and heir should have been.

He had been painted out. I was sure of it. I wondered if there was a family Bible somewhere, with his name also slashed through by an angry parental pen. Well, that seemed an extreme reaction. Was it anger over his marriage? I stared at it for a while, willing it to give up its secrets, but of course that was silly.

Then I stared at the large window, which was not so silly. I had copies of some of Maude's sketches with me. Yes, there were forest animals and tulips, and here I saw similar themes, glowing in stained glass. No coincidence. I felt like I could almost see her, right here, studying the walls just as I was, and envisioning beauty blossoming there. Making sketches. Watching Mr. Tiffany work, while, perhaps, someone else, fascinated and charmed, was watching her?

"Maude," I said out loud, "I am learning your secrets. They don't seem very dreadful, but maybe then it was different. What happened to you after? Were you happy?"

I saw ahead days of slogging through public archives, trying to find the little bits and pieces that would fill in the details. Even in this day and age, only some of it is online. More census records. The city register which might tell me more about where they lived. That marriage license. Death certificates. I would learn everything I could about the once-important Konicks and I would enjoy it. Had they died out, even with that large Victorian family? I hoped that somewhere there was a hint of gossip about the younger Gerard's presumably shocking love affair. Some avid letter-writer or diarist must have mentioned it, or talked about what this prominent young man did later in life.

Or would they be part of the vanished past, one of the many self-important families that had now disappeared utterly? A century later, were the Konicks less real than the characters in an Edith Wharton novel? No one knew about them or cared about what they had done. Except me.

Digging up that particular past was my immediate future. Yes, I needed to impress my bosses with my brilliant historical sleuthing, but of course there was more to it than that. I was making a promise to remember Maude.

I told myself to stop daydreaming and get to work. The place to start was right here, with any cemetery records relating to this building. I looked around for the workmen who had let me in and instead found Bright Skye, sitting cross-legged on the ground right in front of the door, playing a kind of flute, her eyes closed in trance-like absorption.

She sat in front of a jar of lit incense sticks. The stifling scented smoke mixed with the autumn smell of wet leaves made me want to choke.

Other than that, the scene made me want to burst out laughing. I stopped my coughing just in time, and said her name softly. I could not leave without either stepping over her or knocking her to the ground.

"Bright? Uh, excuse me?"

Her eyes snapped open but her gaze was completely unfocused for a moment. Whatever she was seeing, it was not me.

Then she blinked, flushed, put her flute down, and stood up clumsily, knocking the incense over herself. She stepped backwards, away from me.

"I'm not doing any harm! There is no problem here."

"All right," I hypocritically agreed, "but do you have permission? I'm sure there are issues about using matches here, at least."

She continued to look both nervous and defiant. Her head lifted. "It's my right to be here. I consulted with my shaman and my spirit guides and they said, right here there is a ley line for me. This whole place is throbbing with psychic energy. Can't you feel it? But this place is my most connected. I found out I am related to the Konicks. It was in a book I found in my attic."

"Yes. Yes! I think I know how you are connected to them."

"It doesn't matter how. I know it here." She tapped her heart. "But why in the goddess' name didn't you tell me before?"

"Because I just found out myself. But what are you trying to do here? You said you are not interested in your family history."

"I'm not. Screw that. I found my missing papers so I am trying to say thank you. I put the right energy out into the universe and the right energy came back to me." Her eyes glowed. "My shaman back home told me just how to do it. You must know Sedona is a major, major power center and he is greatly respected." She looked up at the sky and back to me. "In fact, you just interrupted me. Now I have to begin all over." Her eyes started to have that faraway look again.

She turned away, and began rearranging the incense, but I was not about to let her get away with that

"You got the letters back? How is that possible? I'm sorry but this is just as important to me and to Ryan's family as it is to you."

"They were gone and then they were there, back in my attic. That is all." She smiled. "Now I am at peace and I can sell them and have something useful from my useless family. It's a gift from the universe."

I thought fast. "Let me help you. I could work with you on getting fair value for those documents. A museum exhibit would certainly increase the price. And I know experts. If I could only take another look at them."

"Help? You? Not a chance."

The light went out of her eyes. She turned even further away, carefully rebuilding a pattern with the incense sticks. She pulled out some matches, and a sheet of music.

"Did you ever read them?" I plowed ahead anyway. "They are just fascinating, charming, really. I feel like I know her. It's a wonderful picture of the life of an early career woman. And I've learned some new and important things just today. Does it mean anything to you that…"

"I already told you." She stared at me like a stubborn child. "I told you. None of it means anything to me. Not. One. Thing. I grew up in that falling-down old house, full of dust and mold and gloom. My mother and my grandmother just loved it—loved it!—and put every penny they could scrape up into it. 'No, dear, no going away to camp, we need a furnace.' 'No, dear, no car, we need a new roof.' I was out of there the day I turned eighteen." She took a deep, shaky breath.

"I finally—finally!—ended up in Arizona and when I saw all that sunlight and empty space, I knew I was home for good." Her whispery voice had grown louder with each sentence. "That is why Amanda is helping me go through all that—that junk!—so

I can sell it all. I only want the money and I definitely don't want any of the damn memories."

"I'm sorry. I didn't mean to offend you." I had no idea what I was saying. Her only response was to turn her back to me, and begin playing her flute. The more I talked, the faster and louder she played.

"Is Amanda Mrs. Mercer? Is she here today, with you?"

She finally stopped playing to take a breath. She waved her fingers.

"Off wandering. She does that a lot. She's been working here forever and she knows this place backwards and forwards and upside down, too."

She went back to playing and I thought I'd keep an eye out for Mercer while I walked down the hill, the breathy flute music following me. Maybe Mrs. Mercer could be persuaded to answer a few questions.

As it turned out, I didn't have to look very long. She was right around the next bend and we almost collided.

"Why, Ms. Donato! What brings you here?"

"I'm still researching the Konicks and their mausoleum. In fact, I just met Bright Skye there." Deep breath. "In fact, she mentioned that you know everything about Green-Wood. I hadn't realized that before."

"Oh, she flatters me, but, yes, I do know a great deal. Perhaps I can help you in some way?"

Her friendly offer took me by surprise but of course I jumped at the chance. "I have been taking a good look at the Konick mausoleum, now that it is finally open again. There are a few mysteries there."

"Oh?" She looked at me with curiosity. Or maybe the sun was in her eyes.

"What do you think? Is there any chance the archives here might have an old photo or sketch?"

She rolled her eyes. "Oh, they might have one. Chances that they know where it is? About zero." She paused and then started over. "I don't want to give you the wrong impression. They are making huge efforts to get all the backlog catalogued but the neglect went on for years. What were you looking for? If you could be more specific?"

"I'm almost sure that a name was removed from the wall where there is that carved scroll and the family names."

She nodded. "The east wall. What makes you think that? It would be a very odd kind of vandalism."

"Ah, I didn't mean vandalism. I have some information that suggests that it happened. And I took a good look. Of course it's so dirty and neglected, I hope what I think I saw wasn't just a century's worth of grime!" I smiled, trying to say it was a kind of joke, that I wasn't being critical.

She did not smile back. "People certainly don't desecrate their own memorial chapels. That crosses so many lines, I can't even imagine such a thing."

She didn't look as if she was trying to imagine it. Her expression was skeptical and disapproving.

"You said mysteries, in the plural. What else is there?" She didn't say it in words but I was pretty sure she was thinking, "What other insane ideas do you have?"

I had nothing to lose. "If you know this place so well, what have you heard about the window that was stolen?"

She looked shocked. Good. So I went on. "Yes, I know about it. Dr. Flint does, too. The Konick chapel wasn't closed because of an accident. It was closed because of a robbery. And I thought maybe you had heard something? Anything at all about what happened here that night? Even gossip?"

"I never gossip." Frost dripped from her words." And I don't know anything, except that someone criminally desecrated a place of peace and respect. Hard to understand, isn't it?" She wasn't looking at me as she spoke, and not at our surroundings, either, but off somewhere else. "These islands of serenity deserve to be protected, don't they? Cared for and cherished? Probably those thugs chose to pick on this memorial because it is so neglected. That is the crime, isn't it, as much as the theft?" She turned back to me, her face infinitely sad. "Maybe they thought there was no one to notice."

She turned and walked away. Our conversation seemed to be over.

I had things to do, too. I went to the records department and learned the boxes I would need to see were in deep storage. They would be ready if I wanted to come back in a few days. I didn't want to wait, but that was the best they could do.

Later, at home, puttering around, the phone rang. It was Darcy. "I'm on my way over. I have dinner—two shopping bags full. And Washington Pinot, as promised. Or sparkling—I had a good trip, we can celebrate."

Oh my stars. I'd completely forgotten about her promise to come over and bring a meal. I could barely stammer out that I didn't care which wine.

"What's the matter? Did you start drinking without me? You sound strange."

"It's a long story. I'll overwhelm you over dinner. "

"I'm looking forward to it. I'll be there in ten."

She was ringing my bell in eight, laden with shopping bags. She claims to be tired of cooking, after raising four children, but she sure knows how to buy a banquet.

I had to force the rusty bolt on my door, with a lot of noise, so she came in saying, "What the hell was that? And this?" She pointed at the hammer in my hand. "And you look like hell, too. What is going on?" She held up a hand, palm open, the universal "stop" gesture. "Let's wait, I don't want food leaking though these bags. "

I cleared space on my overloaded dining table, and we set up the dinner—fancy crackers and cheeses so exotic I did not know their names, lemon-roasted chicken, three containers of salads made with rice and chickpeas and herbs and dried fruit, with not a leaf of iceberg lettuce in sight. Two bottles of wine. A plate of tiny cupcakes in many colors.

She shook her head when she had it all spread out and said, "I still think I'm shopping for a family. Good, you'll have a couple of decent meals this week. Have you eaten anything lately?"

"Uh, no. I guess not." I think I whispered it.

"I believe it. You look like hell. Dig in and no heart-to-heart until you have fueled up. I will do the conversing for now." She was heaping up a plate for me as she spoke.

She chatted away about her successful appearance at an industry convention, the weirdness of Las Vegas, the beauty of Seattle, the likelihood that she had brought in a big new client for her firm, and how she liked business travel less now that it no longer meant escape from a house of teenagers.

She is a vice-president for a company that sells advertising time. I don't exactly understand what she does—our friendship began at a PTA cupcake sale—but it seems somewhat glamorous. She often assures me that it isn't. As she spoke, she refilled my wine glass and added food to my plate.

"Now," she said at last. "Now tell me what is going on with you. I got a message about Chris. Do you want to start there?"

"Yes. No. I don't know. So many things are going on I don't know what I want to say first."

"I have all night. Start anywhere. Start with why in the world you are banging your door lock with a hammer."

"Oh." I rubbed my forehead, where the headache was not leaving even after a good meal. I reached for a second cupcake, and told her the whole story.

She was appropriately shocked and sympathetic. She argued with me about reporting this to the cops immediately. Funny, I did not resent it from her as I would have from my father. I admitted, with unusual meekness, that maybe it could have been handled more wisely.

"So, you see," I concluded, "that's why I feel safer with the old rusty bolt locked, but I can't budge it with just my hands."

She looked at me as if I had suddenly become mentally defective. "You know there are these guys. They are called locksmiths. They will come and…"

"Charge me a lot of money."

She reached for her phone, punched in just one button and started with, "Hey, Ernie. This is Darcy. No, no, everything is fine but I have someone, a very dear friend, very dear, who has an emergency need for better locks. Probably change a cylinder in one, and add another? Yes, what she has is pathetic. And I know you can manage a good price for her right? A very, very good price? Yes, she's right in the neighborhood." She gave him my address. "Yes, yes. Of course, yes. You're a hero, as always."

She turned back to me with a smug smile. "All fixed."

"You have a locksmith on speed dial?" I was flabbergasted.

"Helps if your husband owns a few office buildings. I'm sure we put Ernie's oldest through dental school. He'll have someone here crack of dawn tomorrow. What's next? Chris?"

So that was another monologue, embellished with a few tears and one or two expressions of fury, complete with inappropriate language.

Darcy sort of laughed, even while she was giving me a hug.

"Listen up. Lily spent her preschool years threatening to move in with Grandma. Sally did move in with her college student cousin for a while when she was in high school. Tommy went to college and didn't come home for three years. Only Katy never pulled that. Guess what? They all survived and we are all even on speaking terms now."

I knew that. I had been at her home for holidays. She had four normal, affectionate, successful, grown children.

I put my head on the dining room table. I might have thumped it a couple of times.

"The key is not to take it so much to heart."

"I don't know how to do that!"

"I'm not saying it was easy. Hell, no. I really thought we had lost Tom for a while there. But your Chris? Did she hitchhike across country? Run away with a biker gang? Disappear into some cult? No. She hopped right into Grandpa's arms. On a rebellion scale of one to ten, that would be maybe a two."

She just looked at me, steadily, with, I suspected, a smile lurking underneath.

"Just remember, they do grow up eventually. If you don't kill them first, of course. Right?"

Then we did laugh. Just a little.

She said, "Does that cover it? Should I open the second bottle?

"I'm also in a mess at work."

"Hand me the corkscrew."

She filled our glasses again. "I'm even better at office crap than parenting. Are you in school now, too?"

I shook my head. "I'm on independent study this term. That's why this has to work out. The job is my project and I have to make it work or I lose a whole semester. I just can't, can't afford that. "

"Tell all."

It took me a long time.

"Good God, why didn't you call me? You found that poor boy dead!"

"You were away. It was a business trip."

"Oh, yes, and you no longer have my cell phone number?"

She saw my eyes fill with whatever it was—exhaustion, wine, stress—and quickly said, "Oh, honey, I'm not trying to give you a hard time. I'm really trying to give you some support." She gripped my hand for a second. "My kids are good for the moment, Kevin and I are okay, job is okay. So turn to me if you need me and stop being Wonder Woman! Honestly, though, it does sound like you are working your way through this work crisis. Apart from these deaths, which is not your job, anyway."

She stood and began clearing the table. "Your eyes are going to close in about a minute. I'll clean up and head home, while you, my friend, head upstairs to bed."

"Leave the dishes. You've done enough—way, way more than enough—and you're right, I'm crashing, too. Tomorrow."

She was already stacking leftovers in the refrigerator and loading the dishwasher. As I let her out, struggling again with the extra lock, she stopped.

"I just thought of something that may actually be helpful. Do you want to meet a charming old man named Konick?"

"What? Are you kidding me? Of course I would. "

"I don't know him very well, but we occasionally play bridge with him at the club. I can call him. Maybe he can fill in some pieces for you. Would that be useful for impressing your bosses?"

"Yes. A hundred times yes." I shook my head, trying to take it in. "Do you know everyone? You've found me a pediatric eye doctor and a seamstress and I always thought you could find a performing seal if I needed one."

"Of course I could. And yes, I know everyone. Including the crazy boyfriend I introduced you to. I'm still trying to make up for that."

I hugged her. "Completely forgiven, especially if you know a Konick."

"Go sleep. Maybe that will sweeten up your dreams."

Chapter Twenty

I woke up with a monster headache. It must have been that second bottle of wine. Damn Darcy. She had a tolerance for alcohol developed over years of business cocktail parties and after-tennis drinks, I guess. She was a bad influence on me. Not that I wasn't grateful. My head might hurt but something inside was better after the evening with her.

Overnight a photo had landed on my screen, courtesy of *Brownstone Bytes*. I had somehow signed up for one of their threads. How did that happen?

It was bad and blurry—I was pretty sure that was the photo and not my eyes. I went to splash water into my eyes and on my face. When I looked again, I stopped breathing. It was labeled, "Green-Wood Cemetery entrance at night." The date was the night of the robbery. The night Dima was killed, somewhere if not there. There was a car. A van really. It was far too dim to see the make or license but it was inside the gate in the wee hours of the night.

> "What happened at historic Green-Wood Cemetery Monday night? Sources tell us that all was normal on Monday at closing time, suitably, 'as quiet as the grave.' That night this car was seen, parked there after-hours. On Tuesday morning, visitors were told that there had been an accident. Really? During the night? Because the graves opened up, releasing zombies? Or what?"

That woke me up pretty damn fast. There were two things I could do right now.

First, I sent it to my new friend, Detective Henderson. I wrote in caps, DID YOU KNOW ABOUT THIS PHOTO? Then I had a second thought, just in time as my cursor was already pointing to Send. I rewrote it without caps and said—without the multiple question marks I had in my head—"Could it be real? Could it have something to do with Dima?"

And then I added a cordial hello and good-bye. I read it again and hit Send. Twice, just to make sure. Then I took a deep breath, went downstairs to find coffee and my purse and scrounged around, increasingly frantic, until I unearthed the card of the blogger. I had told him I would toss it into the garbage, but I was pretty sure in my heart that I had not.

His name was Kent. Just Kent without the Clark. I had to laugh at that. No one could say he lacked self-esteem.

I gulped coffee, burned my mouth, thought hard. I wanted to know where that photo came from. I thought Henderson would have tools to get that information, not physical tools, but threats of subpoena and so on, but I didn't know if he would share it. And though my scattered knowledge did not make enough sense, not yet, to bring to him, I felt somehow that I was closer to snapping the important puzzle pieces into place.

Or maybe I just wanted to know because I am a nosy person and was fed up with none of this making sense.

Leary had told me that everything newspeople know doesn't get published. Sometimes it's not an important enough story, or a more important one bumps it. Sometimes the information remained incomplete. Sometimes it just wasn't ready in time. If the blogger knew more, it was worth it to me to deal with him. I could shower the slime off after.

I gulped and thought some more. This Kent fancied himself a newsman. Even if he was actually just a gossip hound, inside information was his life's blood. And I had some, even if I couldn't put it to work. Maybe I had something to trade.

"*Brownstone Bytes*, Brooklyn's real news just for you. Talk to me."

"This is Erica Donato. We met at Green-Wood Cemetery a few times and you wanted to talk. I'm the…"

"Ms. Donato. Of course! I remember you. This is Kent. Lucky you got me. I was just about to go into the field."

That meant snooping around, I thought, but I did not say it.

"You have something for me today?"

"Maybe. But I want something from you."

"Yah? What would that be?"

"That photo of Green-Wood gate at night?"

"You liked that? It was quite a find, if I do say so. They're stonewalling over there but we know something happened."

"Where did it come from?"

"I'm sorry?" He didn't sound sorry. He sounded like this was making his day. "Did I hear right? You're asking for a source? Sure thing! That and my bank account password and my right arm. I wouldn't tell cops, let alone some random civilian."

"So the cops have asked?"

"I didn't say that! And wouldn't."

I remembered his smart-ass expression overlaid on a soft baby face, and thought he would probably give a determined cop his bank account and his right arm in no time. I hoped Henderson would share whatever he learned, but I wasn't counting on it.

"Mmm. What if I had something to share back? "

"One hand helping the other? I might consider it. What ya' got?"

"What would you say to a hate group, with guns, in Brooklyn? It might be small, I don't know, but…"

"I'd be interested in learning more." His cautious words did not quite disguise the excited tremor in his voice. "Who are they after?"

"Does your news focus go as far out as Brighton Beach?"

"Hell, our focus goes wherever we say it goes. Who are they after?"

"Honest? You go past the gentry in the brownstone belt? Into the real Brooklyn?" Now I was having fun.

"Come on! News is news. What is the story there? I have to know if there might be a story."

"Let's say not everyone is happy with the way Brighton Beach became Little Odessa. You haven't heard about this?"

"Lady, that's common knowledge but a hate group is a whole different thing. As we speak I am scanning the other local news sources. I don't think anyone has heard of this. What would it take to get your details?"

I smiled.

"Everything you have on that night at Green-Wood, published, reporter's notes, the original of the photo, all of it."

"I'm not just sending it off without something from you. My mom didn't raise stupid kids."

We worked out the exchange. It was only slightly harder than a U.N. peace treaty. A little from me—easy, I sent him the address of Dima's angry neighbor—and a little from him. He forwarded the original photo, a little bigger and clearer. Then I sent him a note. "Get this guy off-guard and talk to him about Russians in Brighton Beach. You will find it interesting." And he told me, "Here's the sender's e-mail, plus this—look at the photo real well. Where is he standing?"

So I looked. Damn. He must have been right there. Right next to the car. I could only think of one way that could have happened. He was involved. Who the hell would it have been? Could it have been Dima himself? Or maybe it was a security camera? I had to find out if they had one there.

Okay, so the guy was good for his word.

A following e-mail. "I did some looking. He's not unknown to the police. Going out now to pay a visit. Thanx, thanx, thanx. Want a job on my news team???"

No, I didn't. And I was pretty sure his news team was a group of young unpaid nerds, sitting at a computer all day with fantasies of some kind of digital-age *Front Page* life.

Another e-mail to Henderson, with everything I had been sent and explaining what I had been up to. True, Dima's murder was his job, not the Green-Wood robbery, but if I could wonder whether they were related after all, so he could he. And he would know how to get it to the cops on the Green-Wood robbery. At least I hoped he would.

I wanted to start my real day now. I wanted to not talk to anymore crazy people or even any moderately weird ones.

I began again with my most normal routines. I got as far as food and shower and typing up my plans for learning Maude's last secrets, before my phone rang.

"I wonder…"

It was Bright Skye. I almost dropped the phone.

I waited, so she went on.

"I've thought it over. Maybe I was too quick on the trigger?" I guess she heard my little gasp of surprise. "That's kind of an Arizona expression. Maybe I could use your help after all."

Her voice dropped to a whisper but this time it sounded deliberate. "I don't want her to know about this though. Amanda. She would be hurt and, I mean, I've known her since I was little Louise Maude."

"What did you say?"

"She's known me since I was little."

"No, I mean your actual, that is, your old name. It was Maude?" That could not have been an accident. Could not have been. "Why did you never tell me?"

"I never think of it. It's not my name now and hasn't been since I was twenty but sometimes Amanda forgets and calls me that."

"So you were suggesting?"

"Yes. I guess you could come over and look around. There are more boxes of papers in the attic, quite a lot more in fact."

"Yes! You bet. Anytime at all. But I am surprised. I don't understand."

"Amanda has been helping but I am a little worried. She knows antiques…she even had her own shop, but I don't think she knows about letters and you know, professory things like that. Why shouldn't you look? I sure don't want them."

So it fell into my lap. Maybe there was something to this putting it out in the universe after all.

"She has an appointment tonight, so that would be good. How does seven sound?"

It sounded like Christmas morning. Or, as in our house, the first night of Hanukah. Or more fall-season appropriate, an unusually great score from trick or treating. True, Ms. Skye was extremely strange but she was finally, sensibly, helpfully, offering what I had needed all along and what she didn't even want.

Between the material that was already coming in from Illinois and Skye's unexpected offer, I thought I was pulling the threads, as Leary had said, very well today. I couldn't fail to find something that would matter, that would help me at work or open up the mystery of Ryan's death.

In a burst of optimistic energy, I cleaned my kitchen, washed my hair, and knocked out half a chapter of my dissertation.

On my way to Skye's house that evening, I took a short detour past the cemetery. I had *Brownstone Bytes'* photo of the gate and car with me. Of course the cemetery was closed, but I drove up to the gate and moved around until I was viewing the same angle. I couldn't have said why. I just wanted to see it for myself.

The thieves went into a deserted cemetery at night to commit a crime. I am not remotely superstitious. I have seen parts of long-dead bodies in a long-ago archaeology class. I have seen the bodies of two people I loved, just after they died, and knew the body was an empty shell, just like the carcass of a crab on the beach and the person was gone. I knew without a tremor of a doubt that a cemetery is just a piece of land with various kinds of stones and statues scattered around. Or in this case, a masterfully landscaped park with art and architecture. It once rivaled Niagara Falls as the most-visited tourist attraction in the country. I am a hard-headed Brooklyn girl and I know there are no ghosts.

But still, cemeteries are considered sacred ground. This is the place where we can see and touch something concrete and remember what is gone. My young husband and my mother are lying under granite stones but they don't live there. They live in my heart.

But still. What kind of person goes into a cemetery at night, disturbing that peace, to steal something? Obviously, that would be someone who is not afraid of ghosts, someone without nerves whose vision only registers things as valuable and vulnerable.

So they broke into the cemetery. How? Not at the front gate, but maybe somewhere in the back, a weak spot in the fence? Unless, of course, someone let them in. Someone who hid there at closing time. Or someone who worked there. Damn.

They came in late at night, in full dark, no moon. I imagined Green-Wood as I was seeing it now, but later. Dark and deeply quiet. So late, even the surrounding city streets were quiet.

They carried powerful flashlights, I assumed. Their leader was the guy with no nerves, but was any of them uncomfortable with what they were doing? Scared? Superstitious?

They trudged through the dark lanes. No, they must have driven in a van or a panel truck, something large enough for the window. That's what was in the photograph. And someone let them in.

Did they have camping lanterns, easier than flashlights, to put down while they worked? Did one person hold the light while the other worked? Or did they use the vehicle headlights? It was a difficult job to remove something so large and fragile in the dark. They needed equipment, too, a large ladder and movers' blankets to wrap up the prize. Maybe they even came with packing materials to crate it up right there.

I felt as if I were there, nervous and twitchy, trying not to mess up the job and let the others down. Trying not to get caught. I wasn't looking at the beauty of the windows, that's for sure, and neither was anyone else. Fearfully looking over my shoulder in case someone was coming. Did someone come? Did Dima?

I shuddered and shook my head to clear my thoughts. It takes some imagination to do the kind of history I do. It is what makes dead facts breathe, but my imagination was heading into overdrive tonight. I was not there with them. I was here now, all alone, outside the cemetery, in my own cluttered economy-size car. I turned on the engine and the radio and left, but the feeling stayed with me.

Before I headed off to Bright Skye's I saw there had been a call from Henderson. Damn. The message only said he'd tried to reach me and would try later. I tried calling back, did not reach him and did leave a message. So much for the convenience of gadgets.

It would have to wait. For now, I was prepared for whatever Bright Skye was going to show me.

Chapter Twenty-one

She greeted me with an offer of all-natural juice or herbal tea. I politely declined. On a cool fall evening, warm cocoa or a glass of red wine are the only choices. She chattered on as she showed me to the staircase. Having finally decided to work together, she seemed to have jumped right into the deep end.

"I hope your climbing legs are in shape. We have two flights to the top floor, and then a little one to the attic. It's hot up there, too, no ventilation, you may want to leave your jacket here." She hung it on a hook, part of a built-in Victorian monster near the door, complete with a mirror, a bench, hooks for coats and a shelf for hats. In other circumstances, I would have loved to have taken a good look at it but not now. I was here to work. Skye was already leading the way upstairs and I was happy to be following right along.

"Now watch that worn spot on the carpet. It's tricky. Turn here." She patted the peeling wallpaper. "Too bad about this. Best as I can remember, it was once kind of pretty."

I bet it was. She did not seem to know the peeling shreds were silk but I did. Judging from the faded pink color, it had once been a rich crimson.

The broad staircase, too, would have been worth a look in another time.

As Skye was explaining at length, it was in very bad condition, with most of the varnish gone, many treads wobbling under my footsteps, and several lights not working. She talked all the way up, even through her labored breathing. "Ah," she finally gasped in front of a door on the third floor landing. "The attic is right up here." She flipped a light switch. That one worked. "Up we go. I'll try to orient you through the mess and then leave you to it."

I was looking at a hundred years' worth of—well—of stuff. I suspected some would be valuable, some interesting, some pure junk. There sure was lot of it. There seemed to have been some attempts at organizing, with similar items near each other. Old wooden skis with two rusty bikes, and an overflowing toy box once painted with faded circus designs. I was tempted by that. There was an ancient dressmaker's dummy with some decrepit, sticker-covered leather trunks. Was that a Vuitton pattern? Were they filled with turn-of-the-last century clothes? How could I get Bright Skye to give all of this to the museum? The toys alone. What a great presentation for visiting school classes.

No, I was there to focus on the boxes of papers. Skye pointed me to them, stacked up in a corner, the missing ones now returned, piled up next to a stack of others.

She switched on some low-watt light bulbs. "I'm so sorry there is nothing better. And I know it is hot here. There is no way to bring in air-conditioning but I believe there is a fan somewhere." She puttered around and eventually dragged out a tall standing fan. She could plug it into an overhead outlet, but it was too high for my short computer cord.

"Now then, are you set up? I know. You could use that old school desk!" She immediately started pulling a desk from behind some other piles. I had to help; it was solid wood and weighed, well, a lot. A seat that was too low for even a small adult, with an attached armrest writing surface, and, I bet, a storage space underneath. It was old, very old, layers of dust old. I assured her I would be fine perched on one of the trunks. Really, I couldn't wait to get to the cartons that had been lost. Between the excitement and the attic dust, I could hardly breathe.

Yes, these were the missing cartons, and these were the missing papers, Maude's letters, her sketches, her small items. Everything. All safe, all complete. I won't lie. My eyes teared up a little.

I carefully carried them over to the door. These were going right back to the museum with me.

Now, at last, I had my chance to prospect for other treasures and I was going to make the most of it. I could not trust Bright Skye not to change her mind and cut off my time.

I did a quick look through the other boxes, applying a scholarly form of triage. This box, full of household financial records from 1920-1935, probably useful to some historians, but I was not one of them. Set aside. A box of income tax forms from the 1940s? Same. A box of—what? Sentimental keepsakes, I supposed. Christmas cards, Valentines, a few dried and crumbling corsages, piano sheet music from around 1912. Long-forgotten popular tunes, I guessed, and here was a brand new hit. It said so right there on the cover. "Alexander's Ragtime Band," the first of Irving Berlin's lengthy list of classics and not at all forgotten.

Here was something I had never actually seen, a dance program, with a tiny pencil attached by a silk cord, and names written in for each dance. What fun. It was not useful at the moment, but I made second stack of "go back to later."

And then there was sturdy box with some leather-bound books, dark and heavy, with gold-edged pages and paper in surprisingly good condition. I absently noted that, thinking "acid-free paper." I lost my breath again.

They were the earliest histories of New York. *Journey into Mohawk Country* by Joost van den Bogaert, one of the first books about this new Dutch possession. Another, similarly rare, *Description of New Netherlands*, by Adrian van der Donk. There were records of the Dutch Reformed Church of Philipsburg, which was now Tarrytown. Which was where the Konicks once had considerable property. Why here? I had no idea. A very old copy, perhaps an original, of Washington Irving's *Knickerbocker Tales*. These should absolutely be in a museum rare book collection, I thought. Here is where Bright Skye would find her valuable inheritance.

They all had a fancy book plate in front with a ship I could swear was Hudson's *Half Moon* and the name Gerardus Konick

III. Aha. They went into my Important pile. And at the bottom of the box, the biggest book of all, a leather-bound Bible with a family tree written in front. Just as I had guessed. The name of Gerardus Konick IV was covered with angry slashes of ink.

So there it was. It gave me a little chill down my back.

I had to go back. What was the name on the tax pages I had set aside? Only Updike, Skye's maternal grandparents, and it told me nothing, but some of the holiday cards said, "To darling Maude" and were signed "Your loving husband."

Well, great. Maude was loved. Was it Gerard Konick as I already thought? By then, I was stiff from sitting on the floor. I had to stand up and stretch. And walk around. Now would be a good time to look at some of the frivolous items.

I opened an unlocked trunk covered with colorful destination stickers. It was empty but the second was crammed with elaborate old-fashioned ladies' outfits. I live in blue jeans but I am a sucker for those beautiful clothes. The label on the trunk said, "Mrs. Gerard Konick,"—again!—but lost inside was a tiny book of poetry inscribed "Maude Konick." Aha. The last piece of that puzzle slipped into place.

I took notes madly, took phone photos, though I they knew would not come out well, and stacked items I wanted next to the door to downstairs. I was covered with a layer of dust clinging to a film of sweat. I had to go talk to Bright Skye about borrowing it all. But before I did, one more stroll around the attic to see if I'd missed anything. Got that, got this, and oh, the third trunk, I'd skipped over it in my excitement.

It was full of stylish men's clothing of a bygone era. Plus fours. White-tie evening wear. Snappy straw boaters with bright grosgrain hat bands. Historically important but not as interesting as the women's clothes.

And there, stuffed in behind the golf shoes, was something odd, a narrow metal box. Odd because of all the things it was not. Not old. Not physically interesting, not beautiful, but cheap metal in an Army green shade.

Of course I picked it up. I was mindlessly curious, but also determined to be thorough in what might be my one-time access to this place. The box was locked but a key was taped to the bottom. Now that was not smart. Unless the former owner of the box was someone who lost little keys a lot. I could understand that.

It held a few folded papers. They seemed to be notes on business transactions, and fairly recent. At first I could not make sense out of it and was only looking to rule out that it was of interest. It was certainly modern. The papers were all typed and some were printed from a computer. The most recent was dated last month.

That's what didn't fit. Skye's mother had been ill, Skye had left. Who was storing business papers in this house?

I moved into better light. The newest one was marked "Deposit in advance of delivery." It listed the dimensions of something without naming it, and gave a lot of money—a gasp-worthy lot—for final delivery. There was a letter attached, written in Arabic.

The rest of the papers were similar but were stamped "Sale Complete." The money involved was startling, at least to me, an impoverished grad student. The attachments were written in various languages, one in Russian, another in Japanese, I guessed. There were tiny photos attached and they were artwork. A statue of a winged angel and two stained glass windows. That's when my hands started to shake a little.

The one in elaborate script seemed to be Spanish. Yes, the inner address was Cali, Colombia. I had a couple of years of Spanish in high school and I lived here in New York, where many public signs are in Spanish and English. I gave it a try. *Promesa* was easy. It was promise. I recognized *ventana*, the word for window. Could *cementerio* be anything but "cemetery?" I hoped it wasn't "cement factory?"

Oh, crap, this is ridiculous. I was getting caught up in something I couldn't do and really should not even be taking the time to do. I needed to go discuss the old books with Skye. Then I made out, through the elaborate script, the word Tiffany. Now I wasn't in such a hurry. I managed to make out the names of a church and maybe a cemetery. I didn't know the Spanish but I sure knew the names. By then I was breathing hard.

On the Russian page, none of it meant anything to me and the Japanese was even more mysterious. Except for the place where in English it said, "Heavenly Rest." I knew that name, I thought. Wasn't it one of the small, out-of-the-way cemeteries where another Tiffany window had been stolen?

What in hell had I stumbled onto here? I wasn't sure and couldn't be sure until I had some translations. I could see the receipt or bills of sale or whatever they were had been carefully written to reveal nothing so I would need to translate the other pages.

Could I fold them up small enough to hide in my laptop? Not quite, with the photos, but I could put them there, leaving the laptop not quite securely closed, but in my tote bag, under my notebook, and under the rest of the old books I wanted to take. Safely hidden. I hope. Stealing? Umm, maybe. Or maybe it was evidence. I thought I should call Henderson again, right now while I had complete privacy. Nope. My phone was where it belonged. In my purse. Which was hanging from a hook in the front hall, along with my jacket.

I headed downstairs with the huge family Bible in my arms. Off-balance from the bag full of books, and with no free hands, I tackled the short but steep staircase very carefully, one cautious step at a time.

When I reached the second floor, I heard voices coming right up the spacious stairwell. There were voices? TV? Radio? No. I stopped, held my breath, listened.

Amanda Mercer. "Who is here? I saw a car in the driveway. I've told you and told you not to talk to anyone."

"Oh, Amanda, don't be so upset. There is nothing to be angry about. That annoying Ms. Donato said she could help me value those letters, but she wanted something back, a chance to come over and look at the attic. So I thought I'd just let her, and then she'd be done and out of our lives."

I wasn't going to move a muscle.

"I don't believe you." She sounded angry. No, furious. "You cannot trust her and now, behind my back, even…"

"Oh, 'Manda, not behind your back. After everything you've done for me, how could you say that? She is so persistent, I just had a moment—well, I got fed up. I would never let her near the valuable antiques but she doesn't seem to want them anyway. She likes papers, not, you know, jewelry or silver. I thought I'd let her take a look, and she'd go away for good. Wouldn't that be best? She won't find anything we care about."

Well, I thought. That sounded like my entrance cue. I struggled down the last flight, one step at a time, lightly calling Bright Skye's name.

By the time I got to the first floor, they were both in the hall, waiting for me. Skye was fluttering over Mercer, and Mercer looked red-eyed and angry.

"I found something wonderful! I am so grateful to both of you." Stick to what I want, I thought. Don't be part of their argument. I could see it confused them. Good. "Bright, you had an old family Bible there in the attic and a few other wonderful books." I held the Bible out with both hands. "I don't think it's valuable as a book—its condition is very poor—but something in it supports my ideas about Maude which makes it priceless for me. And the other books I am guessing are very valuable. I was wondering…"

"No." Mercer snapped it out, not Skye. "No way. Absolutely nothing leaves this house with you. After what happened to the other items Brighty gave you? No way."

How could I answer that?

"But Amanda, she says she found things that could be valuable?"

I put the heavy Bible down on the bench near the door. It gave me a minute to think. Leary had said, pull the threads until something unravels. Between this dumb, emotional crybaby and this angry, bossy woman, I was more than ready to do some unraveling here. Though I felt the hidden papers telling me to get out as fast as I could, I still needed the information in the Bible.

"Oh," I said, as I turned back to them, "I did. I certainly did. Look at the family tree here." I opened the Bible to show them, but Amanda had her eyes on my bulging canvas bag.

"What else have you taken from here?" She sounded belligerent.

"Just a few books. With Bright's permission, of course. Wait. I'll show you, "

I slid the bag off my shoulder, but she was not in the mood to wait. She grabbed for it and all the contents went tumbling out. I winced when the laptop hit the floor with a crash. And then the hidden papers flew out after it.

Bright Skye, puzzled, picked them up. She looked lost as always, but Mercer turned red.

"That is private property." Her voice became louder. "It has nothing, nothing whatever to do with your historical research. What nerve." She gasped. "They were thoroughly hidden, you sneaking snoop. I never, never thought anyone would find them."

When she stopped to catch her breath, Bright, who had been looking at her intently said, "How can they be private papers, Amanda, if you know about them and I don't? In my own house? We collected all that to give to the lawyer. What is she talking about? Was there something that was not given to him?"

"Why, I have no idea! She hasn't shown us anything, has she? Maybe she is saying it just to create distrust?"

Bright looked down at her feet. "I have lots of distrust of everyone by now. Even my oldest friends. I guess that's what they mean by older and wiser. Right now I am not even sure about you, because the first thing you said was 'that is private property.'" She finally looked straight at Mercer. "Just like you knew what she meant."

Mercer looked right back at her, tears in her eyes. "How can you talk to me like that? I have been so good to you. And your mother, too. All these years, helping out. Keeping you company when you came back. Dealing with this monster of a mess."

At that point, her face was in her hands.

I watched, barely breathing.

It was Skye who stepped over to her, pulled Mercer's hands from her face and said in a vicious whisper, "Tell me the truth. Now. No more games."

The sound of her hand hitting Mercer's cheek rang out. A substantial woman, her smack threw the thin Amanda off her balance and she slipped to the floor.

Skye didn't move. She just stared down at Mercer, panting, her fists clenched, her face a furious red.

Had I told myself not to step into their argument? Did I have a choice? I moved to help Mercer to her feet but Mercer, seeing an opportunity, jumped up and ran to the door. I grabbed her, swung her around and landed a right-cross squarely on her jaw. I hadn't done something like that since I was ten.

It was enough. She fell. By then Skye had pulled herself together and helped. She had the body size to hold Amanda Mercer down.

"You're not getting up until you start telling the truth," Bright announced. Mercer moaned. "Did it hurt? Good."

Mystic, spacey Bright Skye had vanished and someone else had shown up. Perhaps the girl who was raised in a deteriorating neighborhood in Brooklyn and learned some playground scrapping. Just as I had. Or maybe she learned some physical skills out there in cattle country along with the mystic chanting.

I took the other shoulder but Skye didn't really need my help. Mercer was well and truly pinned.

"Let me up and I'll tell you."

We did and she wrapped her shaking hands around her body. "I need a glass of water."

"After you tell us about the papers I found."

"I don't know what…"

"I have them right here, if that would help your memory." I reached one hand into my canvas bag.

At that sight, something in her collapsed. She suddenly looked old instead of somewhere in middle age.

"How can I make you understand?" she began. "There are beautiful windows all over New York, statues too, that are neglected and forgotten. Don't you know that?" She addressed me. "Art, great art, treated like trash." She put her hands on my arms in a begging gesture. "Old churches that had the money to commission them, back when, and now barely have the money to keep the roof patched. And old monuments, too, with no family left to care."

"Like the Konicks?"

"Like the Konicks. Many years ago, there was a case. An expert stole some art with the help of a cemetery employee. So I was so tired, getting old, desperate for money, I had the daydream that it could be done again, and I could be both the expert and the employee. And I met someone who knew the right people. He could sell to those right people, safely right out of the country, who would take care of them, clean them, protect them. Rich people who wanted a real Tiffany window of their very own for their new mansions. And it worked. For a time, it worked. The first two times, at other places, it went very well."

"But no one else would ever see them again? Instead of the art being available to everyone? And you actually stole from Green-Wood Cemetery?" My indignation was in my voice. "Where you worked all those years?"

Her face hardened. "Worked? I might as well have been a volunteer, for the pathetic amount I was paid. And they never gave me a job that matched my expertise. I know everything about that place." She gave a creepy little giggle as she added, "I know where all the bodies are buried! Now that's an appropriate joke. But of course I don't have those credentials that they respect so much. I was always just that strange old lady with a history hobby. Well now I have some money in the bank after all!"

I took a deep breath. "You said an employee. Was Dmitri Ostrov involved?"

"Dmitri? No." She grinned rather slyly. "No, he was too much of a goody-goody. But he was my connection to someone who could get the jobs done. Not that he ever knew that."

I didn't like that smile. Not at all. I shook her. "Were you there when he died? Was he killed there after all? Was he?"

"No and yes. Yes he was. Me? I was safe in my bed where I belonged." She looked at me with surprise. "Do you think I did the labor myself? Look at me! I am a lady and the brains of it all. I was not there to get my hands dirty." She giggled again. "My little pun. 'Hands dirty.' In both senses. I had big, strong men, of course. With tools. Dumb, but strong. Too dumb that night." She came to a dead stop and looked at me, and then Bright, and then at me again. "Most people look at me and see the mask, the sweet, eccentric old lady with gray hair." Her smile had a bitter edge. "Vladimir knew me for what I was almost immediately. It went well until it didn't. Nothing lasts." She stopped again and glared at us. "I don't have to say any more. I should not have said anything but you were hurting me. I'm done."

"No, dammit, you are not. I want to know about Dima! And everything about the stolen window. And I want to know what you know about poor Ryan."

"I want to know why you kept the papers in my house. I don't understand this at all," Bright said.

Mercer looked at Skye with some sadness, and said one last thing. "But don't you see? Your junk shop attic is the perfect place to hide anything at all. And that way, it wasn't connected to me."

Then she shut her mouth, folded her arms, and looked down at her knees. I was considering slapping her.

A phone shrilled into the silence and we all jumped. It was mine. Irritated, I let it go. There was no one I could talk to right now. Ah, yes there was. I jumped up to dig it out of my purse and caught Henderson just as he was leaving a message.

I told him where I was and why. "Come quick."

Then Bright Skye never moved. She sat there in awkward silence, guarding Amanda Mercer, who was not actually trying to get away anymore. She had closed her eyes and may even have passed out. She was still breathing and smelled of alcohol.

Skye finally said with her voice shaking, "I used violence. After all these years of daily spiritual practice. I will have to talk to my master about how to cleanse my spirit."

"I'd say she had it coming. After all she's done? And she was trying to run away!"

"That is her karma, not mine." Her expression was resigned. "I did not have to take on her wrongdoing." She was silent for a long moment. "I can't wait to go home. I hate this place, this house, this city."

I kept my mouth shut. Sedona might have a few flaws, too, but it was obvious that for Bright, it was home. Myself, I'm with Billy Joel. My mind is always in a New York state.

It wasn't long before Henderson came through the unlocked door, followed by a colleague and uniformed cops. He seemed surprised to see us on the floor, hands still on the elderly woman who was breathing but not talking.

He knelt next to me and with a few quick questions had a complete grasp of the situation. He called an ambulance for Mercer and moved us so his team could handcuff her. He talked to me and to Skye and saw we confirmed each other's statements and would swear to it. I gave him the papers I had found, and told him where to find the metal box and he summoned another cop to go up to the attic with me and bring it down.

The situation was finally in good hands. I realized I was shaking but I knew I had finally found some answers. I was sure there would be more.

Chapter Twenty-two

Eventually Mercer did have a quite a lot to say. As Henderson described it to me one night, when he pointed out that there might be murder charges, and they could certainly make a charge of accessory stick she saw that she'd better tell her story her own way.

"Could you have made it stick?"

"Maybe. That's the DA's call. But don't forget, as I was happy to tell her, there is still the not-so-little matter of the thefts. We had a few different departments involved." He grinned. "Gridlock in the interrogation room."

He had explained to her how easy it would be to get rough translations of the documents. "Of course we'd have to have them all translated officially, nice and conclusive, but we could have started on it right away. I told her we had a Russian-speaking secretary on duty in the morning and my friend Sergeant Diaz already said the Spanish paper is documentation for the purchase of a Tiffany window. We knew she provided both the art and the background information—it seems there are photos attached—and someone paid her a whole lot of money."

"What did she say? What could she possibly say?"

"That it was not so much money."

He met my incredulous gasp with a grin.

"Oh, yeah, she protested that." In a little lady voice, he went on, 'But I had a team to pay off, and it was split with the go-between who found the customers.' So then we had a conversation about that mystery man, but that wasn't me. It was the art-squad guys. They're salivating to get his name. So right then was the point where she started thinking she had said too much, and we laid out for her the benefits of full cooperation."

This was cop talk over dinner with Henderson, whose first name was Mike. I loved getting the whole story at last. There was an advantage to dating a cop.

"And Vladimir? What was his role? Was Natalya right all along?"

"It's a definite yes and no." He grinned and I smacked his hand. "Of course the macho Vladimir spent a long time telling us he knew nothing and we were only harassing him because he was an immigrant. So we told him how we were harassing Mercer. That threw him and Mercer's story did him in.

"They did meet through Dima, one time when Vladimir was visiting him at the cemetery. Mercer sized him up and saw her chance, and it didn't take long for a deal. He provided the muscle and tools."

I put my fork down, suddenly unable to taste the lasagna. "Did he kill Dima? That was your real job, wasn't it? Dima."

He put a hand over mine, still gripping my fork, and said, "Not exactly to the first question, and yes to the second. His story was that he wasn't there that night. He wasn't about to rob his own brother at work."

"But I bet he knew all about the place because of visiting Dima."

"Ah, clever girl. He did the planning and collected the men, but he wasn't there himself."

"That's a mighty fine line!"

"Yah, well, these guys don't exactly think like the rest of us. The deal was they weren't even supposed to use guns. Vladimir's no dope. He knows the difference between larceny and homicide. However, one bozo got nervous and brought a gun and used it. We've got him, too, by the way. Evidently Dima tried to be a hero, when he stumbled on them mid-job. Poor bastard. You can imagine what Vladimir said about his good, stupid brother!"

And I could.

"So he was happy to give up the guy with the gun and explain that he'd stayed in touch with Mercer, planning more work, so he could trap her and get his own revenge."

"What? That's ridiculous! Did you or anyone believe him?"

Mike shrugged. "Kind of yes and no. Because he kept notes, like a diary, of his findings about Mercer and his plans. Kind of backed up his story and they're very useful to us. Seems he blamed her for the whole thing." He helped himself to salad. This disturbing discussion didn't upset him at all. "That's because she was there that night." He saw my surprise. "Yes, she lied to you. She was there that night. According to Vladimir she liked the excitement almost as much as the money."

"What's going to happen to him? Volodya?"

He shrugged again. "The legal eagles will be working that one out. Not clear for now."

"So Dima died because some stupid punk got nervous?" I felt sick.

Natalya did too when she found out. I was there, and not by accident. Mike had given me a heads-up that he was calling on her that day and I was able to just drop by for a little mom time.

Mike described the botched robbery, implied Dima was a hero for standing up to them, expressed admiration and sympathy. I could tell he had done this before.

Natalya, turning pale, then red, cut to the core.

"My Dima died for that?" Her voice seemed to get higher with each word. "Because a criminal couldn't even do his own crime right? It is that stupid?"

Mike nodded, warily.

I wasn't sure what she would do next—maybe start throwing things—but she surprised us by collapsing into a ball on a chair and weeping, silently at first, then with great sobs. Finally she stopped, accepted the box of tissues I handed her, and sat up straight.

"I am done. I thank you, Detective. And my dear Erica. I am done for now. He will go to jail for a very long time?"

Mike nodded again.

"Good. You will make sure of that? Perhaps someone will kill him there for just such a stupid reason—that would be justice—but for now, he is not my concern. Erica, come. You have time for lunch? We will talk about our children. Or fashion. Or house decorating."

Later I learned the NYPD found the stolen window while searching Bright's house for more evidence. It was wrapped in moving blankets and stashed behind a massive Victorian wardrobe. It was a perfect place to hide it until it was time to ship it out to a customer in Qatar.

So it seemed Mrs. Mercer's friendship with Bright Skye was even more calculated than I thought. Bright's house provided a perfect hiding place, right next door where Mercer could keep an eye on it. And I thought all along she merely planned to profit from the sale of Bright's antiques.

After those discoveries, I heard a different team of officers went to work on Mercer about Ryan. When forensics put her there at the scene, she finally admitted to everything. She had been tracking him online, me and Flint too, wanting to know everything we learned from Skye's letters, and she saw Ryan's own foolish words. There would be a fortune in her pocket if she could lay hands on a lost Tiffany window. She already had an interested buyer. She hoped some of the information was at Flint's house and she knew Flint was socializing. She insisted Ryan was never supposed to be there. She even claimed to feel badly about it. There was a tussle, she said, that ended with his head hitting a corner of the elegant marble countertop, entirely an unfortunate accident.

And she'd slipped the boxes of letters back into Bright's house because, after all, she was fond of her and wanted her to have them after she'd made copies. Or so she said. Perhaps it was part of her fantasy that she was a good person. Bright Skye still believed there were higher powers at work.

I went over to see Natalya and Alex one Saturday. We walked along the beach and Alex skimmed rocks on the surf while

Natalya laughed at him because it was too windy and called him "You American boy!" When our hands turned blue in the cold fall wind, we repaired to a café for scorching glasses of hot Russian tea and a round of cherry blintzes. The look of sadness in their eyes was still there and I knew it would remain, but I had seen them laughing together that day.

Walking back she told me they had already had a simple funeral for Dima. "I did not invite you because it was all Russian. We got through it, me and Alex together. Just barely, but we did. We will have a memorial service soon, I think, maybe at school, for all our American friends. No, I mean, for all Dima's American friends. He had a lot." She paused. "Alex told me Dima and Volodya were sort of working on making up. So," she shrugged, "we will see. It was Alex saying it, so I had to believe him. You know? Even if I didn't believe it. It's my son talking."

"I know."

I certainly did know. My own offspring came home one day, just like that. She walked in, dragging her big duffle bag, and said, "I'm back. Don't ask me questions. I don't want to talk." She went upstairs, cranked up some music and that was that.

I was too surprised to ask her anything then, and later my father claimed he had no idea. Chris had simply asked for a ride home. I was torn between begging her to talk, forcing her to talk (the power of the allowance might help there), and just letting her slide back into normal life, hers and mine. Was it cowardly to choose the latter? Maybe, but I was exhausted by all the recent drama in my life and glad to have her home. For a time, she made a special effort to be thoughtful to me, and I knew it was her way of apologizing. I'd take it.

One day Dr. Flint sent me a link to a page at Pratt's website. Yes, Dr. Flint. I assumed he must have found a new assistant. It was a memorial page for Ryan. His funeral had been back home in Nebraska, but there was a contact for his parents. I wrote to them on dignified writing paper, a hard note that took me many days to get right. I received a printed thank-you and that was that.

Almost. Because one day Flint showed up and said, "Come with me now. I have a driver." Ah, the old Flint was back.

Our destination was, I hoped for the very last time, Green-Wood. I followed him to the Konick mausoleum. He had a bag of equipment and he measured and tapped and used some small tools, conferred with a man who met us there. The focus was the white-washed side wall that threw the whole design off so oddly. He finally explained with a big smile, "It's a false wall. It hit me just the other day that it might be." He shook his head at his own stupidity. "I must have stopped thinking for a while. It's so obvious now."

The other man, an architect, had a couple of workmen with him to take the wall down, very, very carefully, and there it was, emerging bit by bit: the lost Tiffany window.

It depicted a tidy Dutch garden, with tulips streaked with flames of color and others shaped liked lilies. There were carnations, and perhaps roses. Or peonies. There was a windmill in the far background, to tell us we were on Dutch land. Just beyond the low brick garden wall was the great untidy wilderness, with trees and wildflowers and a few animals peeping from under the leaves. I recognized the tulips, the iris, the ironweed, the wild turkey family and the fawn from Maude's sketches.

It was a work of art, of craft, of history. It told a story about the planned and the wild, the neat and the natural, two kinds of beauty. Maude didn't show us which side of the garden wall she was on. Perhaps she wanted both.

It was dusty and grimy and had a few cracks and it was beautiful. We all stared and stared as the last piece of the wall came down. The two men conferred. There would be cleaning and stabilization of the frame and who knows what else. I just looked at it and whispered, "Nice work, Maude. You did it."

A full-size reproduction of the window became the highlight of our museum exhibit about Maude. We called it "Lost Tiffany Girl, Lost Tiffany Window" and it was quite a success. I had a credit, assistant curator, and I did most of the work.

And then of course I behaved like a scholar (or scholar-to-be) and wrote a scholarly paper, too, my first publication. Dr. Flint, in an unheard of fit of modesty, did not want to be my co-author, and so I mentioned him as a consultant. Ryan was listed as the co-author. I sent a copy to his parents and hoped they found some meaning in it.

And I found my own parental meaning in this: Chris threw me a birthday party. She planned it all herself, with some advice from Darcy and, I suspect, financial help from my dad. Natalya came with a warm hug for me, and a huge cake; Alex and Melanie, Chris' best friends; Mel's parents; and Darcy, with fabulous stylish shoes for a birthday gift. Joe came without that redhead from the glass shop, and just shook his head when I asked him about it. I caught him looking at me when Mike Henderson came in with a big hug of his own and a bigger bouquet of roses. My dad was there and he actually brought a funny card from Leary and a book of old newspaper cartoons.

That wasn't quite the end though, because Darcy had another gift for me, a phone number for the Konick descendent she knew.

"He's expecting to hear from you."

He heard from me that night.

So a week later I had tea, tiny sandwiches and all, at a very old private club in Brooklyn Heights, with a very old, charming man, James Gerard Konick. He told me a story about his uncle who was the skeleton in the closet when he was growing up. How no one would explain what had happened to his father's oldest brother and the less they said, the more curious he was. How, when he was all grown up, he had an interest in genealogy and tracked Gerard to a beautiful house in a suburban area of Brooklyn.

Gerard and his wife Maude turned out to be charming and warm, not at all like his parents. They encouraged his interest in art and his dream of studying in France. Gerard had a successful career as an architect and she painted all her life and was active in arts programs for schools. He remembered how she chided him when he expressed doubt about uncultured, foreign public school students. She said—and he never forgot it—"Do you think art is only for the wealthy? Like your conventional grandparents? Art is for anyone who has eyes."

They only had one child, a daughter. They had lost another daughter in the flu pandemic and there were never any others to fill up the big house with many bedrooms. Gerard's parents never spoke to him again after he jilted the Beekman daughter for Maude, but he was not completely cut off from the world of his childhood. Years later their daughter married the descendent of another old Dutch family, John Opdyke. And then I knew that their daughter was Ginny Updike, Bright Skye's mother. Bright was Maude's great-granddaughter.

"So I did go to Paris," he told me, "and I stayed until the war trapped me there. Before I made it home, they had died in the same year, as if they could not live without each other. They were buried in Staten Island, of all places. I really didn't know their daughter and I had no real interest in my Konick connections either, so that was that."

He didn't know how the letters to River Bend ended up in Maude's Brooklyn home and we never did find out. My guess is that they were sent back to her after her mother's death, when the house in Illinois was sold. Or her sister kept them with other family papers and they were sent back to Maude's daughter years later. It was just one of those little family stories that got lost along the way.

One warm spring day, before he went to the shore for the summer, I picked James Konick up in Brooklyn Heights and drove him over to Green-Wood. He was silent in the car all the way up the hill to the Konick mausoleum. It wasn't until we got there that he said to me, "I loved her, you know. Loved her as an aunt and maybe a bit more. She was middle-aged by the time I met her, but still a lovely woman in every way."

Maude's window was in its full beauty that day, the spring sun streaming through the brilliant glass. He had a bouquet of flame-striped tulips to put in front of it and he stood there for a long moment, his hat against his heart.

Afterword

Since *Brooklyn Graves* is a blend of actual history and fictional (but possible) history, here is an explanation of which is which.

Green-Wood Cemetery is, of course, a real place and is even more beautiful and fascinating than I have described here. The facts and most of the physical description are as accurate as I can make them. All the events, personnel and policies are entirely products of my imagination.

The earlier theft of valuable windows and statues from old churches and cemeteries, discussed here, did happen and was, in part, the inspiration for this book. The all-female Tiffany design studio did exist and Clara Driscoll, mentioned here, was its director. Maude and her letters are my own creation.

Erica's museum may resemble a real place in its physical description and location but everything else I have written about it is entirely a product of my imagination.

The Konick family is also imaginary, but grounded in the history of the Dutch in New York, including the centuries-long pride in their heritage and continuing social connection among the descendents.

To receive a free catalog of Poisoned Pen Press titles, please contact us in one of the following ways:

Phone: 1-800-421-3976
Facsimile: 1-480-949-1707
Email: info@poisonedpenpress.com
Website: www.poisonedpenpress.com

Poisoned Pen Press
6962 E. First Ave. Ste 103
Scottsdale, AZ 85251